RESCUED

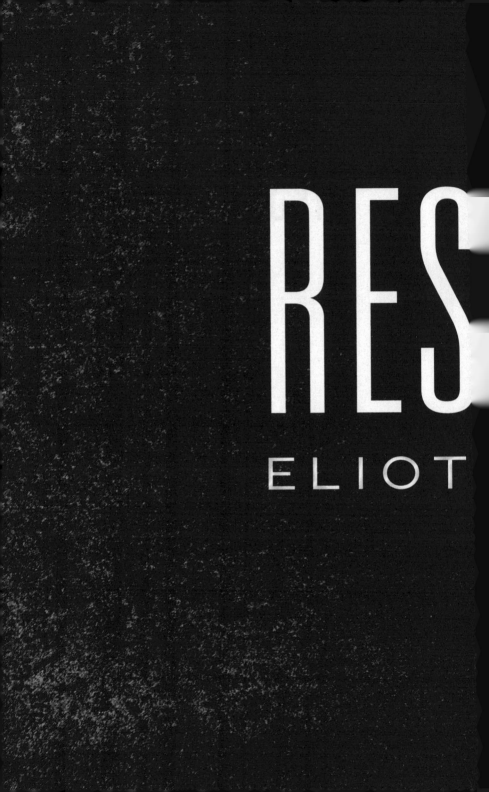

CUED

SCHREFER

SCHOLASTIC PRESS · NEW YORK

Copyright © 2016 by Eliot Schrefer
Photo of Jenny, p. 250: Printed by W Clerk, High Holborn, December 1837/Pigsonthewing/
Wikimedia

Library of Congress Cataloging-in-Publication Data available

ISBN 978-0-545-65503-3

10 9 8 7 6 5 4 3 2 1   16 17 18 19 20

Printed in the U.S.A.   23
First edition, May 2016

Book design by Whitney Lyle

FOR GOKONG

I am twelve years old when it happens. Raja is in a tree outside my window, staring in. He's soaked through with rain, hair dark as ketchup, lips trembling as he watches me doze. My parents would say he looks afraid, but I know he's confused. Ever since he came to our house, he's been at my side, but now he isn't allowed.

Raja putters his lips every time he breathes out, like a little kid baffled by a jigsaw puzzle. He can't figure out what he's done wrong. He can't understand that it's because I'm sick.

I can't bear the look on his face.

I'm lying in bed, drunk on antibiotics and cough syrup. Even though I'm supposed to be on strict bed rest, I kick off my covers and creep to my window so I can be as near to him as possible. As soon as I'm on my feet, my sweat-slick legs turn cold and the useless, honking coughs come, fogging the windowpane. When the glass clears, Raja blinks his golden eyes at me, gives me one of his own quiet, hooting coughs, and places five fingertips against the window. His nose is wet and glistening; he's sick, too.

I put my fingertips over his, touch glass.

"Raja," I say as loudly as I dare, "you have to go back to your hammock. We can play as soon as we get better."

Does he understand that I love him?

I think so. We still get each other. It's my parents neither of us understands these days.

I put a finger to my lips, our sign for *be quiet*. Pleased, Raja puts a finger to his own lips, even as he coughs.

I know Raja doesn't mind being outside, even at night. He loves rain, and will stare up into it and sway — his rain dance, Mom calls it. He isn't getting too wet, anyway, because the tree outside my window has a nice sturdy branch for him to hold on to. He prefers being up high to being on the ground. That's how it's always worked when we play in the dense woods behind my house: Whenever I stop to rest he's right above, staring at me. Only at lunchtime will he climb down and make his awkward wrist-walk to sit beside me.

Now he settles into his spot in the tree and raises a bag of chips he's been clutching in his toes. Rainwater must be pooling inside the bag, because he isn't bringing out chips, just yellow potato paste. He's loving the cold, salty goopiness, though, and scrutinizes each glob before delicately licking it from his fingers. Once he finishes eating, he moves the bag close to the glass, its opening toward me. By our code, this means I'm free to take some. But there's a new barrier between us.

"We'll both be better soon," I tell him. "Then I'll have a chip. Save some for me."

Of course he doesn't. No junk food ever survives unfinished around Raja Solomon. Once the bag is empty, he releases it and watches it flutter to the ground. Mom spends half her day picking up the trash Raja's dropped. Orangutans have many great qualities, but they are the worst litterbugs ever.

Raja eases farther out so the branch bends under his weight. Then he grasps the next tree over so he's spread-eagled between the two. It would be impossible for me to hold this pose for even a second, but he can grip branches for hours.

As Raja sways and stares, I press my forehead against the window and stare back. The glass is too thick for me to hear anything, but I can imagine the sounds he's making: like raspberries with extra lip-puttering. It's been over a week since I've been outside with him.

As the rain falls harder, Raja grasps a branch with only his feet and clamps his arms tight around his narrow torso. He has the whole run of the outside; if he wanted, he could be dry in the hammock on the porch, where my parents have set out fruit and milk. But then he wouldn't have a view of me. I wouldn't have a view of him.

It's a gift he's giving me, that he's always given me. He is making me the most important person in his world.

I cross my arms over my chest, then point at him. Sulkily, staring off to one side, he grips the branch with his feet so he can cross his arms over his chest, then points in my direction. He yawns, which is how I know he's nervous. It's as though he's worried what he'll find in my face.

I sign *I love you* again, slowly and emphatically. Then: *Sorry.*

He points at me then pats his butt. *You poop.*

Sorry, I sign again. Neither of us actually knows sign language, but over the years we've come up with a dozen gestures. Some of them were my invention: Video games are *little* + *Raja* + *thank you.* Nap time is *little* + *sleep.* Raja's combinations usually involve poop. Well, maybe the gesture doesn't exactly mean *poop* to him, but his meaning is clear: He is not happy with me, not one bit. And though I can sign *I'm not poop,* I don't have a combination of signs that says *It's not my fault.* Raja has never been much interested in blame, anyway.

He blows out a long gust, crosses an arm in front of him, and leans his chin on it. That's how I know that he's not mad at me. He's depressed.

I can't leave him like this, wet and sick and alone. I fish a bag of chips from the stash under my bed, unlock the window, slide it up a few inches, and toss the bag to Raja. He catches it with one foot while I quickly shut and lock the window. He wolfs through the bag, and this time doesn't hold the opening toward me. Tilting his head back, he offers his mouth to the rain to wash it all down, giving me a terrific view of his yellow teeth. Once he's finished, he carefully maneuvers the bag so it's hidden behind his back before he drops it.

"Really?" I ask. "*Now* you're shy about littering?"

Raja grouchily refuses to face me, instead giving me a view of his skinny orangutan butt.

Someone knocks on my door — Mom probably heard me open the window. Frantically, I motion for Raja to go away. He stares back defiantly. I get into bed and pull the covers up. If I look asleep, I figure, Mom might leave before she notices Raja on the other side of the window.

Cracking my eyelids, I can just see the door ease open. I turn my head and watch Raja's expression go flat. When my parents are around, I stop being able to read him.

Mom stands over my bed, Raja on the outside of my window. I am between them, blinded under my comforter. Then my mother gasps, my door slams closed, and I hear her pound down the stairs. It can only mean one thing: She's seen Raja.

I hurtle out of bed, reeling from fever, and stagger down the hallway after her, yelling for her to stop.

Wavering at the bottom of the stairs, Mom wrings her hands and calls for my father. Worry washes her face gray.

"John," she says when she sees me, "go back to bed. Now. You're supposed to be resting."

"What are you going to do?" I ask, clutching the bannister. I shiver, even though my pajamas are thick. I have pneumonia, the doctor said, and that word has changed everything. For the last year Raja and I have been trading the same germ, like a game of mucus tag. It isn't his fault any more than mine that we keep getting each other sick.

"I said back to bed!" she orders.

"He got lonely, that's all!"

My father comes out of his study, looking as confused by my behavior as Raja's.

Mom whirls on him. "Your orangutan was outside John's window. Eating chips John must have given him. Breathing the same air."

Father notices me shivering at the top of the stairs and his expression gets serious.

"*Please,*" I say. "Raja doesn't know he's doing anything wrong."

It's hard to detect over the rain patter, but I think I hear fronds snapping. Our only palm tree is by the front door, which means . . . My eye darts to the door, and the stained-glass panel beside it. Two glass-wavered golden eyes are peering in.

Raja raps a one-two pattern against the window. It's the same rhythm he taps against my forehead to wake me up from a nap.

Let's go play.

My parents haven't noticed him yet. *If I go back to my room,* I think, *everyone will calm down. Raja will stop making noise.*

Hands on the wall for support, I lurch back upstairs. The carpet is wavering, colorful mud. Then the world goes white, and I nearly get lost in it while I listen to my parents argue below me.

"It's too much," Mom says. "We can't let Raja wander free anymore."

"What do you want me to do about it?" my father says.

"Why are you acting like *I'm* putting *you* out? *You're* the one who brought him here. *You're* the one who needs to fix this."

This line isn't unfamiliar to any of us.

I crawl into my bedroom and close the door. I press my mouth into my hands and let the pent-up coughs out. When I look up, clammy and woozy, Raja is back at my window. He's fully water-logged now, his eyes desperate.

I love you, I sign, then point toward his hammock on the porch.

He doesn't sign anything back, and I don't blame him. What does *I love you* mean, when I'm letting us be torn apart? When, for all Raja knows, I've sided with my parents?

Raja tugs hard at the window frame. Even though he's half my size, he's stronger than any of us. A corner starts to scrape free from the wall.

"Stop!" I shout. "Raja, please stop!"

I start rummaging under my bed for more chips, a toy, anything to distract him, but a loud scraping stops me. He's getting more and more frantic, and the glass is wobbling in its frame.

I'm worried Raja will cut himself. I try to pry his fingers away, the glass dancing between us. His fingertips are small, rough, wet, *his.* The whole window frame comes free at a corner, and we're suddenly holding hands, warm rain streaming into my room. Raja stops and stares at me, delight and surprise on his face even as the frame cuts him. He's happy just to be touching me.

I know my parents will be here any second.

I know the only way to stop this.

I know I need to let go.

So I do. I release his hand.

Raja cries out, betrayed.

Once he's recovered from his surprise, he leaps into motion, frantically pushing at the window, his slashed fingers leaving bloody streaks. When I push back, the whole frame bends and comes free from the wall. Raja holds it in his hands for a moment, then pitches it to the ground.

I don't move. He has his feet against the gap in the wall, his hands wrapped around mine. Raja's orange hair is so familiar, as much a part of me as my own hair.

But my parents: If they see us together, they'll send him away for good.

I pry Raja's fingers up so I can cast him out and get him back on his branch. But he has his other hand inside now, is crying loudly and making the kiss-squeaking that means he's really upset — a sound I haven't heard since my father first pulled him out of a barrel two years ago, frail and terrified.

Raja's eyes go even wider, and I whirl to see my door open, my parents bursting in from the hallway. When he sees them, Raja opens his mouth and starts biting, battling to get as deep as possible into my arms.

At the sight of his sharp flashing canines, I fall back.

But it's too late. Raja shrieks —

My mother screams —

His jaw snaps —

I can't see the teeth anymore —

His mouth closes on my hand —

He is holding my hand in his mouth.

My mother is still yelling from the doorway, and underneath that distant noise I feel something too intense and too bright to be pain. Raja's face tightens in fear and confusion. He releases me and I fall back onto my bed. My hand is pumping blood onto my white sheets.

I watch it.

Something is impossible.

Raja shrieks. My parents yell. I am silent.

My finger is gone.

PART ONE

IF WE HAD A KEEN VISION AND FEELING
OF ALL ORDINARY HUMAN LIFE, IT WOULD
BE LIKE HEARING THE GRASS GROW AND
THE SQUIRREL'S HEART BEAT, AND WE
SHOULD DIE OF THAT ROAR WHICH LIES
ON THE OTHER SIDE OF SILENCE.

— GEORGE ELIOT, *MIDDLEMARCH*

ONE

Every family's got something weird about it, and mine was no different. We just had to try harder than most to hide it. All it took was someone to walk in the door to see that we had an orangutan. A real-live, orange-brown, TV-obsessed, drinking-grapefruit-juice-from-the-carton orangutan.

Granted, it's possible that Raja wasn't the weirdness itself, but just a symptom of it. I can barely remember a time before my family went all orangutan, so it's hard to get to the bottom of it. It's hard to know a beginning is happening to you, because obviously whatever comes after hasn't happened yet. But here's where it all started, as best as I can see it.

It was summer break before fifth grade, and I'd slept over at my best friend Andy's house. We spent the morning eating cold pizza from the night before and playing video games, then he walked me back to my house so we could talk over strategy for our online rematch later that afternoon. We lived in one of those far-flung suburbs of Atlanta, rural but not poor. To get to my house from his, all we had to do was walk along a two-lane highway for a while, then cross the street.

We were discussing druids versus priests when Andy said something really quickly and dashed across the road. His words were lost, so I just tripped after him.

A truck horn, a blast of wind tossing me along the road's shoulder, Andy's pale shocked face — I turned in the grass and stared down the road, the truck still blaring as it sped off. It was a flooded moment, just as flooded as if I *had* died. Death, near death, racing away down the highway.

"I said wait, you idiot!" Andy yelled. "I said I was crossing but you should wait!"

"I figured you wouldn't . . ." I looked down the road. "That you wouldn't . . . I almost *died*, you loser."

Obedience sounds like a good thing, but that morning I almost died from it. As Andy and I walked home, we were quiet for a while, then went back to game planning.

That afternoon, after Andy had gone back home and my mom had gone out to buy a new mattress, I turned on the TV. Soon enough I flipped to some old movie with an orange ape in it, all eyes and teeth and hair. Even though the movie had the weird washed-out colors of the twentieth century, I settled in to watch.

The ape was hanging out with a grizzled dude in a T-shirt. They had all sorts of adventures, and the hairy orange sidekick was always there, helping the guy beat up some bullies. It even kissed an old lady! Hilarious.

My father was having one of those weekends when he was technically home but spent most of the day in his office, right next to the TV room. One time he came out to use the bathroom and looked up from his phone long enough to see what I was watching.

"Oh, this movie!" he said, rubbing my head. "I loved it back in the day. What's it called again?"

I beamed, as proud as if I'd made the movie myself. All it took was a moment of my father's attention to do that to me. I remember the zap sound his slacks made as he sat next to me. I remember the smell of Speed Stick and coffee, the sound of a beer bottle opening, how it made me feel like a grown man to be near enough my father to hear his beer fizz after he took a long drink.

He was going to spend the whole afternoon with me! I didn't know where that sudden luck had come from, but I didn't want it to ever go away. "I don't know the name of the movie," I said. "But that monkey is *so cool*."

The orange sidekick was pretending to box this mean-looking guy, who was getting really mad.

"Huh," my father said, eyes twinkling. "That monkey *is* awesome. I remember thinking the same thing when this movie first came out. Way before you were born."

"Is it a baboon?" I asked.

"Looks like an orangutan. They wander into our Indonesia operations sometimes. Adorable little guys. I'm going over there next month to scout plantation sites. Maybe I'll bring one home for you."

If my mom had been there, she'd have figured he was kidding. I was only ten, and *I* figured he was kidding.

Even though it was on a channel with commercials, we watched the movie to the end, making ape noises at each other during the breaks and scratching our armpits. As we watched, my father went through a six-pack of beer and I went through a two-liter soda and a bag of tortilla chips my father's company was testing. I didn't like the new flavor — it tasted sort of like hand soap — but my father wouldn't have wanted to hear that, so I hid handfuls under the couch cushions whenever he went to the bathroom or was especially deep into his phone.

Mom had started the day mad that my father was too busy to go mattress shopping with her, and was even more mad about the mess when she got home. It only got worse from there. Officially their fight that night was about how my father had let me spend a beautiful summer afternoon inside watching TV. I remember listening to them from my room, rolling my eyes at my mom. Her anger seemed like proof of how much cooler my father was. *He* didn't care what kind of mattress he slept on. *He* let me stay inside and watch an orangutan on TV even if it was a summer day. *He* never checked for messes under the couch cushions.

My favorite parent at any moment was usually the one who was letting me have my way. The good parent. The favorite parent. Not the same thing.

My mom was always trying to be the good parent. My father? I think sometimes he didn't care one way or the other. But when he did, he was totally gunning for favorite.

When my father returned from his next business trip, he called from the airport to say he'd be a couple hours late. When he finally arrived, he had a large barrel strapped to the flatbed of his pickup.

Mom and I watched from the doorway, confused, while he unhitched the barrel and rolled it along the ground. I asked him what was inside. He didn't answer, just pried it open and pointed.

On tiptoes, I peered in.

Arms and legs and hair, totally still. At first I thought it was some sort of ragged orange toy. But then Raja lifted his little head and looked up.

Curled tight around a pillow, he smelled like pee and farts. His eyes were milky and blank. Mom gasped when my father reached in and wrapped his hands around the tiny creature, lifting Raja as easily as a dropped napkin. The baby orangutan was too weak to keep his head up; it lolled on his neck while he watched the walls of the barrel pass from view. He clutched his pillow tight to him, like it was a branch he'd tumble from if he ever let go. Or like it was his mother.

He didn't look at all ready to fight bullies or kiss old ladies. This was a different, stranger, more fragile thing than the rambunctious sidekick I'd seen in the movie.

"Gary . . ." Mom said warningly to my father.

But it was too late. He'd already placed Raja in my arms.

At first the ape resisted me, weakly but passionately trying to push me away. Then something shifted inside him, and he clutched me with the same energy he'd used to resist. It was the first time I'd held something so delicately alive, something it was in my power to drop or save. I went silent with responsibility. I was only ten, so most things were heavy, but even so Raja surprised me with his weight. He wasn't really as light as a dropped napkin, not at all.

"What *is* it?" I asked.

"An orangutan. And he's your new friend," my father said. "He wanted to come all the way from Indonesia to meet you."

Raja allowed one foot to let go of the pillow and wrapped his long toes around my elbow instead. My father and I took him inside, leaving Mom alone with her shock. It was like my father had given me a new brother. And given my mom a new son. Only she'd had no say in it at all.

By the end of that morning, Raja had forgotten all about his pillow and molded himself to me instead. After he'd napped for a while, we brought him out back. My father sat on the grass beside me, ignoring the wet earth that seeped into the seat of his business suit. As Raja reached his rickety arms around my shoulders, my father grinned with pride. At the time I thought he was proud of me, not himself.

Meanwhile, eyes overcast, Mom wordlessly grabbed her keys and drove to the grocery store to buy baby formula. After she'd returned, I fed Raja his first bottle. He clung tight, fending off my father when he tried to pull him away. So my father stopped, and left Raja to me.

The world that day became an exaggerated and cartoonish place. When Raja was content, it felt like all was peace. When his face tightened in a grimace, and I could tell he was suffering from something inside him, the world had no light in it anymore. No matter what he was, though, fussy or peaceful, he wouldn't let anyone take him off me. I was the one he'd chosen. He slept in my bed that night. The next morning I woke with bruises dotting my arms, one where each of his fingers had clutched.

I woke up with Raja bruises for years. I got used to them. During the school day, when my friends were talking about ordinary things, I'd place my own fingertips over the bruises and think about Raja. I might have looked into where he'd come from, what he'd left behind. But I didn't. I figured it was impossible to know, so I didn't bother to try. What was important was that he was mine. That we had each other for life.

That first morning, it sounded like my parents were on their way to making some bruises of their own. Mom was fighting with my father, their shouts shaking the wall that separated our bedrooms. She kept asking questions, and he kept grunting out syllables that I guess could be considered answers.

Where will we keep him?

Mrph.

What do we feed him?

Formula. Phupt. Fruit.

Is having him illegal?

No.

Can we take him to a vet?

Yep.

What about when John goes back to school in the fall?

Ugh, er.

Can we ever take a vacation again?

Erg.

How big do orangutans get?

Not big. Uripfft.

Once my father got tired of Mom's questions, he launched back:

I don't know what you want from me, because I can't take this back. It's a homeless ape and it wandered into the plantation. What did you expect me to do? John wanted one and now he has one. We have it now. Everyone should be happy. So let's move on, okay?

Whenever my parents' voices peaked, Raja jerked. "Come on," I whispered. "Let's go outside."

As I lifted him from the bed, something dripped and plopped. I realized that we'd need to get Raja diapers. After stripping the sheets and dropping the stinking bundle into the hamper, I grabbed a bottle of detergent with my free hand and took Raja to the tiled patio out back so I could give him the car wash treatment. He loved the water and the scrubbing and the lavender-scented soap, nibbling at the meringue peaks it made on his hair. From that moment on, the back porch was our base. We'd wander off, he'd poop, and we'd trudge back to rinse off. Until he'd adjusted to his new life and his new diet, Raja had frequent bouts of diarrhea — it would come on unexpectedly, and despite his straining he couldn't hold it in. Mom bought me a huge brick of T-shirts, since because of Raja I'd go through about four a day. They all quickly turned a khaki color.

At first Raja drank baby formula, and I'd nurse him in a wicker chair out back. But as he adjusted to life in his new home, he became disdainful of the formula, boxing the bottle out of my hands. Instead, he only wanted what *I* was eating. Fruit, vegetables, all the way up the food chain to Pop-Tarts and brownies. I found out online that copying whatever their mom was eating was how baby wild orangutans avoided eating poisonous fruit. Apparently that technique applied to Pop-Tarts, too.

Whenever we were together he was wrapped on my body, but all the same I couldn't have called him clingy. He'd spend hours on his own while I went into town to get a haircut, or to Andy's house to hang out.

He didn't mind being by himself that much.

A time would come when I'd need to keep reminding myself that.

After a few weeks, my father returned to Indonesia for HappyFoods business, and while he was gone Mom and I figured out a rhythm. I'd play with Raja most days in the backyard, and then I'd get a break by going to a friend's house for a long weekend while Mom took over. I remember returning once and finding her at the kitchen table, the dishwasher thumping through its cycle in the background while she read a magazine. Raja was swirling his fingers through a pile of spilled coffee beans. Mom looked up, smiled, and waved. Raja looked up, smiled, and waved. It felt like I had been on my own business trip, and that I was coming home to my happy family.

Andy thought Raja was way better than any video game. We tried to teach him Ping-Pong, until Raja decided he had more fun when he bit through the balls and buried the husks in the dirt. We tried to teach him slip-and-slide, and that went much better, until Raja got excited and whipped the plastic around, ripping it on a fencepost. Some of our best afternoons were spent finger painting, which went great as long as we were far from anything that was dry-clean only.

Mom said no one could come over besides Andy, for Raja's sake as much as mine. I was secretly relieved that the whole school wouldn't be calling me Ape Boy on the first day back. Fifth grade would be hard enough without a curveball like that.

My parents' blowout fights about Raja had quieted to mutters and bickers, because my father basically had Mom cornered. If she didn't want to break my heart, she had to accept our newest family member. She could call my father reckless and insensitive all she wanted, but that wasn't going to change what he'd done. So she gave up and accepted the situation.

It played right into how my mother and father had always worked. My father did what he wanted, and Mom never calmly told anyone her feelings — any dark emotion only came out if she was fighting. Those were the blazing moments of sincerity; otherwise it was more important to her that everything was good rather than real. She wanted to tell the world the least complicated version of itself. My dad and I were content with that.

The morning of my first day back at school we ate breakfast as usual, Raja restrained in a high chair because of his knack for overturning cereal bowls. Then, while I quietly got my backpack together, Mom went upstairs and brought down my blue stuffed elephant. Well, I guess I should call it *Raja's* elephant. Raja loved that toy animal so much, but normally it had to stay in the bedroom — if we'd let him drag it around the house or up into the trees, it would have gone missing in no time.

I'll always remember the joyful expression he had as Mom approached in her black bathrobe and slippers. She looked almost like a nun, cross shining around her neck as she held the elephant out for Raja, just for Raja. He buried his face in the toy while, awed, I worked my backpack straps over my shoulders and crept out of the house. Over Raja's head, Mom signed *I love you* at me. I signed it back.

The school bus would stop for me anywhere along the road, but I turned and walked until the house was out of sight. If Raja took off after me, I didn't want him to be able to find me easily.

The twin neighbor girls gawked as I joined them at the end of their driveway, but they were second graders and didn't dare question me. When the bus came and I got on, I was relieved to see that Andy had saved me a seat in the back. I slumped down next to him.

"Look behind us," I said through clenched teeth. "Any sign of an orangutan?"

Andy checked. "No, I think we're good."

Relieved, I let myself sit up straight. I couldn't resist eventually looking back, though, and that's when I saw a telltale orange blip at the end of the road, hurtling our way. Mom was chasing after him, all black bathrobe and bare legs. I turned forward, stock-still, terrified that if I didn't act normal another kid would spot Raja and the police would come and shoot him dead. It had happened before — I'd read online about how a chimpanzee this lady tried to keep as a pet got loose in public and was killed. The police had to shoot if an ape escaped. It was the law.

Raja was no match for a school bus, though, and the next time I looked back I saw we'd left him behind. I prayed my mom had already tracked him down.

That morning in school, I couldn't think about anything but Raja until the office lady delivered a note to my desk. *Your mom called and said everything is fine.* My whole body unclenched. When I got off the bus that afternoon, I ran up the drive. "Raja!" I cried when I threw open the front door.

For a long, queasy silence, there was nothing. Then I heard a familiar pattering on the stairs and suddenly my vision was full of orange. Raja catapulted himself into my arms, knocking me over. We rolled on the ground, holding each other tight, Raja sighing happily into my ear.

Mom trudged into the living room, still in her morning bathrobe. I stood up, Raja hugging himself tight against me. No way was he letting me out from under his fingers.

"You never changed clothes," I said.

Mom smiled, though her lips were gray. "It's like when you were young. There's simply no time in the day for me to shower when I've got a little one to take care of."

"I saw him running after the bus," I said.

She nodded. "I thought you might have. I drove all over until I found him."

"Where was he?"

"Huddled by a shed outside one of the houses on State Road Sixty."

I imagined him shivering and scared. I leaned back, and Raja lifted his face so his eyes could meet mine. "He looks sorry," I said.

And he did — he looked pretty wretched, actually. Being alone on that road had spooked him enough that the next morning, when I put on my backpack, he was instantly in Mom's arms for security, his trembling face buried in her chest. At least he hadn't decided to cling to me that morning — I don't know how we'd have gotten him off.

Luckily the first week of school was only two days long, because I couldn't wait to spend the whole weekend with Raja. That Saturday morning, when I didn't put my backpack on, Raja scampered over to it, kicked it, and wrapped his arms around my leg, making angry jealous noises at the pack. As a treat, Raja and I made brownies. He loved the mess and the sweetness, whipping the wooden spoon around his head, flinging a crime scene's worth of batter onto the ceiling.

Mom was not happy with us.

I had to clean it up, and while I did, Raja climbed onto my mother's shoulders, clamping his hands over her eyes. She was irritated at first, but was soon giggling as she struggled to free herself. I remember watching them as I stood on the counter, paper towels in one hand and a bottle of cleaner in the other. Mom would take to Raja, and I'd keep him company as much as I could when I was home. This might all work out.

My father had been the one who brought Raja into our lives, but he didn't spend much time with him. His job was to keep up connections with HappyFoods' local suppliers in Asia, so he was constantly flying to foreign places, calling to say he'd have to stay longer than he expected, that he'd be spending the weekend in meetings at the Atlanta headquarters while Mom, Raja, and I lived our lives an hour away in the countryside.

I didn't mind it that much. My father had always been a question mark to me, and I was getting tired of trying to figure out whether he liked me. I was becoming my mom's son more than my father's.

Me, Mom, and Raja — it felt like enough of a family. We *were* a family.

Until we weren't.

TWO

When the divorce finally went down years later, I believed Mom when she said that the only way forward was in silence, that the way to get through this with the least pain was for no one in our new home to know there had ever been a Raja.

My mom was leaving my father to be near her family in Oregon — my options were to go with her or stay with him. He never asked for me to stay. I didn't ask if I could. We didn't know each other, even after all those years. But everyone knew I wasn't going to stay with him.

It wasn't hard to convince myself I was doing the right thing. We were splitting into two equal halves. My mother and me in Oregon, and my father and Raja in Georgia.

It was my father who had brought Raja home, after all, so he should be the one to take care of Raja now. That was Mom's argument, and she said it often enough that it started repeating itself in my head, too.

Pretending this was the best course for us was easy. Raja had bitten off my finger, after all. It was simple enough to agree with my mother that it was enough to split us apart, and follow her far away.

I was young, but not young enough for that to be a total excuse.

I let go of the animal in front of me. It was surprisingly easy to let Raja go invisible. As easy as not looking.

• • •

Last day of sophomore year. My car was in the shop again, and by the time I finished horsing around with my football teammates everyone with a vehicle had already left, so I had to take the activities bus home. The *Warcrafting* ninth graders were wary of a hulking junior, so they gave me the back row to myself. By tilting my body diagonally across, I could press my forehead against the glass and stare out while lying down. For these ten minutes, I could be quiet with my thoughts, staring at the world going by. Moments earlier, I'd been play-wrestling with my friends. That was the happier me. This one, moody and quiet and *elsewhere* — this was the real me.

As I looked out the window, I imagined an orange shape emerging from the trees and taking off after the bus. I'd have dreaded that very sight years before, but now I had fantasies of throwing open the emergency door at the back and running to Raja, folding him in my arms. It had been two years since I'd seen him, but I knew how much Raja would have loved a bus trip. Hand in mine, he'd have watched closely while the driver ushered us in. Once we'd sat he'd have rubbed the fake leather seat and examined his finger afterward to see if the material had come away, like fruit flesh would. He'd have picked off and eaten the rubber cement plugging a hole in the vinyl, then he'd have been up and down the aisles, into everyone's backpacks, before long wearing one like a hat.

Six years had passed since he'd arrived in my life, four years since I lost my finger to him, two years since my parents' divorce and my move with Mom to Oregon — and the truth was that lately I'd managed to go hours at a time without thinking about him. When life was at its most normal, when I was busy going to classes or playing football or hanging out with friends, I could go maybe half a day without Raja entering my mind. But whenever I was by myself, when I didn't have my new life to fill me, that was when the memories swooped in.

After the joy of imagining him came a familiar punishment: I felt a weight in my chest, a crushing guilt that was always lurking within me, waiting for an opportunity to force its way up.

"Your stop. You getting off or what?" the driver asked, peering at me in the rearview.

I grunted and stood, pressing the bad feeling back down as I threaded my backpack over my arms. My sneakers squeaked on the rubbery floor as I shuffled past the freshmen, who were discussing some sort of warrior pandas. *You remember how upset he was when you left. Mom is right — you'd be breaking both your hearts to visit.*

When my father lost his job last year, the alimony slowed to a trickle. Mom didn't make much from her kindergarten pay, so we'd never moved out of the rental unit that was supposed to have been temporary. We had the distinction, though, of having the only apartment in all of Medford with lawn ornaments. She'd glued Astroturf to the outside landing, where she propped up a painted piece of plywood that looked like a farmer bending over. Next to it was a Christmas angel that stayed there year-round, praying over our apartment even now in June. The front door itself was besieged by lawn trolls, some holding mock watering cans, some tromping through the weeds, some standing and glowering like thugs. I could only imagine what the neighbors thought.

I trudged up the walk, then up the stairs to our door. I sifted my keys out from under the gum wrappers in my backpack.

"Hi, Mom!" I called out as soon as I entered. But she was too busy yelling on the phone to notice me.

". . . can't even imagine it!" Mom was saying. "You have no idea what this will do to him, Gary!"

My parents' preferred medium was the tense email. It had been years since one of their fights had played out in real time. I wondered who the unlucky "him" was. I hoped it was me. Anyone — just not Raja.

I didn't know whether to sneak back out or try again to announce myself. I looked around the apartment for help, but all the apartment did was look back. Our place was all pastel purples and greens, and nothing was lacking a frill or a doily if it could manage it. Lots of Jesus figurines. In a manger, or smiling benevolently with a shepherd's crook in his hand, hand-painted hair and girly lips. He was blessing our house all over the place. Although Jesus definitely represented, he was far outnumbered by bears and geese. Woodcut bears on picnics, bear ornaments hanging by twine above the oven, plump stuffed bears lazing on the baker's rack facing the couch. Then there were the geese: little craft-shop birds clattering from the fridge door, or the rainbow flock circling the welcome mat. Geese holding hearts, geese dangling leprechauns, geese sitting on pumpkins or wearing Santa hats. The geese had bows tied around their throats, every single one — ribbons must have been a goose commandment. I'd always been cheered by the Momness of it all — but all the same, I avoided having any of the guys over.

The only animal in the house that wasn't a bear or a goose was a cat clock in the kitchen. Its big eyes peered left and right while its tail swung from side to side. I imagined it taking in the same kitchen scene while the seconds ticked by, as if it was expecting something new to appear. *Oven, pantry, oven, pantry.*

Mom furiously shook her head at whatever she was hearing, then started talking again. "It's *not* your decision — that is *precisely* what I was saying, if you'd been listening. Shouldn't it be his? He deserves that much . . . Well if you don't, I will . . . Yes, you'd better believe it. You keep saying it's out of your control, but you're the one who *set up* this situation, I know you realize that . . . Yes, I know, and I don't *care.* Punish *me* for that, not him!"

I heard a soft thud as she threw the handset onto the couch.

I was paralyzed. Whatever the news was, I was sure I wouldn't want to hear it. And I was just as sure that I'd end up hearing it anyway. "Hey, Mom," I finally called out again. "I'm home."

She appeared in the doorway. Clearly the phone call had thrown her — and she was a hard person to throw. Even during the most intense moments of the Raja period, she'd been sturdy. Ferociously positive. "Hi, honey," she said automatically. She got two plastic tumblers and filled them while she spoke. That could have been her motto: *When Things Get Tense, Pour Some Water.*

I didn't want water. I wanted to know what was happening. But I couldn't say anything. Not if it would upset her further. There was a yawning sadness within each of us, too big to be able to speak about. The sadness had been handed to me, and had grown larger while it was mine. Whenever it bloomed was when I hit the gym, as if muscles could shelter me. But even as I grew stronger, so did the sadness.

"Is everything okay?" I finally ventured, chasing a magical scrap of hope that she'd say yes.

"No," she said. "I'm afraid it isn't."

"It's about Raja, isn't it?" I asked, lowering my backpack and folding my large frame into a kitchen chair.

She paused, and looked almost confused. I realized why: She was surprised to hear his name. We avoided saying it aloud anymore. She slid into the chair across from mine.

"What happened?" I asked.

Mom loved being a kindergarten teacher — she had lines around her mouth from where she constantly smiled, and her eyes almost always had a twinkle. Every day she wore a teddy bear pin, usually over a comfortable mohair sweater — her "huggy sweaters," as she called them. The teddy bear jangled as she rubbed her face. "Your father is moving. He's out of money, so he has to sell the house. The court's involved. There's no other option."

"He mentioned something about money being tight, but I didn't realize . . . that . . . Um, so what does that mean for Raja?" I asked.

"It means . . . well, it means that he can't stay there."

"I figured." Here we were, sounding calm, but my stomach said that the sky was falling up and the ground was falling down, that I was a pinpoint tumbling in space. "So what's going to happen to him?"

"Your father found a zoo that will take him."

I could feel my face flush — the curse of the redhead, that at any moment of hope or disappointment, our flesh itself gives us away. "We tried all that two years ago, and nowhere would take him."

She shrugged slowly, like she was lifting something much heavier than her shoulders. "It must have changed. I don't think he's lying, if that's what you're implying."

"No, I don't think that, either, it's just . . ." My voice trailed off. *It's just that there's no seeing anything clearly. My thoughts about Raja are under a dome, echoing everywhere.*

"The good news is that he won't have to go through foreclosure, because the house already sold. But the bad news is that this will all happen very quickly. The zoo will be coming in a matter of days."

"Oh," I said.

She put her hand over mine. I looked at it, numb. "He's going somewhere better. I'm sure there will be other orangutans there. He's probably been lonely at your father's."

I nodded.

She looked a little freaked out that I wasn't saying anything, peering at me like she'd just found me under a rock. "I hoped that chapter of our lives was over when we moved here, honey. But maybe it wasn't. Maybe *now* it is. Because Raja's finally going somewhere he belongs."

"Maybe it's over, yeah," I said. The words were just sounds. Without quite knowing what I was doing, I took my phone out and placed it flat on the table. I scrolled to the photos folder, the one I usually avoided.

I wasn't intentionally making myself miserable or anything — it just felt really unfair all of a sudden that Raja was so invisible. That my parents and I were talking about him without having to face him. Not that a photo was much better, but anyway, I clearly wasn't thinking straight.

My mom eased into the seat next to me. "It's been a long time since you two have seen each other, I know. But it's for the best. He's been weaned away from you, and now it's back to other orangutans."

I grunted something meaningless. I wanted to see Raja, that was all I knew.

The first picture to come up was Raja in my scrawny ten-year-old lap. I was sitting on the edge of the bathtub, and he was clinging to me tightly, face pressed against my belly. His eyes were scrunched tight, his diapered butt high in the air. Moist from the steam billowing from the shower behind us, his hair lay flat in wet tendrils. The toes that gripped my bathing suit were slender and delicate.

The bathroom had always been a place of unexpected terrors for Raja. I'd been lifting him from the tub when my face unexpectedly appeared in a mirror — the double-me startled him so much that he peed in fright, scrambling up the shower curtain and clutching the rail, squeaking and shrieking. When I reached for him, the double-me appeared in the mirror again, and he bolted. I was finally able to locate him behind the dryer only by following a Hansel-and-Gretel trail of pee droplets.

"John?" my mother said.

I was in my bathing suit because I'd get soaked whenever I tried to bathe Raja. When I took my shirt off, though, he'd screech in worry. He didn't get that I was just *wearing* the shirt, that it wasn't some body part coming away. He'd recover from seeing me peel part of me off, then it would be time for the shorts and he'd get upset all over again. Then, once he'd calmed, we had to transfer him to my mom so I could take *my* bath. He'd fight and fight to stay on me. Clutching so hard. Bruising.

I looked at my muscular arm, filling the sleeve of my T-shirt. No bruises there, not anymore.

I looked up at my mom, wondering how to phrase what I had to say.

"John?" she asked. "Are you okay?"

For a moment my thoughts escaped their dome, and for the first time since I left Raja I had a flash of clarity. "I have to say good-bye to him, Mom. I'm going back."

THREE

I could go long stretches without thinking about my missing finger. But then something small would happen and it would be back in my mind. At the airport check-in, I handed my driver's license over with my good hand, like I usually do, the four fingers of the other down at my side. But when I pulled my wallet out of my back pocket, I sensed the airline worker's eyes on my stump, on the lightning bolts of scar tissue frizzling the surrounding fingers.

His eyes widened. "Hey, buddy, where'd your finger go?"

It had been four years since I'd lost that finger, and only a day or two would go by without someone reminding me about it with a lingering glance or an awkward question. The hospital had amputated the shards of bone that were left, leaving a clean, neat scar right at the knuckle. Everything that remained was whole and healthy, just the finger was missing. My hand didn't look wounded as much as partially erased.

"You know, messing around," I muttered.

"Okay," he said, holding up an open hand as he handed over the boarding pass. "Didn't mean to pry, big guy."

I put my maimed hand in my pocket. It was the least of the things I had to answer for. But it was the only one that was visible.

The court said I was supposed to see my father three times a year. But there was the hurricane warning the first time, and then I made the special football clinic so spring break was shot, and then my dad was remodeling in the fall so he was staying with his girl-friend. And so on.

As I stepped out of the Atlanta airport and onto the air-moist curb, it hit me: I kept thinking of this as my first time seeing Raja since I left. But it was also the first time I was seeing my father, too. I'd been gone so long, I had no idea what I was going to find in either of them.

He was supposed to pick me up at the curb, but there was no sign of him. I texted and then called, twice. Finally, half an hour later, he pulled around in his pickup truck. He leaned over and pushed open the passenger door, smiling broadly. "Get in, get in!"

I lobbed my duffel bag onto the flatbed and got in.

"I'm sorry," my father explained as he pulled onto the inter-state. "I was sitting in the short-term lot, waiting for a call, but then I realized the phone company messed up and disconnected my line by accident. It'll get sorted out in a few days. See?"

He lifted his phone and pointed to where it said EMERGENCY CALLS ONLY. His hair was frazzled, a couple days of growth on his face. "Okay, okay. Keep your eyes on the road, okay?" I said.

"Yeah, sure," he said. My father prattled for a while about the parking lot attendant he met while he was waiting, then about a documentary he'd seen the night before about the Vietnam War, then the next election and whether a Republican would finally have a decent shot at the White House. As he talked I listened to my bag roll around in the empty flatbed. Shuffle, hit a wall, shuf-fle, hit a wall. Had he become even more . . . impersonal? Or was I just noticing it now?

I wanted to ask about Raja, but as I was working up my cour-age my father said, out of nowhere, "How's your mother doing? She find a magic man yet?"

It felt familiar, this shock snap from superficial to way too personal. My father really saw nothing weird about the question, because the answer meant as little to him as the Vietnam documentary. He showed no interest in me for most of the time, and then would make these deliberate attempts at intimacy that felt like military maneuvers. It was like he was missing whatever mental app would have told him that what he was about to say might startle whoever he was saying it to. Even the personal wasn't personal with my father.

Instead of answering, I said, "It's nice out here." We were close to home by then. One moment it was twelve-lane roads and smog, then the next it was two-lane roads and woodsmoke. That was Georgia for you.

"Yeah, it's nice out here," my father said. "I have to downscale to a city apartment, though."

"Oh," I said. *Good to know.* "Is this Rita's doing?"

"Rita, well, yes," my father drawled. He patted his belly, like that explained something. "She's no longer part of the picture, I'm afraid."

"Sorry," I said.

"It's okay," he said, looking like it really and fully was.

My father and I had no language whatsoever for talking about hard things. I knew he wasn't going to mention Raja, and I bet he was pretty sure I wasn't going to bring him up. We'd be there soon enough and I could see him for myself.

My father brought his hand back idly to his belly. It had gotten big, straining against a ragged HappyFoods polo. Once he'd been a trim executive, wearing moccasins with those little tassels even on the weekend, but he'd lost the job around the time of the divorce and was now "consulting." I wasn't sure what that was, but figured in this case it was a lie unemployed people said to cover their butts. Whatever it was, it didn't pay enough for him to send

Mom alimony anymore. Or keep the house, apparently. He scratched a meaty finger through the salt-and-pepper growth on his cheeks. *You're seeing me for the first time in ages,* I thought. *You might have shaved.* But who'd have thought I cared?

The first thing I noticed when we pulled in was the Realtor sign at the end of the driveway, FORECLOSURE slotted into the top. But otherwise, it still looked like the house I'd grown up in.

My father had bought the house in the middle of the flush HappyFoods years, and it was something special to see. The driveway was ridiculously long and covered in seashells trucked in from some faraway country. Our house was small, but shady and modern and full of glass and chrome, reflecting green because of the mossy trees all around it. It looked impressive, I have to say. Impressive had always been smack in the middle of my father's skill set.

I followed him in. With the personal stuff boxed away, it looked like a fancy boutique hotel. White wall-to-wall carpeting, shiny black wallpaper, a row of black stools at a white counter leading out to an infinity pool with Buddha serenely presiding over the hot tub at the end — a statue my father had brought back from one of his Indonesia trips. Jazz piped through the walls and a frosted-glass chess set weighted the coffee table, frozen one move in.

Dad got a phone call as soon as we went in — I guess he'd managed to pay the landline bill — so I went alone up to my old room to unpack my duffel. Shivering in the air conditioning, I suddenly felt desperate to be back home in Oregon. I unzipped the duffel and dumped everything onto the bed. That was the thing about traveling: Everything had to come out, so anything could. Sifting through my belongings, I realized I'd forgotten to pack a spare shirt. But I found an old oxford of mine hanging in the back of the closet and managed to get it buttoned over my chest. It was good the shirt was there: I'd flown wearing a football tee, and it was starting to smell a little rank.

None of the stuff from my childhood remained in the room. No ruined mobile, no big blue stuffed elephant, no poster of Raja in my arms. Where my dresser had been there was now a table with a sleek little espresso maker. Who knew who that was for — certainly not me. The only evidence of my history in there was a silver scar on the black window frame where it had bent when Raja ripped it off the wall.

Flashes of that evening came to me. Raja hysterically upset at the sight of my blood, my father wrestling him into his arms, his little orangutan head over his shoulder, signing *I'm sorry I'm sorry* while my father carted him off to lock him in the garage. He was left in there while I was in the hospital, and for a week after I was back.

They operated right away, but couldn't reattach the finger because it was . . . gone. So they took off what remained of it.

Apparently while I was coming around I kept asking the nurse whether Raja was okay. From the way I talked about him, she'd assumed Raja was human. "He's fine, don't worry," the nurse had said. "I'm sure your parents are taking good care of your brother." I remember at one point waking up from a hospital-room nap and hearing my parents talking in the hallway. At first I couldn't understand what my mom meant — she just kept saying that they should have the vet take care of it once and for all. That if it was my safety or an animal's, the choice was clear. My father said no way, no way would they do that to Raja.

At that moment, he was my favorite.

He knew that it would have broken me if they'd killed Raja in my name. Even though it was hard to say that I didn't feel broken now all the same, what with Raja locked away.

•   •   •

As I walked back downstairs, I peeked into my father's workshop to see if he was there. He was usually halfway through building a bunch of stuff. Now, though, all the workshop had in it were cardboard moving boxes. Everything had been cleared out, and clumps of dust and scraps of paper were the only things not in boxes. The carpet still had square indents in it, as if the furniture hadn't been sold but turned invisible instead.

When I got to the kitchen, I found Dad standing in front of the oven, reading the back of a box of pizza bagels. It was a little frosty — for all I knew, Mom had purchased that very box two years ago. My father wasn't really the eat-at-home type. When he saw me, he shook the box in the air, like he expected me to leap for joy. I didn't, but I did realize I was ravenous.

"Everything in the house looks ready to go," I said.

"Yeah," my father replied. "Your things are packed away in your old bedroom closet. You should look through. A guy's coming by next week to make a bid for everything that's left. That stuff can't still be here when the new owners move in, of course."

"I don't know what I'd do with everything," I said, "so I guess it's fine if you just sell it."

"Sweet," my father said. "So. You going out back to say hi to Raja?" He kept a taut smile, but his posture went stiff. I imagined the pizza bagels growing warm and wet in their waxy corner of the box.

I got a can of soda out of the fridge, and debated bringing a second one for Raja. He liked anything small and bright, that looked like a piece of fruit. The soda inside would be a bonus. But I left both cans in the fridge. Who knew what he'd do with one — maybe chuck it at my head. He was bound to be pissed. Justifiably.

I walked outside. *This isn't your fault*, my mother's voice said in my head, as it had so many times before. *You know that, right?*

It sort of made me want to cry and sort of made me mad. I wanted her to be right, but everything also definitely *did* feel like my fault.

I headed along the stone trail that passed into the dense backyard. Back during the wealthy years, my father had paid for someone to landscape it. Beautiful urns in vinyl rock, frozen gods and goddesses, plastic satyrs with flutes at their lips. The path twisted past what used to be the rose garden, a delicate trellis with flowering vines crawling in reds and yellows and oranges. Raja adored bright colors, and would have loved picking those roses off one by one and chowing down on their petals. He had done exactly that, in fact, back when he'd had access to them. Now it was a wall of kudzu.

Next along the path was the koi pond. I was surprised to find that some were still alive, fat, wavy fishblobs barely distinct from one another in the murky water. When I was a kid, it had been a natural pond with fish-colored fish. In winter a family of ducks would arrive, which my mom and I would go feed each morning. I'd always try to aim the bread at the smallest birds. I remembered how important it was to me that the littlest ones got fed. After my father had tiled the pond with imported Italian stone and filled it with these bizarre hyper-color fish, the ducks stopped returning.

At the far side of the koi pond, shaded by an old Georgia tree and draped in lichen, I expected to see the chain-link enclosure where Raja had last been. But instead, there was only a camping trailer. The windows must have been broken at some point, and were replaced with nailed-on plywood. The door had a bar across it, with a heavy padlock. The whole thing wasn't more than ten or twelve feet long, and was almost completely sealed off from the world.

Something was thumping the wall. The creature doing it was incredibly strong: The trailer groaned and shuddered.

My ribs turned into heavy bands, pressing my lungs so flat that it became hard to breathe.

My knees hit the soil, and all I could see were my cupped hands and a triangle of grass.

From beyond where I could make myself see, the thumping continued.

My telltale heart, the one I'd left behind.

FOUR

When my parents brought me back from the hospital after Raja bit off my finger, I found out that in order to prevent animal services from coming to our house and putting Raja down, my father had asked Mom to lie to the staff, to say a stray dog had wandered into our yard and attacked me.

For a while, my parents kept Raja in the garage while Mom hit the phones, hoping to find somewhere to put him. She tried every zoo she could, but none of them was willing to take an ex-pet. They didn't have enough space, and apparently former pets were no good at playing nice with other apes. The ape sanctuaries they found were all overstuffed, too, because of the hundreds of primates that get retired from medical testing with nowhere else to go. So the only options were to have Raja stay with us or to put him to sleep.

I never blamed Raja for what happened to my finger, not for one moment. He loved me, and it had made him desperate. He hadn't meant to hurt me. Finally, I convinced my parents that it was cruel to keep Raja in the garage any longer. As soon as I opened the door, Raja climbed up my body and hugged himself tight to me, signing *I'm sorry* over and over. I hadn't cried during the finger incident, even when the painkillers wore off and my phantom finger had started its fiery throbbing, but I cried with relief to have him in my arms again.

For a week or two, everything was fine. Well, the level of fine you get used to when you're living with an ape. Sure, Raja would cause huge messes, but it was always because he was an orangutan. He'd get scared by a garbage truck outside and try to climb a bookcase and send it crashing into the TV. He'd see if the vacuum cleaner would fit in the dishwasher. (It didn't. It definitely didn't.) As he got bigger, though, he'd defiantly pee or poop on the carpets if Mom yelled at him — so often that we had to rip them all out. He demolished our kitchen stools, one by one, so he could examine the stuffing. Things like that.

It was clear Raja couldn't live in the house anymore. My father and I took a road trip over one winter break so we could visit a couple of primate sanctuaries in Florida. We took notes on what was best about their enclosures. What we came up with was basically a big dome of wire fencing, with a small door for humans to get in and out, and a couple of truck tires hung from the ceiling to play on. Raja would be alone during the day, but I'd hang out with him as soon as I came home. Or, that was the plan.

The problem was that Raja was an amazing escape artist. He was always finding new ways to get free, usually in the hour after I'd left for school in the morning. He'd jimmy the lock, or remove the door from its hinges, or, once he was his adult size, bend the wire. I got it — he'd become lonely and did whatever he could to make the bad feeling go away. Could I blame him?

Mom was generally tense those days, but after one escape that involved mud and an heirloom tablecloth she got especially angry. My parents sent me to my room, but I waited in the hallway and listened. My father said he'd done his best and what more could we ask of him? Mom asked him what *that* meant, and somehow by the end of the fight they'd given up on the enclosure out back and Raja was back to sleeping in my bed. But then the next week Raja toppled the grandfather clock when he took the stairs too fast, almost knocking out Mom, and suddenly specialists were coming in to strengthen the fence. They were only able to do it by shrinking it into a cage, lowering the roof and inserting steel posts. Even that was only barely enough to keep Raja contained. By the time my mom moved me and her out, he was spending his days working diligently on a hole in the fencing, slowly making it bigger and bigger.

He didn't want to cause trouble, but he also didn't want to be alone. Up through the very last day I saw him, he'd sign *I'm sorry* the moment he saw me approach his enclosure. I didn't know how to tell him there was nothing for him to be sorry for.

I'd thought his old reinforced enclosure was small, but this new trailer was half its size. It rocked and rocked. One wall shuddered, the floor thumped with two heavy steps, then the opposite wall shuddered. I stared at the tiny shaking structure, horrified to see my old life through my new life's eyes.

It's not your fault, my mom said again in my head.

Sure, anything that happened to Raja wasn't my fault when I was ten. But wasn't it my fault when I was twelve, fourteen, sixteen, and he was living in a tiny space? Wasn't it my fault for ignoring this last week? Wasn't it my fault for ignoring it today?

The banging stopped. I could hear creaking right on the other side of the padlocked door, and knew Raja was listening. For a moment all was still. Then the door rattled. It had a slider at the bottom for passing food through, like in a prison cell. After it raised, out emerged an orange-brown hand, palm up and fingers outstretched. Ready to touch.

Did he know it was me?

Raja's fingers waved.

Raja. You're right here.

Hesitantly I touched a fingertip to his. His hand jerked out of sight and he banged on the door, kicking it so hard it shook. I stepped back.

Are you mad? Do you know it's me?

The shaking continued. It wasn't like Raja to do this. But how well did I know Raja anymore?

The pounding slowed and stopped, and eventually Raja's arms reemerged. He stretched them along the ground, palms up. I imagined what he looked like inside the trailer, head crooked against the metal so he could reach as far as possible. His hair was soft, long and orange, the skin of his arms mushroom-white wherever it parted. He must not have been in the sun in ages. I used to be able to hold those hands entirely within mine, but they were so large now. They could hold mine. Or they could grasp around my neck and give me what I deserved.

I reached out again — and this time he snatched and pulled.

I was caught off balance. Even when he was little, Raja was stronger than a person; if he wanted something, he got it. And now he was fully grown. I fell to my stomach and slid through the grass, my arm disappearing up to the elbow into the trailer.

"Raja!" I called out. "Stop!"

I pulled back as hard as I could, but it was no use. Then I felt what Raja was doing. He wasn't going to tear my arm off. He wasn't going to bite into it. He was running his fingers over my skin, picking through my sparse arm hair. Investigating.

Then . . .

Tickling?

Was it a game? Did he realize who he was playing it with?

When his grip loosened, I pulled my arm back. There was only one way to know for sure.

"I'm going to open the door," I told him. When I overturned a frog statue nearby, I was relieved to find no one had moved the hidden key — it was the same padlock as the old enclosure. I wiped the key clean and fitted it in. As I did, the door groaned on its hinges; Raja must have climbed up it. For a moment, all was still. I held the key in the lock and took a deep breath, ready and entirely unready at the same time.

"It's me, Raja!" I told him.

I turned the key and removed the lock, careful not to make too much noise. I suddenly imagined Raja busting out and bolting for the property fence. What would I do if that happened? I faltered, but it was too late; the lock was already off.

The trailer remained still. I slid the steel door open. It had been used so rarely that clods of rust fell from its casters and into the dirt. I had to muscle it most of the way, the door clanking off its groove.

I couldn't see Raja at first. Then, leaning in, I spotted a huddled form at the far corner of the trailer, facing away from the sudden light. I cautiously stepped inside, the vinyl floor creaking and bending under my feet.

"Raja?" I said.

He faced away from me, rocking.

There was nothing in the trailer except for him. Once he'd destroyed the toys I'd left behind, no more must have come. The familiar weight inside me closed down tight. How could I not have sent more? He had nothing in here for comfort. He had only his rocking. He was his only company.

"Raja?" I whispered. "Can you hear me?"

He continued to rock, face buried between his knees.

It smelled like a cross between grandma's basement and a gas station bathroom where truckers missed the toilet. The stench was strong enough to make my eyes water.

While I watched, Raja's rocking slowed and stilled. He twisted so he could look at me, visoring his eyes against the sunlight. With his fingers straight against his forehead, he looked like he was searching for something far beyond the door. I could tell he was having trouble focusing his eyes — and why wouldn't he, when he'd had nothing to see for so long?

I kneeled on the groaning floor, skeeved out by its sliminess but wanting to get as near as possible to Raja's level. Raja stared over his shoulder. Though he was looking in my direction, his face had no reaction on it at all. He put his head down and started rocking again.

I don't know what I'd been expecting. Raja wasn't like a dog who'd been left alone and got all sloppy and happy to see his master when he returned. He was like a *person* who'd been left alone. He was mad. He was depressed.

I made our *I'm sorry* gesture. He watched me passionlessly, then buried his head between his knees and began to rock again. The skin at the back of my neck pricked — there was something in his lap that I couldn't recognize.

I heard my father's steps outside. Raja lifted his head, and for the first time his face showed some excitement.

"Pizza bagels for good orangutans!" my father called from the lawn.

Raja's expression didn't change, but he did get to his feet and shuffle toward me and the exit.

He'd been much smaller than me when we'd left. But now . . . he had to be one hundred pounds. We'd both become a new size. He was wide in the shoulders and fat in the belly, matted orange hair making him look even bigger. My heart seized when I saw him, and for a crazy moment I thought, *Raja is already gone.* Then he took a step toward me and fear shot me out of the trailer.

I hovered a few feet away while my father approached. He set a broad plastic platter down in the dirt, orange oil glistening on top of the pizza bagels, pooling between hot-pink cubes of meat. Raja lumbered out of the trailer, eyes streaming tears in the daylight. He held steady, blinking rapidly, then his eyes began to focus and move, gliding past me to rest on my father and the food. He wrist-walked over, plunked down, and dug in with one hand. Only a moment later, a great fistful of bagels had disappeared into his mouth. He made a surprised gasp, and I imagined the cheese burning the roof of his mouth. Then, bagel bits tumbling into the grass on either side, Raja picked up the plate with the remaining food.

Finally I saw what he was dragging through the dirt in his other hand: a blue stuffed elephant. *My* blue stuffed elephant. Or at least the one that had once been mine.

As if sensing my attention on his companion, Raja pulled it into his lap and hunched over, shielding the toy from view. Then, ably leveling the tray with the other hand like a waiter in a fancy restaurant, Raja made his way back into the trailer.

I crept over and peered in. Raja was in his corner again, wolfing down pizza bagels. When he saw me looking, he turned his back so I couldn't watch him.

"On a day like today," my father said from outside, "that good boy deserves some special food."

"He does," I croaked. "He's such a good boy. Aren't you, Raj?"

I looked at him while he ate. "Man. He's gotten so big . . ."

"I know." My father groaned, a smile spreading and making his face handsome again as he fired up the charm machine. "I'm like the divorced dad who spoils his kid with cake. Anyway — there's another batch cooking in the kitchen. How 'bout you and I go in and polish them off?"

I shook my head. "I want to spend some more time with him."

My father nodded. "Suit yourself. Just be careful — if there's a wrestling match, you're going to lose."

"Got it," I said, pretty sure he was kidding.

As my father returned to the house, I watched Raja eat. His hair had gotten long, but his shoulders had grown bald; the fringe scooped low, like an evening gown. He still looked young, kind of, but he no longer looked cute. Like me, I guess — we were both technically the size of adults.

I watched through the trailer's doorway as he finished the bagels without ever looking at me, licked the dull blue plastic platter clean, and then nudged it with a finger so it rotated. Once he'd grown bored of that, he crossed his arms and hunkered down.

I eased into the trailer and hunched in the opposite corner, mimicking his position. Slowly edging into his line of sight, I signed *I'm sorry* once more. I pointed at the stuffed animal and made a curving motion in front of my nose, our sign for the elephant.

He stared at me dully, ran his arm clumsily over his strained eyes. Then, slowly and deliberately, he hocked up some phlegm.

"*Raja,*" I warned.

He let it fly. Raja had always been able to aim his hockers precisely where he wanted them to go. At least he'd spared my face and gone for the base of my neck instead; I could feel orangutan goober on my skin, draining into my shirt.

To be honest, it felt good to be spat on. It felt like the truth.

Raja wrist-walked so he was right against the wall, stooping and staring into the crack where it joined the floor. He started rocking again.

"Raja, I'm sorry," I said.

He ignored me. There was no mistaking that he wanted to be left alone.

So I gave him what he wanted. Stepping out of the trailer, I walked as far as the koi pond. Dazed, I watched the hardy fish-blobs sludge along. I wished I could feed the ducks that had once been there, aiming my bread for the smallest ones like I'd done before. I turned so I was leaning my back against the prefab bridge railing, and stared at the trailer.

"Raja!" I called out. Despite being sixteen, I hoped for magic, that this time Raja would emerge as the baby ape I'd known.

A moment later I saw movement at the door, and my pulse quickened. When he stepped into the daylight, though, Raja ignored me and moved right for an empty mulch bag. He held the woven nylon fabric to his cheek and met my eyes, as if to make sure I got the message that he preferred a dirty old bag to me. Then he ambled back into the trailer, the sack in his hand. Remembering old games of tug-of-war, I stepped toward him.

There was a grinding sound, and the door shuddered. Effortlessly, Raja slid it closed.

He'd shut me out.

I padlocked the trailer door, returned the key to its hiding place, and picked my way back to the house. I'd hoped my father might be waiting for me in the kitchen, but he was nowhere to be seen.

I went back to my room and stood in the center of the feature-less gleam, holding my own arm like I was something made of rundown clockwork. Without quite knowing what I was doing, I pulled back the coverlet and got in. I pulled it over my head and put my head on the pillow, but it slipped right out from under my head, like it was oiled.

When I turned over, the billion-thread-count sateen-something sheets made me slide right out of the bed. Actually, it was more unpleasant than sliding out. The bed sort of spat me onto the rug, like a watermelon seed.

I wanted to escape everything, but all the same I couldn't stay in my old room. It wasn't where I'd lived — it was where my younger self had lived, and the longer I sat there doing nothing, the more outraged that old me got. He knew what to do — if Raja was depressed, the young me would try to cheer him up. If Raja was standoffish, the young me would make him pay attention. The young me wouldn't shut his eyes because someone said shutting your eyes made life easier.

Go out back. Find a ball or something. See if you can get him to play.

Whatever was coming down the road, playing right now would make Raja feel better. It was simple, and true.

There was a small shed out back, where there used to be a croquet set. No one had probably touched it in years, but I could dust it off and see if Raja would play. The red striped ball would be his favorite.

I'd only just brushed the spiders away and eased open the shed door when I heard a large vehicle crunching the seashells of my father's driveway.

I knew Raja would be leaving, of course. But I'd thought the zoo people were coming later. Not now. Not yet.

They were here to take Raja away.

I crept around to the far side of the shed so I could see the truck better. It paused at the start of the driveway and then rolled intently toward the house, crushing imported seashells all the way.

My reasoning mind said that everything was fine, but my animal gut said this didn't feel right. Nothing about this felt right.

When the truck came more fully into view, my worry grew. It was pulling a trailer. Nothing about that was too surprising, except that the trailer was a rented U-Haul. Maybe animal transfers happened infrequently enough that this zoo didn't have a trailer of its own, and rented one each time.

Maybe that was it.

Once the truck had crunched to a stop, the two men in the cab kept it idling while they stared at the house. Like they were casing it. Then they got out, one after the other, each stubbing a cigarette against the truck's hood and dropping the butt into the shells. *Raja shouldn't be around secondhand smoke,* I thought — as if that was the worry that had set my heart skipping. But that was the way my heart had become, a stream curving to find the nearest downward path.

I crept around the side of the house so I'd have a better view of the men. One wasn't much older than me, hangover-lean body drowning in an oversize Budweiser T-shirt, cap balled in his fist, his expression buckled-down. The other looked like he could have been the younger guy's father, same spindly legs but with a shirt-stretching paunch, faded cap looser on his balding head. I couldn't see the fronts, but figured their hats had a zoo insignia on them. At least I hoped they did.

Where is my father sending Raja? He'd been cagey about it on the phone, and I'd let him get away with telling me he'd explain it later. But time had collapsed. I'd plummeted right into *later*.

The younger guy rang the doorbell and peered through the stained glass at the side, the way Raja had done years before when he'd been sick and fighting for my company. Eventually it opened, and I heard my father say hello.

"We're here for your chimp," the older guy said.

Orangutan, I mouthed. Sweat dotted my brow, even as my flesh chilled.

My father must have invited them in, because they entered the house and the door closed.

I eased forward so I could examine the truck. It had West Virginia plates. I tried to think of any zoos in West Virginia. Just because I didn't know of any zoos in West Virginia didn't mean there weren't any . . . right?

On reflex I already had my phone out and searched *West Virginia + orangutan*. There was only one kind of link that came up on the first page, and it wasn't good.

The only orangutans I could find mentioned at all in West Virginia were in a research center near Charleston. The center itself didn't have a website, but an image came up of a small windowless cinderblock building. Its monkeys and chimps and orangutans were mentioned as footnotes in PDFs of academic articles published through medical schools. Studies on hepatitis, vaccines, HIV. Another link was a Humane Society alert, only a paragraph long and years old, about apes crammed into tiny cages far below ground, without access to sunlight or room to walk, brought out only to be injected or cut up and then put right back. Apparently using apes for research was being phased out in the United States, but there were a few remaining test subjects.

My heart pounded, and the sky turned too bright. This was where my father was sending Raja? *Medical testing?* It sounded impossible, but at the same time it felt true. When logic began to match belief, my knees turned liquid.

Part of me wanted to find my father right away and ask him what was going on.

But another part of me knew that would be a mistake. He'd say he was stuck. That he was out of money and had to sell the house and didn't have any other options.

My body jolted to life. All the long-building muddiness in my mind vanished. Because I *knew* what to do.

I had to break Raja out of there. I'd put him in the car. And we'd leave.

I didn't have much time. If I wasted another minute, Raja would be stuck in some underground cage forever.

His trailer was in sight. I dropped into a crouch behind a bush. My mother's warning voice ran a tight loop around my thoughts. *He bit off your finger, John. He's strong. There's a reason apes don't wander around free.*

She'd be furious at me for doing this. And so would my father.

But I had to put thoughts of them aside. For once, I had to put them out of my mind entirely. Because this was for Raja.

I stole across the grass toward his trailer. The door was ajar.

"Oh, no," I said as I squeaked across the plastic koi-pond bridge. It was clear to me what'd happened: They'd already gone in for him.

As I got closer, though, the story changed.

A strand of plastic snaked out of the food slot. It had a loop tied at one end, which was snagged around the nose of the frog statue. The frog was on its side in the dirt, its muddy unfinished plaster bottom up to the sun. The key beneath was gone.

Gingerly, I crept to the trailer door. It was empty inside. Even the stuffed elephant was gone.

I crouched over the length of nylon, dumbfounded. It was from the landscaping bag Raja had taken into the trailer with him after he'd eaten his pizza bagels. He'd picked apart the nylon until he had a thread, then he'd made a loop which he'd tossed until it snagged the statue. I examined the mussed dirt in front of the trailer. The statue must have been just barely within reach. For all these months, it had been too far for him to grip with his fingers and knock over. Until he'd had the right tool.

Once he'd gotten the statue over, he must have used the same loop to fish the key. Then he'd opened the lock. By doing it all in secret, rather than running away in front of us, he'd gotten himself a head start. He'd been plotting and planning this whole time. It was like he sensed a storm was coming, knew when his life had gotten rotten enough that it was time to abandon it and strike out on his own.

Whatever the reason, Raja had escaped.

PART TWO

ALL PITY CHOKED WITH CUSTOM OF FELL
DEEDS.

— WILLIAM SHAKESPEARE, *JULIUS CAESAR,*
ACT 3, SCENE 1

Back when he lived in the wild, his view was almost always the same: bristly orange hair, and lots of it.

Most of his early days were spent face-planted into his mother's belly. All he needed was her warmth, the sour sweetness of her breast, the breezes on his back as she carried him through the trees.

As the days passed, he started turning his head. His choices were left and right, left and right. Watch. Mother. This green-yellow spiny fruit was no good. This green-brown spiny fruit was delicious. His mother sank her sharp front teeth into it, jawed open the flesh so it made the same crack as a breaking branch. A stray chunk of that fruit was his first piece of solid food. He gummed it, happy to do anything his mother had done. School was imitation.

At night she made a nest high in the trees, battening branches to form a soft, springy layer of green. There were no boars or tigers up in the treetops. As the sun set, he would wander to the edge of a branch then back, toddling sixty feet above the ground, until his mother's arm suddenly filled his view and he was scooped to her belly. That moment of dizzying open space was enough adventure for the day. He pressed himself deep into her side.

Come morning, there was no time for exploration. His only job as they moved through the trees was to feed and to hold on. His fingers and toes clutched naturally, so staying close to his mother took no work at all. It was letting go that required muscle.

FIVE

I stared into the treetops, listening for crashing branches, the surest sign Raja was in motion. But I heard nothing but the ever-present Georgia cicadas and the burble of the koi pond's artificial waterfall. Either Raja was hiding or he was long gone. He could have left anytime in the last half hour, which meant he might be a mile away by now. I imagined him wandering into an intersection, cars screeching and swerving. Children fleeing, police swarming, helicopters hovering. Raja pacing, bewildered, signing *I'm sorry* over and over as they began to shoot. The back of my neck prickled with horror.

Breaking out was one thing. Survival in the human world was another. He needed me more than ever.

I paced this way and that, staring into the trees. When I heard the back door open, I skirted around the trailer so it blocked me from view. I heard my father and the men approach from the house. "... hosed it down. Meals at eight and three," my father was saying. "Then he doesn't eat again until morning, which is when he likes apples. Give him five apples each breakfast and he'll be as happy as a clam. He'll put them in a row, rearrange them, and then eat them throughout the morning."

The men grunted a response as they trooped closer.

"What the . . . ?" my father said as the trailer came into view.

As silently as possible, I passed into the greenery and ducked behind a tree. I had to figure out a next step. The property went back for about a quarter mile. Then it was county roads on two sides and school fields at the back. Assuming Raja was on the move away from the house, he was going to hit either road or schoolyard eventually. Since it was Sunday, at least there wouldn't be kids out at recess.

As I picked my way through the backyard, I kept thinking about Raja somewhere off in these woods, scared and lost. When it started throbbing I thought, too, about my missing finger. The landscaping soon ended, and dense Georgia scrub closed in. Dry palms and red pines, sharp grasses, the occasional rabbit plunging to safety through the blades. I scanned above and to the sides, pausing from time to time to see if I could detect any sign of Raja. Nothing.

I came to the old wooden fence that marked the far border of the property. It wasn't tall, and plenty of trees overhung it — Raja would have had no trouble passing over and out.

I tried to get back into his mind-set, to figure out what he'd most likely have done. He'd spent almost his whole life on my father's property, and these few hundred yards of backyard were the only home he knew. The most likely thing was that he *wouldn't* run away, I realized: He might have hidden himself high in the trees until the strange men — and I, since obviously he didn't trust me, either — were gone. Stillness had always been his favorite defense.

I worked my way down the side of the property, scanning the treetops. I didn't call out to Raja, as I once would have. While it might have brought him running before, I suspected my voice would do the opposite now.

Still nothing.

If he wasn't in the backyard, he was off on the roads somewhere.

Carefully, I made my way back into the house and sifted through the clay dish by the front door until I had my father's car keys in hand. When I went back outside, I saw the two men were out front, caps shading their expressions. The older one gave a small smile as he caught sight of me.

"Is it normal," he asked, "that your monkey be wandering off like this?"

"No," I said, "it's not normal. I bet Raja's nearby. I'm going to drive around and see if I can track him down. Be back in a minute."

"You hurry," the guy said. "Next step is calling animal control for help, and that's not good for your guy."

Finally, I was close enough to read the cap. It said *FriendlyLand*.

"See you . . . in a minute," I stammered. Seeing that stitched name had thrown me. FriendlyLand sure sounded like a zoo. Maybe my father hadn't been lying after all.

But that didn't change the fact that I had to find Raja before the authorities did.

I walked past my father's pickup and to his car, a little four-door that my mom had once used to drive me to school. I fumbled with the keys, but it was unlocked. When I got in and shut the door, I was instantly hot in the hush, a baby in an incubator. I hadn't been in this car in two years; it smelled like my history.

Before turning on the ignition, I stared through the windshield at the dinged-up trailer with the West Virginia plates. This determination to do *something* to help Raja, this drive that felt so much like anger — and probably *was* anger if only I could get it better into view — had nowhere to go. Even if I found Raja, would I really bring him back to these men? Even if I looked up FriendlyLand and found it was the worst place on Earth, what better option did Raja have?

"What do I do?" I said out loud, rolling my forehead against the steering wheel.

I heard a kiss-squeak in response.

Slowly, I looked into the backseat. Raja was sitting politely, legs crossed neatly beneath him, seat belt on and buckled. He thumbed the belt in irritation, as if to ask what was taking so long. He kiss-squeaked again and sighed. *You poop,* he signed, avoiding my eyes, then gestured vaguely at the world outside. He began to rock himself. The stuffed elephant was politely sitting on the seat beside him, also buckled in.

Raja was ready to go. And he was ready for me to take him.

"Raja," I said, staring at him in the rearview. In the reflection my knitted brows made me look like a parent scolding a kid. Which I guess I pretty much was. "Raja. Look at me."

Sulkily, Raja raised his eyes. He stared into the mirror and stuck his thumb back toward the driveway, his expression calm.

I looked out the rear window. The not-so-friendly men from FriendlyLand were staring over at me.

We needed to get moving.

"What do you think you're doing, Raja?" I asked. At the tone of my voice, Raja finally reacted and looked right into my eyes. His orange hair was mussed, falling over his brow. For a heart-jumping moment his glaze lifted, and he was my Raja again. Then he lowered his head and tugged at the elephant's trunk. He put his feet together so they made a basin, then face-planted into it.

I knew what this meant. "You want to go for *ice cream*?" I asked.

I'd stayed paralyzed for too long. Raja bounced in his seat, tugging at the seat belt and slapping the window. Loudly.

Startled by Raja's sudden intensity, and afraid that the men were going to come over any second, I started the car. At the quiet hum of the engine, Raja grunted and examined his seat belt, unfastening it and clicking it back in. Years before, after a particularly disastrous attempt at a car trip, my mom had decided she'd let go of the gas whenever Raja unplugged his seat belt, until he'd come to believe the car wouldn't move unless he was buckled in and still.

Luckily, he seemed to have remembered the lesson. The last thing I needed was a one-hundred-pound orangutan roaming around a moving vehicle.

If this went like it used to, he'd be making a lot of noise once I started moving. I turned on the radio, which was tuned to some staticky AM nun reciting from the Bible. I didn't have time to change it, so all I did was put the car in reverse and roll along the driveway, scripture blasting. As we neared the men, I started a video on my phone, so it would stay lit, and dropped it on the backseat floor.

Sure enough, Raja leaned over, staring into the screen. Years earlier, he'd once played with my father's laptop, shattered it, and run around the house signing *sorry sorry sorry*. After that, he'd learned he wasn't supposed to touch screens, just look at them.

The men stared at me as I rolled past. I knew how odd it must have seemed, obscure Bible verses vibrating the car's tinted windows. Raja was making sighing sounds of excitement from the backseat while he investigated the video — I could only hope he was keeping out of view.

Once we'd reached the end of the driveway, I backed onto our small county road and drove, keeping my speed slow and constant so Raja wouldn't get too agitated. But I needn't have worried — when I glanced back I saw he was motionless, absorbed in the screen.

As soon as I was around the bend I looked for a place to pull over. Down the road was a long-abandoned gas station, corroded numbers dangling from its sign. Someone had parked an old Caddy with an orange-and-black FOR SALE notice in the front, but otherwise there was nothing around us but rust. I rolled the car to a stop in the crumbled-asphalt parking lot.

"So," I said, turning off the radio. In the backseat, Raja panted in excitement.

Turned out Raja wasn't intimidated by screens anymore. He had the phone in his hands and was licking it. He kept licking even after he'd accidentally pressed the button to make it go dark; Raja must have enjoyed the smooth surface beneath his tongue. The phone would occasionally light up under his fingers, and Raja would gasp, stare at the screen returned from the dead, and start licking again.

I'd have to hope my phone had been designed to withstand orangutan saliva. Cautiously, my phantom finger throbbing, I pulled it out of his fingers and unbuckled Raja's elephant, putting it in his lap in the phone's place. That seemed to work — for now. Raja seemed calm, but I hadn't been around the new him long enough to feel confident about what he'd do.

I did a quick search for FriendlyLand and waited for the results to load. The connection was slow, so the page was appearing line by line, like it was printing. I squinted. "Well, so far I can confirm FriendlyLand definitely exists," I told Raja. "That's a start."

Raja laid his hand on top of the gearshift, palm up. A peace offering. I placed my four-fingered hand over his, and was startled by the strength in his grasp as he easily lifted it to his face, the better to examine the sparse red hairs on the back of my palm. I winced. I was pretty sure that Raja wouldn't intentionally cause me pain, but I remembered, too, the sight of his mouth closing over that hand.

Waiting for Raja to lose interest so I could pull my hand back, I turned off the engine and undid my seat belt while I waited for the screen to load.

The minute I unbuckled, Raja yanked my arm.

There was no way to resist. He wanted me in the backseat, which meant I was going in the backseat. Despite my new football frame, I became the weight of ten-year-old me in his hands. He held me to him, arms tight around my chest. I struggled to see his face, hoping to find friendliness there, or at least playfulness. But Raja looked only serious.

"What are you doing?" I asked him. "It's me. Don't you know it's me?"

While Raja ran his lips up and down my arms, I said his name over and over, hoping to get him to acknowledge that I was John, someone he knew well. The most dangerous thing anyone could be to an ape was a stranger.

Then he was sniffing my ears, my neck. The move was familiar — he was about to do something he'd loved when he was little. A trust exercise. But now that he was bigger, it required more trust than I was ready to give.

But there wasn't any good way to resist. Raja placed his hands on either side of my head and drew it toward his mouth. Before I knew it his jaw had opened wide, and his teeth were around my skull.

I knew Raja wasn't planning on hurting me. But all the same *my head was in an ape's mouth.* My fists clenched, my pinkie and middle fingers poking each other over the empty space of my ring finger. *It's fine,* I told myself. *Stay relaxed. He wants to see if you're willing to let him do this. All you have to do is let him.*

I'd once seen Raja crack a coconut open by biting down on it; the hard shell had simply parted under his canines, milk spraying everywhere. I kept up a smile, even as my stomach tightened. There was nothing I could do; I was at his mercy, and the only way to get to the other side of this test was to let it happen.

His jaws were around the broadest point of my skull now. His teeth were sharp. Sharper than before. My hair was matting inside Raja's mouth.

"Please stop," I gasped.

Raja grunted, causing a line of slobber to drip down my neck. His teeth gripped even tighter. My skull made dentist sounds.

I couldn't stand it anymore. I howled and pressed my hands into Raja's face, my fingers on his chin, in his nostrils.

Raja's canines scraped my scalp — but then I was free. I jumped away and pressed against the backseat door. Raja peered at me, mouth still agape, puzzled by my reaction but with something new on his face: contempt.

I'd failed.

Raja hunched forward, arms on his knees, and studied my expression. It only now seemed to dawn on him that he'd scared me.

For a moment I thought he was going to sign *I'm sorry.* But then he turned against the car door, buried his head, and started rocking himself. He picked up the stuffed elephant where it had fallen to the floor and clutched it to him.

Carefully I maneuvered over the gearshift and back into the front seat. Buckling myself in tight, I stared forward, body shaking. I was too rattled now to have any idea of what to do next.

My phone was dark on the seat. I picked it up and lit it.

The FriendlyLand site looked back at me. Seemed legit. I scrolled down, and as I did Raja turned so his back was fully against the front seat and pressed. It pitched forward, so I was sitting perfectly upright. I struggled to keep my phone in my hand. "Cut it out, Raja."

He relented, and I could look at the screen again. It buzzed, and FriendlyLand disappeared. MOM CALLING. I considered the screen for a moment. I could easily imagine what she would say. *Your father called. This is not your problem. This is not your fault. Let him deal with Raja. Come back to me.*

I opened the glove box, placed the phone inside, and returned my attention to the backseat. Raja was tugging on the elephant's trunk, pressing its head against his, giving the animal a big openmouthed kiss.

As I turned forward I caught a flash of movement through the rear window, the grill of a truck glinting in the distance as it turned onto the roadway. Heading away from us.

The zoo men were leaving.

At first I was relieved, but then I realized I was screwing up.

Raja was family to me, and he'd had my head in his mouth plenty of times before — but this time had felt different. It felt like Raja had been deciding whether to release or punish me. What if he tried that same move on strangers, as a way of getting to know them? I knew, or thought I knew, that Raja wouldn't intentionally harm someone who hadn't harmed him first. But the rest of the world didn't know that — as soon as we left my father's property, he was in danger.

I hated that Raja was going to FriendlyLand, but maybe it was his best chance. It would be better than living in that trailer by himself. He'd probably meet other orangutans in a zoo.

I would have sat and waffled, but the guys with the truck were leaving — if I wanted to catch them, it was now or never. I turned the car on. At the noise of the engine, Raja looked at the steering wheel then at me, mystified. *Why aren't we moving yet?* I lifted my seat belt and pointed to it exaggeratedly. Raja got the message right away. He faced forward, reached behind him, and stretched the seat belt over his fat belly. He forgot to latch it, though, and it hung at his side. He pressed the tab between the seat cushions so it would appear fastened and glanced at me: *Did I do it right?*

I shook my head. Raja tried again, this time managing to get his seat belt clicked in. He leaned over the dirty old elephant, working to get its belt attached, too.

Here I was, putting safety first when I was about to send him away to be imprisoned. What a weird and two-faced thing, my mind. Suddenly furious at myself, I gunned the accelerator, the wheels spinning in the dirt before they gained enough traction to jolt us forward. Raja made a startled squeak and frantically clutched his belt.

The car fishtailed as I pulled into the roadway, but then we were under way. The road was practically empty. As I accelerated toward the disappeared zoo truck, I stole guilty glances at Raja in the rearview mirror. Did he have any idea what was about to happen?

I scanned the road for the truck. The next time I glanced at Raja, his eyes met mine in the mirror. *I'm sorry*, he signed, finally. The gesture was so small that I might easily have missed it.

Sunlight glinted on metal, pulling my attention back to the road. The U-Haul hadn't gotten far; soon enough its painted back panel was in view. Once I was near enough, I honked. When I saw its brake lights blink, I flashed my headlights until the truck pulled over.

I brought my father's car to a stop behind it and lowered the windows as the men got out of the truck's cab. When he saw me, the younger one scowled and spat into the dirt.

"What do you want?" the older one asked.

"It's okay," I said. "I found Raja. He's in the backseat."

The older guy broke into a smile and nodded to the younger. "He's got 'im."

"Yeah, I heard," the younger one said, still scowling. "They're lucky we're still here." He flipped a lever on the back of the U-Haul and raised the gate.

Raja stared at me, making his nervous kiss-squeaks while I got out, closed the door, and approached the older guy. "Raja is the best orangutan in the world," I said. "You guys take good care of your animals, right?"

The younger guy snorted at that.

The older one went to the back window and cupped his hands against the glass so he could see Raja, still buckled into his seat. "It's a zoo, so they have to take care of their stuff," he said.

"Don't you work for them?"

The guy shook his head. "Nah, they contract out. We just have to get this guy there. Today." He pointedly tapped the spot on his wrist where a watch would be.

"Okay," I said, my heart thumping. The situation felt wrong. But how *could* it feel right, when I was handing Raja over to strangers? "So what do we do next?"

"You step back and let us take care of it," he said. "Is the car unlocked?"

"Yeah," I said as the men took up positions at the back doors. Through the tinted window I saw Raja looking between the two of them, the elephant gripped tight in his lap. His mouth opened in an anxious yawn, and I knew he was making his confused squeaks.

The men tensed, then one signaled to the other and they both dropped into a crouch, like they were beginning some special ops mission. The older guy opened the car door and sprang backward, ready for combat — but as soon as the door was open, Raja unbuckled his belt and elegantly stepped out, like he was using a valet service. The elephant still clutched tight to him, he looked at me, then held his hand out to the older guy. To be stroked. Comforted.

The man stepped back nervously, pointing to the open trailer. "Go in there!"

Raja held still, baffled. *Really?* I thought. *This was their big plan for getting him in there? Asking? I'd be confused, too, if I were Raja.*

I sat on the lip of the trailer, trying to project calmness despite my storming heart. *Come here*, I signed.

After a long reappraisal of the situation, Raja cautiously wrist-walked over. Easily pulling his large body up into the trailer to sit beside me, he placed the dirty old elephant in my lap, I guessed because he figured I might enjoy a turn with it. Raja rocked his legs in the open space, like a kid at a picnic bench. I looked down at the elephant gift. I felt sick.

The younger guy stepped toward us, but I put up a hand to stop him. "Could you give us a minute?" I said. "Raja needs a little time to get used to the trailer."

The guy stopped, and I returned my attention to Raja. Strangely enough, some part of me was enjoying the moment. Me and my Raja enjoying the fresh air, shoulder to shoulder. This felt like a better good-bye, at least, then our sulky time at the backyard trailer. Raja looked at me, then down at the elephant. I gave it a squeeze, and he looked away, satisfied that I cared about his companion, too. He seemed almost bored, like he thought this moment might go on forever. My gut fell away. It would take all my concentration not to betray the boiling sickness inside me.

It's for the best, my mother's voice assured me.

There's nothing else we can do, my father insisted.

Inside the U-Haul, a large plywood box was strapped to the floor. It was probably eight feet on each side, banded with two-by-fours and stabbed through with airholes. It looked like a giant wooden cheese grater.

"He needs to go in there?" I asked. The zoo guys nodded.

Sighing, I leaned back and placed the elephant in the crate. Raja looked at me and rolled onto his side. Careful not to let any part of his body touch the mysterious plywood, he hooked the elephant with his long forefinger and returned it to me. I looked down at the oily, dirty fabric and gave it another hug, for Raja's sake. Then I tossed the elephant farther, so it hit the back wall of the crate. Raja grunted in pleasure, sensing we'd happened upon a game. He rolled to the edge, and then gingerly placed a foot inside. Then he got down onto his belly and stretched. He managed to reach the elephant, and pulled it in tight to embrace it. He tossed the elephant to me and waited for me to return it, his arms outstretched.

There's nothing else I can do, I thought. I was about to be a junior in high school. My mother and I lived in a small apartment and didn't have much money.

So I did the wrong thing, because there was no right one. Feeling every part the villain, I grasped the crate's hinged plywood door and swung it. Raja's foot was still outside, so I shoved it at the last moment so his leg was entirely inside just as the door slammed. He whirled, and his surprised eyes were the last thing I saw. While I heard Raja scurry, I pressed all my weight against the door, legs and arms straining. "How does it lock?" I cried as I heard Raja grunt and squeak. Good thing I'd had so many football workouts — if I'd been any lighter or weaker he would already have gotten out. "Hurry!"

With a thump, the younger guy was in the trailer and beside me. He fit a padlock over a hook bolted into the plywood and snapped it shut.

The door shuddered under my body as Raja hurled himself against it, crying.

Because he wanted to be with me. Or not. Maybe I didn't matter to him anymore. Maybe he just wanted to be free.

I staggered out of the trailer as the door continued to pound, Raja streaming angry kiss-squeaks. I missed my footing and fell to the side of the road, the stuffed elephant tumbling to the dirt alongside me. I gasped and stared, the wind knocked out of me.

As I got myself to my feet, the trailer's grate rolled closed behind me. My head hung low; I couldn't manage to lift it.

The older guy was on his cell phone. "Yep, we've got it," I heard him say.

I wanted to say, *Take good care of him, please,* but when I opened my mouth what came out instead was, "I want to follow along behind."

When the two guys gawked at me, I stammered forward. "I'll call my father and let him know that I'm coming to help Raja settle in at FriendlyLand."

The older zoo guy closed his phone, shaking his head. "Absolutely not. That's very clear in the contract. You know that."

Of course I didn't know that. My father was the only one who knew everything about everything.

Never again, I found myself promising.

Raja was still crying inside the U-Haul trailer. "Please," I said.

"No," the man snapped. Though the younger one kept scoffing at me, the older one's face softened. "It's better for everyone this way, trust me. You've said your good-byes."

The younger guy was already at the truck's door. "We can still make it before dark if we head out now, Dad," he said.

They're going to a zoo, I told myself, *and zoos are good places.* I wanted to say something to these guys, to do anything if it meant I wouldn't be standing there like a tool anymore. But to say anything more I'd have to get my head to lift, and I hated myself too much for even that. I signed *I'm sorry.* But of course the trailer door was shut now, so Raja had no idea what I was trying to say.

The truck's engine rumbled, and the trailer pulled away. I watched it go, stunned.

You did this, I scolded myself. *You let this happen.*

Sweat had soaked my shirt, ran from the pits down my arms. The heat radiating up from the pavement made me dizzy, even though the perspiration on my brow was chill. I bent over, hands on my knees. I could feel the cords of my neck stand out, straining. Getting ready to start my stomach, at least, back at zero.

I heaved in air, and it sounded like a sob. Then it was a sob. Something huge and dark and terrible came out of me, something that had been tamped down for so long that it had become even more huge and dark and terrible.

One last sob came out of me, then all was quiet.

There, slumped in the dirt, was Raja's old blue elephant.

I felt unsteady as I walked up to my father's front door. Would he be furious at me for rushing away, or relieved that I'd found Raja? He wasn't either. Instead, he had this bland expression on his face, like we were about to discuss the news in a foreign country.

"The zoo men called," he said when I dropped his car keys into the dish by the door. "They told me you found Raja."

I nodded numbly.

"Well, I guess that's that," he said, raising his phone to his ear and turning toward his office.

I shambled upstairs. The moment I was in my room I lay flat on the fancy-slippery bed, hands over my face. But the tears had all been used up. I only cried something like once every two years. Maybe I was out of crying shape, like it was the off-season for tears.

I'd dropped the stuffed elephant to the floor when I walked in, and in a fit of weirdo remorse I propped it up on the foot of the bed. Seeing that slumped stuffed elephant, the ache reopened underneath me. Somewhere on some interstate, Raja was shut in a trailer on its way to FriendlyLand. He didn't even have his stupid toy friend to keep him company.

To give my mind someplace to be, I shut myself in the walk-in closet and pulled down cardboard boxes. Three containers, printed with fake wood, contained all that remained of my childhood here. It wasn't much: stale erasers, a cracked incense burner, my name spelled in block letters — nothing worth flying back to Oregon. Except for the poster tube. I couldn't bear to pull it out and look now, but knew it contained a picture of Raja and me. I placed it to one side.

I pulled my phone out to charge. When I turned on the screen, I saw it was still on the FriendlyLand home page.

Now that I had time, I looked closer. FriendlyLand seemed to be mostly carnival rides, but the website said it also had over two hundred *Fun Animalz 4 U for just 10 dollarz extra or 8 with a Monster can!!* It was right along the highway, and an image search showed a random mix of captives: toucans, hyenas, goats, and one patchwork baboon, all in tight, small cages.

I typed *FriendlyLand* into a search engine. The third link in the list led to a photo of two foxes curled around each other. It wasn't until the text finished loading that I realized those foxes were dead. An animal rights group had been trying to get the zoo shut down; apparently its captive animals regularly died or disappeared.

This past winter, the text said, activists from a local school's environmental club had snapped pictures of dead sloths huddled in the corner of a cement cage — their heater broke during the zoo's annual closing period and no one had been checking on them.

This was Raja's new home.

Back when my parents had divorced, and I'd found out I'd be moving away, I'd tried to get him into a real zoo. I'd written and called everywhere. But no reputable zoo in the States would take an ex-captive orangutan, and the primate sanctuaries were all full. Why should that have changed? The truth was that it clearly hadn't — my father had given Raja away to whoever would take him. Raja had tried to escape, to save his own life, but I'd been the one to trick him into the crate.

I'd made it happen.

Now I'd have to be the one to make it right.

PART THREE

HUMANITY HAS IN COURSE OF TIME HAD
TO ENDURE FROM THE HAND OF SCIENCE
TWO GREAT OUTRAGES UPON ITS NAIVE
SELF-LOVE. THE FIRST WAS WHEN IT
REALIZED THAT OUR EARTH WAS NOT THE
CENTER OF THE UNIVERSE, BUT ONLY
A SPECK IN A WORLD-SYSTEM OF A
MAGNITUDE HARDLY CONCEIVABLE . . . THE
SECOND WAS WHEN BIOLOGICAL RESEARCH
ROBBED MAN OF HIS PARTICULAR PRIVILEGE
OF HAVING BEEN SPECIALLY CREATED, AND
RELEGATED HIM TO A DESCENT FROM THE
ANIMAL WORLD.

— SIGMUND FREUD, *A GENERAL INTRO-
DUCTION TO PSYCHOANALYSIS*, 1920

He was clutching his mother as she crashed from one tree to the next, whipping them forward through the jungle. It was the hottest day yet, and for once the warmth of his mother wasn't a comfort but an irritation. He dozed with a grimace, his little fingernails digging into her ribs.

The snake was a surprise.

He came suddenly awake when his mother screamed. Clutching even harder, he opened his eyes in time to see a length of sinuous green ribboning down to the ground. His mother pulled herself close to the trunk and held her hand to her mouth, sucking the webbing between thumb and finger.

She held the tree only with her feet so she could focus all her attention on the hand. He left her side and shifted to another branch to better see what she was doing. Sweat matting his orange hair into tendrils, he poked the back of the hand that was taking so much of his mother's attention. She squealed and turned away from him, hunched over.

It was the first time he hadn't been able to see the front of her. Huddled and afraid, he watched the knobs down his mother's back, waiting for her to return to him. Then, impatient, he worked his way over to her. He was new at moving on his own, and he went in slow animation, as if the air were something far thicker. He made his way around to her front, cheeping, fear stretching his mouth into a grin.

When she saw him near, his mother took her good hand and wrapped him close. He snuggled in, relieved.

They didn't travel any farther that day, instead resting in the tree. His mother didn't have enough energy to build a nest, so they were open to the sky above and below. *She was still for a long time, but as the sun fell she began squealing with pain, poking frantically at her arm, swollen from hand to elbow. Shivering against the night breezes, he snuggled tight as he could, but never felt warm enough. Except when his mother shifted in her tormented sleep, bringing her bitten hand right beside his face. That hand was as hot as if it had been blistered by the sun.*

SIX

I shut off everything on my phone besides the GPS and drove.

I could imagine the voice mails accumulating. My angry father. My mother — concerned at first, then angry, too. Maybe a friend from home, calling to see if I wanted to catch a movie or watch a game, wondering why I wasn't responding to texts, having no idea that I'd gone away. No one knew where I was. I'd never existed that way before.

It felt ghostly, to be unfindable. I stared at the cars driving alongside me, wondered where they were heading, wondered if they wondered where I was heading.

Eventually, no matter how loud I blasted the radio, my eyelids stayed only half open. Worried I'd get myself into an accident, I pulled my father's car over at a rest stop. At first I thought it would be impossible, but once I'd laid myself out on the backseat, Raja's elephant under my arm and his sour orangutan scent in my nostrils, I fell asleep. I washed up in the rest stop sink after, and with only one more stop for a bathroom and snacks, I was in West Virginia. For a long stretch, there was nothing on the interstate but my car and the occasional tractor.

I kept the phone off.

An hour into West Virginia, I spotted the first FriendlyLand billboard. It was a picture of a little girl reaching out a finger to touch a flamingo that had clearly been photoshopped in. Neon text declared FriendlyLand to be *the best tourist attraction in central West Virginia.*

I wondered what other tourist attractions there were in central West Virginia.

The air began to reek, even though the windows were up and the air-conditioning was on. The landscape was dotted with farms — not the kind you see on milk cartons, but long gray buildings belching waste into the air. They looked like prisons. The only way I knew there were animals inside was because of the logos on the buildings — even though we were in hog country, I didn't see a single pig. I wondered how many animals there were inside, and how they were treated. There was no way to know. They lived their entire lives out of view.

Soon after, my phone directed me to exit onto another highway, this one surrounded by low scrub, dry grass, and sparse pine trees. I passed another FriendlyLand billboard: a tiger's face, lips pulled back from long white-yellow teeth. After that, every few hundred feet was another sign with animals printed in saturated, hyper-real colors. Someone had tacked a piece of wood to cover the elephant in one billboard, the tip of a trunk giving away what had once been beneath. I guessed that meant the elephant wasn't around anymore.

I'm coming, Raja. Truth was, I had no idea what I was doing. I had to believe that when the time came I would be able to figure it out.

As I pulled into the zoo's entrance, I grew nervous that maybe my father had realized where I'd probably disappeared to and had tipped off the zoo, that I'd get arrested the moment I drove inside. I oversmiled as I paid a couple of dollars to the parking attendant, but she waved me through like anyone else. I found an isolated spot among the rusty trucks and motorcycles in the muddy field of FriendlyLand's parking lot. After I'd turned off the car, I sat still for a second, overwhelmed. My life up until now had a map to it, and I'd fallen off the edge.

Somewhere out of view, people screamed as FriendlyLand's roller coaster released.

"Make it right," I told myself.

I sounded convincing.

With a deep breath, I opened my door and stepped into the humid day. Immediately my sneakers were half submerged in mud. Embedded in the sludge were cigarette butts, drink lids, zoo tickets. While I picked and slurped my way to the entrance, the roller coaster released again, sending up another wave of screams.

At the end of the parking lot was a ticket booth with a lone cashier, a sulky kid who looked like he was still in middle school. "Have a Monster can?" he asked. I shook my head.

After I bought a full-price ticket at the window, I passed into FriendlyLand. A sign said I should go left for animals and right for rides. I went left.

It looked like a ministorage joint more than a zoo, dirt corridors separating three rows of low cement buildings. At the entrance was a gift shop offering up a row of exhausted and slumping stuffed animals. Next to them was a food stall selling chicken fingers seeping oil into wax paper boats. A tiger — apparently the FriendlyLand mascot — was painted on a plywood sign that announced three-for-two T-shirts.

It looked like most of the families at the zoo were breaking for lunch. The picnic benches were filled with men, women, and children digging into hot-dog specials and baskets of tater tots.

Where are you, Raja?

I passed toward the cages. The first thing I came to was a stand of potted silk plants, with a lion painted onto plywood, its head sawed out so kids could put their own in and take a picture.

With the sun directly overhead, only the very backs of the cages were shaded, so most of the animals were baking on the cement of their cage floors, which were covered in continents of stains.

The first animal I came to was a leopard lying on its side, eyes closed, rib cage pumping as it panted. The ground must have recently been hosed down; the tang of fresh poop was in the air, and steam rose from the concrete, wavering my vision. I kept shuffling forward — I needed to see everything but couldn't handle lingering.

Next was an otter in a bathtub, half in and half out of the few inches of greening water, eyes scrunched shut. A lone fox was next, one who must have survived the two I'd seen dead in the online photo. It paced its cage in tight circles, hair so pale it was almost khaki. At least it was able to move: The camel that came next stood stock-still in its narrow pen, chewing slowly, eyes glassy, resolutely ignoring the toddler playing xylophone on its bars.

So clever at finding its versions of *Everything's Fine*, my mind told me the next row of cages would be better. Maybe there was a luxury ape section, with velvet rope and a plucky band of charming gorillas, orangutans, and chimps, arms entwined as they fed one another grapes.

I stopped a teenager in coveralls with a name badge. "Hey," I said. "Do you guys have any orangutans?"

"No clue," the guy answered. "I just work in the food shack."

I turned a corner and found Raja, suddenly in perfect view. His cage was slightly bigger than the trailer at my father's house had been — at least there was that. He was by himself, behind thick bars that were rust-colored wherever the silver paint had rubbed away. Raja had his chin on his knees while he hunkered down and rocked himself. Though his eyes were closed, his fingers wandered the hot concrete, like if he kept doing it they might chance into something soft to touch. As I watched, one of his fingers happened on his own foot. Surprised by the unexpected contact, he held it close to his lips and kissed it.

Suddenly the last thing I wanted was for Raja to see me. He might think I was there to take him away, and he'd get his hopes up that we could go back to normal.

I ducked around the corner, hiding on the other side of a large birdcage. Peacocks crouched in the dirt next to me, like coop hens.

This place was awful. I couldn't avoid it. That was a fact.

But it was impossible for me to take Raja away. Also a fact.

I sighed.

In response, I heard a familiar kiss-squeaking noise and clanging metal. *Oh no.*

I peeked around the corner and found golden eyes staring at me. Raja had his hands and feet against the bars and was facing me in midair, like a toy suction-cupped to a car window. As soon as he saw me looking back, he switched to holding on with just his feet and made a flurry of signs with his fingers.

I'm sorry. You poop. I poop. I'm sorry. His cage rattled and groaned.

I wouldn't have thought it possible, but he'd recognized my sigh. After all this. After everything that had happened to him over the past twenty-four hours and the past two years, six years.

"I can't help you," I said. What could I do, other than tell him the truth?

But the truth clearly wasn't good enough. He began to cry out louder, rattling the bars of his cage.

"When I get home, I'll call every sanctuary again," I promised. "I'll make my father do better. I'll get my mom on it, too. I'll try PETA, the Humane Society, the ASPCA — all those places."

He watched me try to talk myself out of it.

A curious family made its way over to us. I didn't want them to ask what I was doing and attract attention, so I stepped away.

Looking for a plan, even the lamest one, I decided that since I hadn't eaten much in hours I should get a basket of fries. Maybe I'd be able to figure something out by the time I finished it.

Closing my eyes to Raja, I headed off — but didn't get too far before I heard a scream.

Not Raja's.

A woman's.

This wasn't good.

I heard more yelling, and the sound of rushing feet. Radio in hand, a zoo employee bolted past me, toward the ruckus. As I turned to the noise, I found a crowd rushing toward me. Away from Raja.

I pushed my way back to him. As I neared his cage, I slowed to a stop, blocked by the people who weren't fleeing. Children clutching parents, parents clutching children. Phones were out, recording. One little girl was squatting on her heels, face in her hands, sobbing her heart out.

Because Raja was out of his cage.

Two of his rusty bars were bent into parentheses, and he must have slipped through the opening. Not easily, either; when I finally spotted him, I saw his sides were all scratched up and his brow was leaking blood. He stood in the dirt walkway, pivoting, the crowd giving him a wide berth but inadvertently sealing off any exit routes.

On one side of Raja, two caged baboons clutched each other and screamed, and on the other side a badger watched expressionlessly as the drama unfolded. Raja scanned the tops of the cages, clearly debating whether to climb up. But that would mean scaling the bars in front of the hysterical baboons. He decided against it and instead stepped toward the crowd. As he neared the panicking tourists he balked, doing an about-face and trying the other way, only to freak out another set of tourists.

While I struggled to push through the horde, Raja took matters into his own hands. He lumbered toward the peacock cage, tourists tumbling to either side. He seized the bars and started climbing, easily pulling himself over onto the top. The hot cement roof must have burned his hands and feet; he grunted and fell onto his butt, holding the soles of his feet to his lips and kissing them.

"Raja!" I cried.

He was back onto his feet immediately, ignoring the pain as he stood up and peered around. When he saw me waving, he kiss-squeaked and lumbered across the tops of the cages to the one closest to me. Animals squawked and growled as he passed over.

"He's coming after us!" a nearby woman warned. A huge bearded guy protected us all by hurling his soda. It went wide, but some of the drink sprayed Raja's face. He blinked, surprised.

"Stop," I told the man. "He's heading for me. I know him. He's not going to hurt anyone."

The big man seemed to have intimidated Raja, who changed his priorities from finding me to getting away from the crowd. Raja wrist-walked across the cage tops to the far edge of the zoo, where there was a spindly pine tree. He leaped from the cage to the trunk, catching it in both hands and feet. The tree bent far to the ground, creaking and cracking. Then it slowly righted itself, with Raja swaying in its highest branches.

While the crowd gasped and jostled, I noticed a guard approaching, baton in hand. By the time I'd moved near the tree so I could coax Raja down, the guard was beside me. "What the hell is going on here?" he asked. He looked maybe a year older than me, and totally in over his head.

"Looks like your new orangutan escaped," I informed him.

He looked up at Raja, who had buried his face in pine needles. "Did you let him out?" he asked, eyeing my biceps.

I pointed to the bent bars. "Dude. Do you really think I could do that?"

The guard let out a stream of curses as he peered up the tree. "Hey, monkey! Here, monkey!"

"Don't hurt him," I said. "Please. He's mine. If you can get all these people away, I think I can get him down safely."

The guard looked baffled more than anything else. "He's yours? I don't know what you're on about. But all I have is a baton, so I don't think you have to worry about *me* hurting *him*. If the police get here, that's a different story."

"Has someone called the police?" I asked.

The guard shrugged. "Probably."

"Raja!" I called, a chill passing down my body as I held my arms open. He peered down at me. "Come on down!"

He stared down. His expressions were always so transparent to me: I knew he was judging whether to trust me. Then he gave me my answer by climbing higher. There wasn't much tree left, and the thinning trunk swayed again under his bulk. The soil nearby cracked and boiled.

Raja seemed to figure out that the tree wouldn't hold him much longer. He started down the swaying trunk then held still, clutching it tight. He began to kiss-squeak. Because he needed help.

"Can you get all these people out of here?" I asked the guard.

He turned and faced the crowd. His mouth opened and closed helplessly.

Okay, I thought. *Up to me.*

I yelled to the tourists with as much authority as I could muster. "Could you all go away?"

No dice. I might have been kiss-squeaking, for all they cared.

"How did it even get out?" the security guard asked.

"He must have gotten excited," I said. "Please, just help me out here."

"Help you out what?" he said, seeming to remember himself. "That's the zoo's monkey. You need to get back. Everyone needs to get back!"

"Yes, they do," I agreed. "Because if any of them get hurt, they are going to sue you until the only thing you own is that baton."

That seemed to click for him — they probably had lawsuit-prevention exercises as part of the training at FriendlyLand.

"Everybody back!" he roared, deputizing a nearby dad to usher the tourists farther along the row of cages. They moved warily, hands in fists, like at any moment Raja might bound down and attack.

They didn't go too far, though, after a dozen paces stopping and holding their phones out again. From somewhere in the huddle I could hear that little girl still sobbing.

"Farther!" I called. "Get them farther back!"

Raja stared down at me, chewing his lip as he mustered his nerve. Then he stopped crying, dangled one of his feet into space, and wrapped it lower on the trunk. He did the same with the other foot.

"Good job, Raja!" I called up. "You're doing great."

While he made his slow, tentative trip down the tree, my mind calmed enough that I could make a plan. The moment Raja was beside me, we'd make a beeline for my father's car. If we got out of here before the zoo people got organized, they might not interfere.

Raja continued his achingly slow descent. He'd clearly lost a lot of his tree skills; as often as not, he'd grab a branch instead of the trunk, and it would break away. He paused whenever that happened, staring in surprise at the loose piece of tree in his foot, then look at me for reassurance before continuing down.

Police sirens sounded in the distance.

"Hurry!" I called.

But he'd heard the sirens, too. He stopped descending, ear cocked toward the sound. "Raja," I pressed, "I need you to come down right now."

He looked at me, then out toward the parking lot. He squeaked, uncertain. Then something seemed to click, and he double-timed it down the tree, practically barreling his way. When he reached the bottom I was there waiting, arms outstretched.

Raja ignored my arms and got down the last few feet on his own. He seemed surprised by the feel of the ground under his hands and feet, the soil tracked in dried clumps of gum and maps with smiling cartoon tigers. He lifted one foot and then the other, staring at the soles, as if trying to figure out whether some of the litter had come off on him. I forcefully took his hand in mine. He looked up at me, startled again. It made me nervous to keep surprising him — in case he started surprising me back, I guess — but we didn't have time to go gently.

I tugged him toward the park exit. As we approached the line of tourists they scattered, most of them scared dumb, but some shouting words my mind was too frantic to process. I prayed no one would stop me, that the sight of us would be too weird for them to do anything but watch.

As we neared the parking lot, the guard tripped forward out of the crowd. "Hey!" he shouted. "Where are you going?"

At the sound of the guy's barking voice, Raja wrapped his arms around my waist, head buried into my side. His legs kept going, though, so now he was the one blindly dragging us vaguely toward the exit.

The turnstiles were in view. I expected a manager to appear, or for the guard to physically try to stop us, but we seemed to have surprised them enough that we might make it all the way to the car.

Two boys were cowering by the turnstiles, their mother hovering over them protectively. "It's okay," I said as Raja dragged me toward them. "He might be big, but he won't hurt anyone."

The mother didn't move.

"We have to get through that exit!" I said, frantically waving her to the side.

Numbly, she shuffled her boys away, then, as one, they seemed to realize what was happening and ran into the gift shop for cover. "Good enough for me," I muttered as we shuffled toward the car.

I clicked the UNLOCK button on my father's car key. We were still far from the car, but I kept clicking until I heard the reassuring *thwick* of the doors releasing.

Raja let go of me and went into a full sprint when we neared the car, getting there first and thumping the back door with his fists. I heard yelling behind us, a woman's voice shouting "Stop!"

"Handle, handle!" I yelled to Raja. While he stared at me in confusion I ran to the car and flipped his handle, opening his door then opening mine. Raja was instantly inside, door closed by the time I'd taken my seat.

I started the car. Raja went completely silent in the backseat, buckling himself in while I backed us out. We rolled toward the parking lot exit.

But it was chained.

Beyond it, blue and red lights strobed the trees. My pulse raced and my mind screamed, *They're going to shoot us!*

Two police cruisers blocked the way. Each had a door open, officers shielded behind steel. They waved us down, as if we had any option but to stop.

I needed another option. Fast.

But there wasn't one.

I slowed to a stop a short distance from the barricade. One officer yelled to me, her hand up in the air. "Stay in the car!" she called. "The zoo has called in its emergency staff. Please stay inside your vehicle until they arrive."

Emergency staff. That didn't sound so bad. I stared forward, engine idling, doors locked and windows up. "I guess it's over," I said while Raja panted in the backseat, hand pressed against the window as he gazed out, wide-eyed.

I put my hands on the sleek wood-paneled dashboard, my missing ring finger throbbing harder than ever. I sort of hated myself for the feeling, but I was relieved to have the next steps out of my hands. Maybe it was for the best if Raja was taken away again before he or someone else got hurt.

I lowered my window.

"She asked you to stay in your vehicle!" the male officer yelled.

"We *are* staying in the vehicle!" I called. "I just want to know what you're planning on doing to him."

"The zoo staff will be here soon. Roll your window back up."

I did as he said. Raja, probably figuring we were about to finally get moving and head home, clasped his hands in his lap and faced forward. He looked so lonely and hopeful back there, like a shy little kid whose parents had forgotten to pick him up at school. Not wanting him to be alone right now, I climbed into the backseat. Raja watched me, relatively calm, as I took his hand in mine.

We settled in to wait.

I doubted he'd go with them peacefully. He'd be confused at first, for sure — hadn't I brought him to safety? Once he realized that he was going back to the cage, he'd resist. The thought of it — of Raja screaming and fighting as he was roped and hauled back to that awful row of isolated cages — had me overwhelmed.

"I don't want them to take you," I said quietly, running my hands over Raja's coarse orange arm hair.

His breathing slowed, and he relaxed into my side. He was almost calm, and all it had taken was my presence next to him. Company. An ally.

I hated that I was putting him through losing that again.

Another betrayal.

Another abandonment.

Another failure.

Could he have any idea what was about to happen? Or did he think this peaceful moment in my father's car might continue forever, that our worlds weren't destined to change, to break and re-form? Unable to do anything else with what I was feeling, I buried my head in Raja's shoulder. Although I felt like I was crying, no tears came. I breathed into his rough, sour hair, my mouth open and chest silently heaving.

He cast his gaze to the window, facing away from me. A sparrow was shuttling back and forth over a nearby car's luggage rack. We watched it together.

He loved watching other animals — that had always been true. Suddenly reminded of the stuffed elephant, I groped around, found it, and put the reeking, grimy creature in Raja's lap. He squealed in glee and pressed it tightly to him, burying his nose in one of its soft ears.

I was filled with a strange satisfaction. Whatever happened next, at the very least Raja had gotten his treasured old toy back. Even if I accomplished nothing else, maybe I could make sure they let him keep it this time.

A white van pulled up beside the police cars. A uniformed woman got out and rummaged in the back, emerging with a sort of pole-and-noose device and a large canvas bag. The police officers stood by their cars, weapons at the ready, while the zoo worker approached. I rolled down the window when she got near.

"Can you safely get out of the car?" she asked, stopping a dozen feet short.

"Yes, definitely," I said. "Do you want us to?"

"Slowly. Leave the animal inside," she said. Her voice had a quiet confidence to it.

"That's going to be pretty hard. 'The animal' is hugging me."

The uniformed woman got near enough to the car to catch a glimpse of the inside. "Oh, wow," she said. "That's a big orang-utan. Is he the one that just arrived? You were delivering him? I haven't even done his intake yet."

I was encouraged by her calm, and that at least she knew what kind of animal Raja was. "He's not causing any trouble," I told her. "He'll go wherever we lead him, now that he's settled down."

The woman cocked the pole and noose against her hip. She had kind eyes. Tired eyes. "The police are involved. There's a zoo full of people that can't get to their cars. We can't walk an ape around in the open. That's simply the way it is."

"Do you have to take him back to his cage?" I asked.

She rubbed her face. "Of course I do. He's FriendlyLand property."

Property. The woman fished what looked like a gun from the big canvas bag.

"Wait. You're not going to shoot him, are you?" I said, craning so I could make eye contact through the window. "He's totally calm back here."

"Don't worry — it's a tranquilizer dart."

"If you let me, I think I can walk him right to your vehicle, or to the cage. There's no need for anything like a tranquilizer."

She considered it. "Yes, okay," she finally said. "I'm going to inform the police what's happening, and then I'll signal when you can bring him over to me."

We watched as the woman marched back to her van, frequently looking back over her shoulder. I pressed Raja's cheek against mine. "Whatever happens next, you be good, okay?" I said.

After discussing the plan with the police, the woman gave us a thumbs-up. When I opened the car door, Raja stared into my eyes, clearly curious about precisely what I intended to do. As I eased out of the car he eased out, too, pressing against me for comfort. Within moments we were standing in the mud, Raja's hand in mine. He slipped, the quick shift in his weight nearly toppling me before we recovered. It had always been hard for him to stay on two feet.

"Now!" the zoo woman yelled, "I need you to step away from him."

Hand in mine, Raja watched me closely for clues. "I can't step away from him," I called back. "He won't let me. Let me walk him all the way to you, like you wanted."

"I'm not asking, and it's not up for discussion."

The woman had the dart gun at the ready — either in case of an emergency or because she planned on using it as soon as I was out of the shot. I stood there, struck still. Raja was clutching me too hard for me to move. He made a frightened cry.

Instantly, the police had their guns raised. Raja seized up even tighter, fingers digging into my torso. He squeaked in terror, and I gasped in pain as he clutched me harder and harder. Fear shot through me, greasing my nerves.

"Please put your guns down!" I called. "There's no need for that."

"They're not planning on shooting him. But the animal can't leave the zoo," the woman said, voice quavering. "Do you understand? They will kill him if he crosses the property line."

"They can't!" I said. "He's my brother!"

She paused, totally still. "What did you say?"

When I didn't answer, she moved so she was between Raja and the zoo exit. We were trapped — police officers at the gate, zoo woman one step nearer, FriendlyLand and its rides and cages behind us.

"How do you know him?" she asked. "Why did you call him that?"

Raja had been quietly assessing the situation, and now was when he decided it was time to take matters into his own hands. Clenching tight to the four of my fingers he could reach, Raja took a big sideways step and climbed onto a car. I heard the officers shouting, but all I could think about was how easily Raja was dragging me. He hauled me up the side, my cheek squeaking against glass. Before I knew it I was in Raja's lap on the roof of the car; I was tight in his embrace, the stuffed animal pressing into my side. Raja's breath pounded with the exertion.

My pulse slammed through me and my vision narrowed. The police wouldn't shoot at us while I was in Raja's arms. Would they?

"Do you need to hand this over to us, Dr. Jackson?" one of the police officers barked. Their loudspeaker sounded tinny and crackly. I noticed a line of cars forming on the other side of the police cruisers, more FriendlyLand customers waiting to get in. They peered at us from behind their car windows.

Raja tensed, and his grip grew even tighter. It was getting hard to breathe. "Ask them not to use the loudspeaker," I said to the zoo woman, Dr. Jackson. "It's scaring him."

She was talking into her phone, one hand up to tell the police to stay where they were. Her other hand was fumbling with something at her side.

Suddenly Raja's hands were off me and he was groaning. The elephant tumbled from his grasp and I caught it on reflex, confused. I turned to see Raja had something in his hand. A dart. He looked at it in irritation, then flicked it to the ground. Lifting his arm to his mouth, he sucked on his elbow. I whirled and saw the zoo vet, one foot on a car bumper so she could raise herself high enough to see if she'd made contact.

She'd darted Raja.

I was scared he'd pass out right there, that he would fall off the top of this car and I wouldn't be strong enough to stop his weight from slamming to the ground. But he was staring at his elbow in confusion, periodically sucking on the knob of bone. Did it matter that the dart had hit him at a joint? Raja looked alert and irritated, not sleepy. He took the elephant back and wrist-walked to the edge of the car roof, staring angrily at the vet.

Dr. Jackson raised the dart gun again.

Raja wasn't going to let himself get struck a second time. He bounded down from the car and advanced on the vet on all fours. She fell back, but Raja was so quick — he was on her in moments, passing out of view behind a line of cars. My heart pounded, my absent finger throbbing.

The vet screamed out, but a second later Raja had disengaged from her and turned toward me. He had something in his hands — the dart gun. As soon as he was a few paces away he grasped it in both hands, sat down, and stared into the end of it, trying to figure out how it had fired. His fingers were dancing over the trigger; I imagined him releasing it by accident, sending a dart into his eyes. I jumped off the car and started toward him.

"It's okay!" I called to the vet where she crouched on the ground. The simple truth of the situation, that I'd found it so hard to articulate before, now came out of me rapid-fire. "He's trying to figure the gun out. He's curious. He's not going to hurt anyone. I've known him for years. He wound up here by accident. I'm here to take him home."

"Home?" she asked, her voice shaking.

"Stop!" called the police officers. They remained beside their patrol cars, guns drawn.

Raja glanced their way, then returned his attention to the gun. He put his mouth over the end of it, his lips tight against the black metal. That dart would shoot right into the roof of his mouth.

I put up my hands. "I swear, he's not trouble, officers. Please don't hurt him."

"Walk to where we can see you," the male police officer boomed.

The man's voice triggered something deep in Raja. He reared back, as if he'd been stung by another dart, and hurled the gun in the officer's direction. It went astray, denting the side of a truck. Then Raja was loping away, passing between cars, back toward the zoo, putting as much distance as possible between him and the police.

I moved toward him. The police officer yelled again, "Stay still!"

When their guns trained on me, I stood motionless, hands clenched. Raja moved away and out of view.

As the female officer circled her vehicle so she could keep Raja in her sights, the zoo vet got to her feet and crept in the other direction. From where they headed I figured Raja was fleeing through the parking lot, in his own slow, meandering way.

Shouting, then a hush. The remaining police officer took a step toward the noise, indecisive. "You can go," I called, staying motionless. "I'm not going anywhere."

That was all he needed. Weapon held ready down by his waist, he sped to his partner on the other side of the lot.

I heard a kiss-squeak and a thump from far away.

A gunshot rang out.

An anguished cry came out of me, swung up into the bright blue sky, like an uppercut. Suddenly the world was clear and vital. I wasn't waiting for it. It was waiting for me. Like Raja was waiting for me.

I ran.

SEVEN

Cars were not cars but blocks of color at the edges of my vision, black and silver and blue and black again. Mud sprayed under my feet, and all I could think of was Raja laid out and bleeding. When I came up short against a fence, I turned the way Raja would have gone. I followed the roadway as it planed upward, ending with a taller fence that marked the zoo's boundary.

I watched as the police officer fired again, the gun recoiling in her hands. After the boom made it to my ears, the world was ringing, only ringing. The police had fixed on Raja, and didn't appear to notice me as I pressed my back against the grill of a truck.

Beyond the zoo was a wide-open lot, weedy and neglected, separating FriendlyLand from a strip mall. Old abandoned bricks were stacked beside a lone tree, and that tree was where I finally located Raja, clutching the only branch strong enough to support him. Before my eyes it bent and broke, dropping him the few feet to the ground, where he held on to the piece of wood in shock, the wrecked branch tight in his grasp.

A brick near Raja was shattered, its insides bright like flaked rust. The police fired again, missing Raja and demolishing another brick. Sprayed by the shards, Raja startled and dropped his branch, lumbering away from the police. As he saw the wide-open lot, with so many options for where to go, his courage dissipated. He returned to the tree and crouched at the far side of the trunk, crying, the weedy branch doing little to shield his body from view.

Everyone at the strip mall must have fled indoors at the sound of the gunfire. An office-supply store, a chain coffee shop, a bank — all had closed doors and faces pressed against glass. A car peeled out as its owners made their escape.

All of them were terrified of this one-hundred-pound King Kong on the loose in rural West Virginia. Terrified of my Raja.

I wanted to help him, but couldn't approach and risk getting shot. Instead I stepped toward the officers, hands up in surrender. "Hello," I called, keeping my voice as low and nonthreatening as I could manage.

One of them kept his gun trained on Raja, but the other faced me and lowered her weapon. "Keep back!" she ordered.

"I can help you," I said, my voice hitching as cold sweat ran down my chest. "I've known this animal for years. Radio the other police officers in the area. Tell them I'll return Raja safely to the zoo if they stand down." I wasn't sure I could follow through on it, but it was our best course for the moment.

The police officers looked at each other, then back to me. One lowered her gun a fraction and nodded, then started speaking into her radio. She looked relieved — I'm sure she hadn't loved the idea of shooting an animal that was clearly scared out of its mind. "You'll head over the fence. Then if you get him to come back this way, we'll get the vet and she'll be waiting. Can you handle that?"

I nodded.

"Here's the situation. We have to begin shooting again if it looks even remotely like he might be a danger to the public. Escorting him back to the zoo is his only chance." She listened to some burbling from her radio. "Wait, how old are you?"

"Eighteen," I lied.

She relayed the information, then shook her head. "Sorry, kid, scratch that plan. You'll stay here."

"Please," I said. "Let me help. Or call my mother. I'll give you the number. Maybe she can help."

The officer returned her attention to the empty lot. Raja was motionless, huddled under the broken tree. "You'll stay back here is what will happen," the officer said.

I didn't think Raja was wounded, but he certainly seemed overwhelmed, and maybe a little sleepy from the dart. I knew a tranquilizer could take time to take effect. If he passed out now, then the crisis would be over.

"Hey!" the male police officer shouted. "He's on the move!"

Raja had cast away the fallen branch and was on his feet, peering around the lot. He made soft hooting sounds, and I knew just what they meant.

He was searching for me.

The blue elephant back in hand, Raja went down to all fours and took a few steps toward the strip mall. The police officers raised their guns. "Stop!" I cried. "Please don't shoot!"

Raja's attention snapped in my direction. He peered up and down, trying to find me — his distance vision had never been very good and seemed only to have gotten worse during his time in the trailer. Once he decided where I was, he rushed over, dragging the elephant along the ground. He went surprisingly fast, soon disappearing from view. Maybe the police officers would have shot, but their sightlines were blocked by vehicles as Raja lifted himself up the fence. He came into view after a long moment, leaping to the roof of a car. He jumped from that roof to the next, heading straight toward me — and the police officers. They barked orders at each other, guns drawn.

"No, no. You have to stop," I said.

"He's coming straight for us," I heard the male police officer say, panic in his voice. "Permission to fire?"

"It's okay, he just wants me!" I shouted, holding my hands in the air.

But the officer was taking sight with his pistol. Raja had only a few feet left to go until he'd be on us. He tripped on a car's luggage rack, and teetered. He reached a hand down to the surface, to get to a more stable position, and was crouched like that when the officer fired.

The bullet hit Raja in the leg, and the impact of it sent him spinning. Blood misted in the clear summer air as he tumbled, falling out of view on the far side of the car. I could hear the thud he made as he struck the ground, even beneath the new ringing in my ears. The officer held his pistol out, ready to fire again, shaking as he maneuvered to get Raja back into his sights. But his partner stopped him.

"You've disabled it," she said. "Animal control can take it from here."

Disabled it.

They'd *shot* him.

I watched in anguish as Raja dragged himself into view. He crawled forward on all fours and then stopped, turning on his back and pulling the stuffed elephant to him, curling his body around it. When I didn't see blood pumping onto the ground, I began to hope that maybe he hadn't been too gravely injured.

The officers circled around to get him back in their sights.

Raja sprang up and took off. He headed away from all of us, holding his wounded leg tight against his torso. One of the police officers fired again but the shot went wide, sending up a spray of mud. Raja was gone, off toward the strip mall, leaving a trail of spots behind him.

"He's hurt," I said, breathless.

Nobody could hear.

I knew his only chance was if I got to the car and tracked down Raja before the police did.

They were too busy radioing in to notice as I took off between the cars. When I turned the last corner, my father's car was right there — and so was Dr. Jackson, the vet.

She looked totally undone. The dart gun was in the mud by her feet, and she was standing with one hand pinned under an armpit, phone up to her ear as she waited for someone to answer. When she saw me, she ended the call. "What are you doing?" she asked.

The tired kindness in the vet's eyes made me take a gamble. "They're going to kill him if I don't get to him first."

"But where would you take him?" she asked.

"I don't know. A sanctuary. A different zoo. My father wasn't supposed to give him away."

Her eyes flitted in the direction the police officers had gone and then back to me. "Nancy Jackson," she said.

"What?" I was at the car now.

"When you're out of here," she said, "have your parents look up Dr. Nancy Jackson. Me. Good luck."

Mystified, I got in and started the car. I backed it out and turned toward the exit. The interior smelled like Raja.

I took a service road toward the strip mall. I had my shoulders low, forehead against the windshield as I searched for any sign of him. I couldn't see even a glimpse of orange hair, though. As I rolled through the parking lot, anxious people stood murmuring at every window. At the end was a dry cleaner, where the owner had the door open wide enough to stick her head out. She was on her phone, and staring down the street. Toward a cemetery.

I pulled up to the cemetery entrance and found a chain drawn across it, dangling a USE OTHER ENTRANCE sign.

I'd have to go in on foot.

"Raja!" I called as I ran into the cemetery. But there was no answer. The place was quiet and leafy, dappled with sparse sunbeams, chill after the heat of the zoo. No sign of the police or zookeepers here yet — though I imagined they were either on their way or entering through another gate.

I sped down the meandering main path. "Raja!"

I still didn't hear him. But as I continued along, the ringing in my ears died and I did hear something: an old woman yelling, not too far off. I took off running toward the sound, leaping over gravestones and darting between trees. There was no more yelling, but I didn't slow. There were many reasons for a scream to stop, and some of them were not good at all.

I passed down a rise and vaulted a low wooden fence to find an old woman kneeling, narrow body beside a broad grave marker, hands clasped in prayer. Her eyes were focused on the far side of the tree before her.

Raja was there, sitting on the ground, leg in his hands. He stared deep into the hair of his thigh, fingers grooming desperately to try to find the source of the pain. He dabbed his pinkie to his lips, tasting the blood. My missing finger throbbed in empathy.

I stepped forward, hands open. "It's okay, ma'am. He's not going to hurt you."

She turned toward me. Her limp gray hair was in disarray, fingers trembling as she clasped a cross at her throat. "Am I seeing a monster?" she asked in a rickety voice.

"He's an orangutan," I said. "An ape from Indonesia. Not a monster."

"What is he doing here?" she asked.

"I don't know," I said quietly. And I really didn't. Even though I knew the chain of events, it was hard for me to say why Raja was here. I'd thought about it sometimes, what Raja left behind and what his life would have been if my father hadn't brought him out of the jungles of Indonesia and into my world. But though that nagging wonder had always been with me, I'd never sat with it long enough to understand it. What *was* Raja doing here? The question floored me. Or, here's what floored me: No one had asked it before.

"He won't hurt you," I said, advancing. "I can promise you that."

"He's injured," the old lady pointed out.

"Yeah," I said. "Someone hurt him. He's not supposed to be here, so he's in danger."

I was near enough now for Raja to notice me. He chirped in joy and got to his feet. His injured leg tricked him, though, and he crumpled back down to the ground. He kiss-squeaked in confusion, eyes never leaving mine as his fingers became a flurry of motion, begging me to come near.

"It's okay, Raja," I said, moving forward in a crouch, making myself as small and unalarming as possible. "I'm here now."

He tried to get up and crumpled again. I could see his wounded leg better now. The hair on his thigh was matted in blood. "Raja," I said, "I'm sorry I let them hurt you."

As I neared, Raja clearly couldn't wait any longer. He got on his hands and knees and dragged himself toward me, using his forearms to leverage himself forward. Once I was near enough, he unsteadily got to one foot and wrapped his arms around me for balance.

The old woman stayed kneeling, holding her cross tight and staring at us in amazement. She put a hand to her forehead, eyes tightly closed, streaming tears. Like someone in an old religious painting who had seen a vision.

It took all my defensive-lineman skills not to fall over as Raja pressed himself to me as tightly as he could, hands muscling into my lower back, holding on for dear life. He lifted his wounded leg into the air.

I kissed the top of his head. "It's okay, Raja. We're going to get you out of here."

He swung his injured leg around dramatically, as if to make sure I realized he'd been shot. He'd always been one to play it up, my Raja. "I know," I said. "I know they hurt you. We're going to get to the car, and then I'll look at your leg."

The hand against my back trembled. He must have lost plenty of blood already — his body was sturdier than mine, but I wasn't sure how much more it could afford to lose. I put an arm under his shoulders, like I'd do for a teammate with a twisted ankle, and staggered forward. Raja did what an injured teammate would do, too, giving me enough of his weight so that we could both move forward. After a few paces he paused, teetering on one leg while he signed. *I'm sorry.*

Tears filled my eyes. *I'm sorry,* I signed back.

He teetered as he scooped the stuffed elephant up from the ground, then our arms were back around each other. Raja hopped with me over a rise, shifting left and right to pass between gravestones.

"Go in peace," cried the old lady in an awestruck tone, knobby fists clasped at her chest. I wondered what she thought, whether it was an angel she'd just met, or a devil.

As we kept going, Raja's breath came in wheezy gusts. He had to be near his limits, but even with his wheezing, he was keeping pace with me.

The cemetery gate came into view, my car the only thing on the other side . . . for now.

When I opened the passenger door, Raja tossed the elephant in first and then gripped the lip of the roof with both hands so he could swing in. I got in the driver's seat and slammed the door shut.

Raja dutifully put on his seat belt.

As I peeled out, I looked over at him. *I'm sorry*, he signed, staring down at his leg, bleeding onto my father's gray vinyl seat.

At first I drove without direction, turning and muttering and turning again, trying to get us out of the town and onto the interstate but not able to afford the time to look up the route on my phone. Then we finally made it onto the highway, sprinting in the center lane, cars whizzing by, honking or silent, drivers on their phones or singing along to their radios, unaware that a shot ape was in the passenger seat of the car gliding beside them.

Raja was the only thing on my mind. It wasn't just the leg wound. Some of the fencing must have had jagged edges, since he had razorlike slashes along his shins and forearms. The wound where his elbow had been darted was ragged and clotted, the blood mixed with dirt to form a kind of paste that was probably helping to stem the bleeding. A wad of blue gum had stuck to his forearm; I was able to roll away some of it and flick it to the floor with my spare hand, but the rest was too matted for me to deal with while driving.

Either the dart had released some of its tranquilizer, or Raja was too exhausted to remain conscious. Soon his eyes were closed. His head lolled so far over that the crown touched the door, and his legs were turned out and splayed like a frog's. His breathing, though, was hearty and regular.

I pulled over at the first rest stop I came to. Cautiously at first, then more freely once I saw that Raja wasn't reacting to my touch, I examined his leg wound. The bullet had taken a chunk out of the muscle of his thigh, about half an inch from the surface, like a mini-trough had been carved out. I could see thin and intricate veins, and muscle turning black where it had been exposed to the air. It was all clotting and hardening, thankfully, but still I peeled my T-shirt off and dabbed it at Raja's leg. It came away a grisly rainbow: purple with dried blood, red with fresh blood, brown with dirt, and green with crushed grass. I dabbed again and again until the shirt came away sort of clean, then wrapped it around the wound. I hoped the fabric would be enough to keep infection at bay.

I started the car back up and continued our journey. There was only one direction to go, and that direction was *away*. I kept looking in the rearview mirror, expecting police at any moment. I reminded myself that it was an animal on the loose, not a serial killer. The police weren't going to suddenly blockade I-64, and I was pretty sure there wasn't a simian equivalent to an Amber Alert.

I knew I was in trouble. I knew, theoretically, that I'd stolen the zoo's property and broken the law. But, all the same, it didn't feel like a theft.

That's exactly what most thieves would say, my mother's voice chided in my head.

Which was why I wasn't calling her. Or anyone else. It was just me and Raja this time.

I ran my hand through his sweaty hair. He must have been dreaming about something; his eyes moved under their lids and his fingers and toes twitched.

We'd reached a point of no return. Now that the police had decided he was dangerous, if they found him they wouldn't put him back in a cage. They'd kill him, just like they would kill a dog that bit a postman.

Don't think about that, I told myself. *Focus on the injury. Before you can save Raja from being killed, you have to make sure he's not going to die.*

My father's upholstery was pretty wrecked, but it didn't look like Raja was bleeding out anymore. Infection would be invisible until it was too late, though. I couldn't exactly take him to an emergency room, so I'd need to buy some rubbing alcohol and bandages and clean him up myself.

Raja still passed out, I drove until I came to a neon-signed chain superstore. After the murk and confusion of the day, the chilly fluorescent brightness of it cheered me, made me feel like it was possible for the world to be orderly again. I picked a spot near the back of the lot, put the car in park, and turned it off.

"Please stay asleep," I whispered to Raja. As if to calm my doubts, he shifted into the fetal position, face against the seat back, the stuffed elephant tucked tight into his belly.

First step in not attracting attention: Stop being shirtless. I rummaged a fresh T-shirt from my bag in the trunk, put it on, and headed into the store. It felt otherworldly, rolling my shopping cart alongside the moms and screaming kids, when wounded Raja was unconscious right outside. I hurried down the aisles, grabbing toothpaste and toothbrush, a three-pack of under-wear, chips, and cookies before heading to the pharmacy section. There I bought rubbing alcohol, cotton swabs, and bandages. I grabbed a few sale dish towels on my way to the register. Then some cinnamon gum for Raja. He wanted everything in his life to be red.

After my few minutes of normal life, I went outside to rejoin my orangutan brother.

While we drove to a nearby motel, Raja woke and sat up grog-gily. He looked at me for reassurance and then leaned heavily into the car window, pressing his forehead and lips against the glass. Even in his pain and exhaustion he was fascinated by this new world; I wondered if he thought there were orangutans in the other cars, if he would search them out if only he knew how. I wondered if he thought we might someday come across other families like ours.

A sprinkling rain had begun, and Raja was sucking his mouth against the window, I guess to lap up the water he didn't realize was on the other side. Anyone driving past us that actually bothered to look would see orangutan lips and teeth behind the glass. But that was the thing: No one ever did bother to look.

The Glades Motel was dingy, with a nearly empty lot darkened by overhanging trees, views of a gas station on one side and a shuttered community pool on the other. Filthy and overlooked: perfect for us. I drove directly around back and parked in the far corner. After the car sighed to rest and the wipers stopped, Raja and I sat in quiet.

"Okay," I told him. "Here goes nothing. Which may end up being literally nothing. I don't know if hotels even rent to teenagers."

Raja rasped in response and started chewing on his arm hair.

At reception, I got lucky. The clerk asked me no questions, so I told him no lies. The credit card was tied to my father's account, so he could easily use it to track me — but I had barely any cash so I had to take that risk.

Once I had the key, I drove the car to the parking space nearest to our room. Unbuckling my seat belt, I turned to look at Raja. He was so *deliberate* in his not looking at me: He'd peer at the window, the dashboard, pick at the seams between the cushions, scrutinize the ceiling. Finally he allowed his golden eyes to meet mine. It almost made me gasp, the worry I saw there.

I'm sorry, I signed.

Raja picked up the elephant, put it in his lap, and dove his face into it.

All he and I had to do now was cross a few feet of asphalt — I figured that shouldn't be too hard. I ducked out of the car and opened the room's door, then returned and opened Raja's.

He stared furiously into the seat, and for a moment I worried he'd refuse to go. But then he placed the foot of his good leg on the pavement. I nervously scanned the parking lot.

"Come on, Raja, no one's here. Let's get a move on."

He stared down at his foot on the damp asphalt, and I wondered again what was going through his mind. Then he rolled out, two hands and one foot on the ground. I offered an arm for support but he refused it, instead using the side of the car for balance as he hopped. I was about to close the door when he squeaked in irritation. I paused, then realized what the fuss was about when he reached in to rescue his grimy elephant.

Raja went down to all three good limbs and wrist-hobbled into the room. I made to follow him, but then the door closed soundly in my face. I stopped, stunned.

Luckily the key was still in the knob. I turned it, but the door wouldn't budge.

"Raja," I called warningly.

A black pickup truck pulled into the motel lot. Even though it was a different model than my father's, my heart missed a beat as I watched it park. The owner got out, walked up to the room next to ours, and paused. He looked at me as I stood stock-still, staring at him.

"You okay, son?"

"Oh, yeah, I'm fine," I said with as much cheer as I could muster. *Hanging out in a motel breezeway after getting locked out by an ape — what's going on with you?*

I tried the handle again, and this time the door opened.

Raja was sitting on one of the two beds, his body weighing the skinny mattress enough that the springs nearly grazed the carpet beneath. The bedspreads and sheets had tumbled into the middle, so Raja looked like the cherry on top of a bedding sundae. I slipped in quickly and shut the door, dead-bolting it.

"Hey," I told him sternly, "no more door shenanigans, you hear me?"

I looked out the peephole, fastened the chain lock, and drew the curtains shut. The room went black until I flicked a switch and desperate yellow leaked from one of the bedside lamps. "Ah, motel life," I said.

Truth was I'd always liked motels: the adventure of the almost-working remote, the strangeness of the Bible in a particleboard drawer, the scaly mysteries of unfamiliar showers. But I realized now that motels were only enjoyable because they were temporary. This time, with nowhere to go and wounded outlaw Raja in tow, it felt more like a prison with pay-per-view.

Raja got off the bed and limped to the TV. He rapped on the screen, and the heavy TV rocked back alarmingly, nearly tipping forward on the rebound.

"Hey, hey," I said. I picked the remote off the greasy glass-topped desk and handed it to Raja. He returned to the bed, reclining against the headboard, wounded leg crossed over the healthy one. Pointing the remote the wrong way, he raised it to the television and started pressing buttons.

I took the opportunity to examine his wound again. Considering how deep it was, it had scabbed over really fast. Almost like Raja was Wolverine or something.

Raja brought the remote close to his face and studied it, then went back to pressing buttons, remote still facing the wrong way. Not quite Wolverine.

I assembled the goods on the other bed. Snack food (a bunch of it from a HappyFoods brand), toiletries, bandages, and rubbing alcohol. I took a deep breath. Renting a hotel room at sixteen was one level of intimidation. Patching up a gunshot wound was another.

The remote squeaked away. Raja had always loved colors, and was now focusing on the red POWER button. Too bad he was facing the transmitting end right into his armpit.

"Give it here, Raja," I said, hand out. "I'll make it work."

He defiantly avoided my gaze, continued to press the creaking buttons. *I will do this on my own.*

"Fine, have it your way," I said. Despite myself, a smile crept over my face as I watched him press away. I nudged forward, then wrinkled my nose. "Man, Raja. You *reek.*"

Standing over him, I reached for the remote. When Raja narrowed his eyes and flipped back his lips to show his teeth, I raised my hands in surrender and headed for the bathroom, trying to walk off the adrenaline tremoring my thigh. Getting a wounded and suspicious orangutan washed and treated was not going to be easy.

I closed the tub drain and turned the water on high; soon it was billowing steam. Then I wet my arm and picked up a packet of motel shampoo. I soaped up my arm and stood in the doorway, working the lather into my sparse red hair. Raja kept resolutely pressing buttons, but at telltale moments his attention flicked to me. I put my arm to my mouth and tentatively licked the shampoo. My tongue curled; that was some nasty blue goo.

As if he didn't have a care in the world, Raja put down the remote and ambled over to me. His eyes lit when he came near the running water, the billowing steam, and the shampoo packet. Moving gracefully despite his weight and his wounds, Raja hopped past me and belly-flopped into the bathtub. He placed his injured leg and head on the rim, as if to prevent them from getting wet, then gave up and went all in. He winced only the first moment the hot water hit his wounds, then started wiggling his butt and sighing in pleasure.

"Okay, Raja," I said, kneeling at his side. Most pets look smaller when they're wet, but under his wet hair Raja was broad and muscled and fat. I'd wait to examine the gunshot wound; I figured it was better to warm him up by starting with something I knew he'd love. Once I saw he was calm, I drizzled some shampoo onto his arm and started lathering it in. The last time I'd bathed him like this, he'd been the size of a large teddy bear. Now he was a beast. But here was our old ritual, happening again like no time had gone by. I worked the shampoo into a foamy lather, and as soon as it was frothy and peaking like frosting Raja started lapping it up. He put his arm in his mouth, sucking on the foam, then worked some more soap in and licked it away, like soft-serve ice cream. It was a race — I was working to get him at least a little washed before he ate off all of the shampoo.

He tried to slurp the shampoo off his wounded leg, but to do that he had to support his weight on the towel rack; it wrenched free into his hand, raining plaster. He looked at me, giving a worried yawn.

"It'll be okay, Raja," I said. "You're not in trouble. We'll, uh, leave an extra tip."

He was fascinated by the towel rack, peering into either end, shaking it in the air and watching as bits of plaster fell out and floated in the bathwater. I took advantage of the opportunity to start working on his leg. First I shampooed and rinsed the nearby hair. Then I cupped water in my hands and gently released it over the injury. Raja glanced at me, then went back to his examination of the towel rack. Bits of dirt streamed away, and I saw the gash was clotted and purple, blood no longer seeping out.

I gingerly positioned Raja's leg so it was hanging over the side of the tub, then dried it. Dousing a dish towel in the rubbing alcohol, I cautiously approached the wound. As I did, Raja made a big show of facing away and scrunching his eyes shut. Eyes trained on his face, I gently pressed the fabric to his injury.

He didn't react at all.

Emboldened, I used more alcohol on the wound, then patted it dry and wrapped a bandage around it. Raja opened his eyes and watched in fascination as I taped it closed.

Then he must have decided he was done with his shower. Still soaking wet, Raja rolled himself up and out of the tub.

I could only watch as he limped out of the bathroom and down the length of the motel room, leaving trails of soap bubbles wherever he stepped. Returning with the remote in one hand and the stuffed elephant in the other, he brushed past me to get back into the tub. After dunking the elephant and then the remote, he bashed them together, rasping happily. I sighed.

The unlucky remote sat in the tub's standing water while Raja got to work scrubbing the elephant. He picked up the same shampoo packet, squeezed out the last few droplets, and began to rub. Starting with the arms, he switched to the legs and finally did the body and face — the same order, I realized, that I had washed him.

After Raja had finished scrubbing the elephant, he got out of the shower sopping wet and carefully positioned the stuffed animal in the sink. The air conditioning blew directly on Raja there, though, and he started shivering. He looked up at me, at a loss. I wrapped one of the motel's threadbare towels around him and rubbed him dry. Raja resolutely stared at the ceiling, avoiding my eyes, dutifully raising one arm and then the other so I could get the towel beneath.

Once I'd finished drying him, Raja looked pointedly at the elephant, as if to make sure that it, too, got the full spa treatment.

Soon a scrubbed-clean Raja was sitting on his bed, his orange hair dried stiff and sticking straight out, puffball-style, as he watched TV. Newly cleaned and dried, the elephant was nestled in cheerfully at his side. The remote was useless, and I couldn't get the channel buttons on top of the TV to work, so Raja would have to settle for public access.

While he watched TV, I took in the damage. The carpet was soaked, and there was an inch of standing soapy water on the bathroom floor. Bubble foam was on the wall, the lamp, the dresser. The towel rack and the TV remote had seen their final day. But at least Raja's wound was clean.

While he was occupied, I plugged my phone in to charge and did some research. The websites were all familiar by this point. There were a half dozen ape sanctuaries in the States, most of them in Florida or the Southwest (apes and snow: not a good mix). I figured I'd call them all eventually, but in the interest of time I'd start with an email I could send to each one. So I wrote a letter and cut-and-pasted it to each sanctuary's email address. I told them that I had an ex-pet orangutan and that I would do whatever it took to find him a place to be.

I knew what to expect back, because Mom and I had tried for years to get Raja placed: no response, or testy *What did you expect to happen?* emails. I couldn't blame them — sanctuaries were all underfunded and overfull. Apes were kept as pets or used in movies when they were defenseless and cute, then ditched at sanctuary doors once they were strong and ugly. The operators probably saw me as another in a long train of irresponsible people. I attached an old photo of cute little Raja to each email, to try to convince them of what an amazing creature they could have. Looking at him burping while he watched public access, I realized I was probably as delusional about his specialness as a parent gushing over a monster toddler.

On a whim, I looked up Nancy Jackson and found the webpage for a private vet practice. She must have worked at the zoo only part-time. I found her contact info and started an email:

You asked me to reach out, and here I am. Raja is okay.

I looked the message over. Even if she was setting us up, nothing I'd written would give her a clue of where we were. It seemed safe. I sent it, adding my phone number at the last minute.

Raja farted long and loud as one public access show switched to the next, this new one something about a guy making meals from random stuff in his freezer. My phone rang. I stared at it. A West Virginia number.

"Hello?" I said.

"Is this Tiger99?" asked a woman's voice.

"Yes. Well, John Solomon. That's just my email address."

"Yes. Well. Hello, John. This is Nancy Jackson. I would have been your orangutan's vet at FriendlyLand." Her voice sounded tired, like she was at a desk at the end of a workday, making her way down a checklist. But she didn't sound angry.

"His name is Raja. I'm looking at him right now." I flailed my arms, motioning for Raja to turn the TV off. He watched me, confused, then held up the elephant in case I wanted that.

"I'm relieved you were able to find him. Is he safe?"

"How do you mean?"

"Is he in physical danger right now, or could he put someone in physical danger?"

I thought about our day, then chose my words carefully. "Yes, he's safe. He's not causing danger. Are you tracing this call?"

She chuckled, a world-weary sound with no amusement whatsoever in it. "No. I don't exactly have that kind of technology."

Nothing in her tone sounded upset, but I imagined heaps of accusation behind her words: *You have a smuggled orangutan on the lam, with no thought for his welfare. FriendlyLand is awful, but is a road trip with you that much better?*

"An orangutan is the only ape that's gentle enough to have tagging along in the human world," Dr. Jackson continued. "A chimp or gorilla, and you'd be in a totally different situation. I did a zoo internship in veterinary school, but my main job is the small-animal vet in town. FriendlyLand's full-time vet quit, and while they search for another I've stepped in to help. That's why it took me a while to get there — I had to rush over from my clinic. I wish I had been there before you arrived. A lot of that crisis might have been averted."

"Raja got shot," I said, the words enormous as soon as they were out of my mouth.

"What? The police thought they didn't connect."

"Oh, they connected. I'm looking at his wound right now."

"Is he okay?"

"The bullet only grazed him, and it's not bleeding anymore. I cleaned it out good."

"You should bring him to my clinic. Or I can come to you."

I didn't answer. I wanted to believe her, but I had no way of knowing that this wasn't a ploy, that she wouldn't throw him right back into solitary confinement at FriendlyLand.

"I care about animals, John," Dr. Jackson said, "and I'll tell you that I hate how they're treated at that zoo. But if I didn't come in to care for them, no one would, and their lives would be much, much worse."

It dawned on me that she was worried that I was judging *her*, not the other way round. I started to feel safer.

"I'm actually involved in some of the animal rights move-ment," she said. "Have you heard of the chimp personhood cases?"

"No."

"A well-known lawyer has been arguing in court that some animals, like apes, have a consciousness that is developed enough that they deserve a basic right to life, happiness, and — most importantly — liberty. Just like humans. That, particularly in the case of the great apes, those rights have been violated by many medical facilities, some private owners, and some zoos. While so far he's only identified chimps as personal plaintiffs —"

"Wait, you mean, like, owners of chimps?"

"No. The apes themselves. That's why this is such an extraordinary moment. He's arguing that their incarceration is a violation of habeas corpus, that they are being unlawfully detained. He might succeed. What I'm suggesting is that he could add Raja to that list."

I looked at Raja, imagining him behind the witness stand on an episode of *Law & Order*. "What would that do?"

"As far as where you can bring Raja now, nothing. But if Raja's listed on the brief as a plaintiff, it will complicate FriendlyLand's claim to him while the case is argued."

I knew all her words should make sense, but after the day I'd had, I couldn't make them come together in my head. "I'm sorry, what does this mean for me and Raja, like, practically speaking?"

"If Raja becomes part of the class in these proceedings, you won't have anyone trying to bring him back to FriendlyLand. You could argue that you were protecting Raja's rights as a person by liberating him from unlawful detainment. I can't guarantee what will happen with the case, and I'm afraid any final Supreme Court decision is a ways off. Can I ask — how old are you, John?"

"Eighteen," I lied.

"Are your parents there?"

"No. I'm the one taking care of Raja. I'm on my own with him."

"Where are you?"

"A motel."

"Wait. You have an orangutan in a motel?" She had the same tone of voice you'd use for *You have a toddler in a strip club?*

"Yes," I admitted.

Dr. Jackson said something to someone in the background, her voice so muffled that I figured she had her hand over the receiver. I wondered again if I was being set up.

"I need you to give me your parents' phone numbers, John," she said once she was back.

"I can't do that. They've given up on him."

"I can imagine how you got into this situation, and it can't have been easy for you. People buy these apes as infants, and they're adorable then. But once they're strong adults, they get locked away. Is that what happened to Raja?"

"Yes," I said quietly. Some part of me was relieved and some part of me was saddened. *There are other people who have done this. My family isn't the only one.*

"I'll drop a line to the lawyer and email you his info. Have your mother or father reach out to him."

"Can you think of any place I can bring Raja, that might have room for him?"

She paused for a moment. "Honestly, no. Your family was lucky to have found even a roadside zoo willing to take him, and as awful as FriendlyLand may seem, it's actually in the middle of the pack as far as animal welfare is concerned. Most roadside zoos are moving away from apes. With the Internet and people posting pictures, it's too easy for the world to see the bad conditions. So most captive apes are in seclusion, in university studies or testing facilities, hidden where the public can't see them and get upset. The luckiest ones are in sanctuaries. But those are all dangerously overcrowded already. I doubt you'll find one that has space for an adult male orangutan."

I got it — the people trying to do the right thing were overworked and underfunded, and for the welfare of all of their animals, they couldn't take another. But I had Raja to worry about, not all the rest of the apes. "If I showed up on one of their doorsteps with Raja, would they turn us away?" I asked.

She sighed. "You shouldn't put them in that position."

"I'll try to avoid it," I said. And I meant it. But I had no idea what else to do.

"John, take my advice. Do whatever it takes to get your parents involved. They have to find a solution, and quickly. You don't want to be wandering the world with an ape. People get scared, and scared people are dangerous people. For Raja's sake and yours, he needs to *be* somewhere. Even if it's not where you'd like him to be."

"I understand," I said, staring at Raja. "And thank you for calling me. For caring about Raja."

Nancy sighed. "My instincts are telling me I shouldn't be touching this situation with a ten-foot pole."

"Well, I'm grateful you are."

"I can tell how deeply you care about Raja. That comes through loud and clear. It did from the moment I saw you clutching him — or, actually, him clutching you — in that parking lot. Apes are excellent judges of character."

I thanked her and finished the call.

"Sounds like that was a bust, huh?" I said to Raja. He flickered his attention to me, then back to the TV. "But Dr. Jackson said that you like me. Much as you try to play it off."

Raja kept watching, but moved over a few inches on the bed so there was room for me to sit next to him. I lay down, the sagging mattress instantly pressing us together. While Raja continued to watch TV, I looked back at my phone and saw two more missed calls from my mom. I sent her a text: *I'm okay. I'll explain as soon as I can.* Then I shut off the screen.

It wasn't much past five, but fatigue washed over me, sudden and heavy. I lay on the bed, still in my jeans and shirt. The mattress bent farther under my weight and I rolled into a valley in the middle. That groove felt like a permanent part of the bed, and I sensed I'd be in it until morning. Raja and I both. There were two beds, but this was the one I wanted to be in.

"Don't go anywhere, okay?" I said to him.

He made a sound I couldn't recognize. I had to hope it meant he agreed.

As I dozed off, Raja put his arm around me, like I was his stuffed elephant, and my heart filled with gratitude.

EIGHT

Raja spent his first night of freedom dreaming hard. Whenever I came back from peeing, I'd find him in a new position, sometimes on his back snoring and sometimes somersaulted, head under his legs. What never changed, though, was the hand gripping the headboard. It brought back memories of when we'd shared my bedroom — there, too, he'd always clutch something while he was sleeping, as often as not a part of me. At first I'd thought it was some tenderness on his part, that he wanted to feel close. But then I'd learned that orangutans slept in trees in the wild, and I realized it was probably a hardwired impulse to prevent himself from falling.

The Glades Motel clearly wasn't designed for orangutan sleeping habits. When we woke up in the morning, Raja was laid out flat, snoring away, the headboard ripped from the wall and wrapped in his arms. A fine layer of plaster dusted the scene, making it look like he was holding a giant piece of cinnamon toast.

"Raja," I said as I nudged the dozing ape awake, "we're going to have to have a talk about manners."

I checked my phone. My mom had texted: *I won't be angry, call me.*

It was time to stop avoiding her. I dialed my mom's cell, and she picked up right away.

"Hi, Mom. I'm sorry to call so early," I said. With the time difference, it would barely be daybreak back in Oregon.

"John! Oh, honey. You're okay — thank the Lord you're okay. Where are you? What happened? I thought we said you'd call every night."

"Well . . . I'm in a motel."

"A motel? Why aren't you staying at your father's house? He told me yesterday that the zoo came for Raja, but he hasn't been picking up the phone today."

I couldn't believe it. She didn't know a thing.

I could imagine my father not wanting to pull her into it until he had more information. That for a few hours, at least, he'd figured it was best if she didn't know Raja and I had going missing, so she wouldn't flip out at him before he had good news to share.

It would have been easiest to lie and pretend that everything had gone as planned. But that wouldn't be fair to her.

"Actually," I said, "I'm here with Raja."

There was a long pause.

"That zoo, Mom. It was horrendous. He'd have been trapped in a tiny cage his whole life."

"They let him go?"

"Not exactly. But sorta."

"John. This is unbelievable. I'm going to call your father so he can fetch you and return Raja. You sit tight. He'll come to you, wherever you are. All you have to do is lock the door and wait."

"I met a vet from the zoo who offered to help, Mom. She said we can get Raja onto this court case that would say it's not legal for him to be cooped up in terrible conditions. That he has a right to freedom."

She paused. I could hear the wooden beads of her necklace clack as she twisted it around her neck. They were broad, flat squares, painted like letter blocks. Her kindergarteners loved them. Raja would have loved them, too. "What does freedom look like for Raja, John? Can you tell me that? No one's ever been able to tell me that."

"I'm still hoping for a sanctuary to come through this time."

"This isn't safe. You know that. For my sake if not for yours, you need to come home. Please."

"I can't bring Raja back to FriendlyLand. That's why I've got him here."

I was relieved that, for the moment at least, she wasn't going to question me on that. "Do you have money? Are you safe?" she asked.

"Yeah, we're safe," I said. "Just don't cut off my ATM card, okay? I'm using Dad's credit card for now, but in case he shuts it down."

"I'll make sure he doesn't," she said. "John? How is he?"

She wasn't asking about my father. I looked at Raja. He'd woken up and rolled over onto his side, and was poking at his wounded leg, grimacing. "Raja seems depressed. A little weird. More like scared, and working hard not to show it."

"You're in huge trouble once this is all over, you realize that?"

I found myself smiling. Huge trouble sometime in the future — that I could deal with. "Yeah, I get it," I said.

"For now, I want you to concentrate on taking care of yourself. You're the one who has to get through this safely. That's most important."

I didn't think that was true, that I was the only one who mattered here. But all the same I was glad to hear my mom say it to me.

"We're always going to see differently on this, I know that. Just don't put yourself at risk. Do you promise? If you have to choose between you and Raja, promise me that you'll choose *you*."

"Okay. I will. In return, can you call this lawyer guy? I'll email you his info. Maybe he'll know some way to help."

She sighed. "It won't hurt to call him. I'll tell you what he says."

"Thanks, Mom. I'm going to go now. I miss you. I'll be careful."

After I ended the call I looked at Raja. He'd dropped the headboard beside the bed and was huddled in the sagging middle. He glanced at me, glanced away, then picked up the stuffed elephant and started kneading its fabric. I sat on the edge of his bed. He still smelled like blue motel shampoo, like metal flowers.

"We have a long car trip ahead of us," I said, gently poking him in the chest. "Are you going to behave today?"

Raja hugged the elephant, then rolled off the mattress. He stared at the rumpled sheets, then at me, waiting for me to make the bed — back when I was a kid, that was the first thing we had to do each day if we didn't want to get Mom mad. To appease Raja, I flung the comforter over the plaster-dusted sheets. As if to help, he handed me the headboard, which I propped up against the mattress. It balanced for a moment, then slid down. Raja tried holding it up. It slid again, but this time Raja turned around before it had finished falling, playing it off like he hadn't noticed anything. I turned around so I could play it off, too.

As I started packing, jamming snacks and clothes into my duffel bag, Raja stood in the middle of the room, watching as I scooped the toiletries up in one armful and dropped them in a plastic grocery bag. Catching on to what I was doing, he dropped to his belly and reached under the bed, emerging with the T-shirt I'd been wearing the day before.

"Thanks, Raja," I said, reaching for it. But he surprised me by putting it on. At first he decided to wear it as pants, his feet and legs emerging from the sleeves, but after a minute of struggling he'd maneuvered it over the top half of his body, though back-to-front.

He was still favoring one foot, but this morning he seemed able to tolerate the toes of his injured leg grazing the ground. His bandages were holding on firm, and their outsides were still white — he hadn't bled through, which I counted as a success. I hesitated a moment with my hand on the doorknob, afraid of what I'd find on the other side. Then I turned it, opened the door, and looked out.

The coast was clear.

I stepped outside, gesturing for Raja to follow. He only slowly emerged from the dim motel room, checking twice to see if anyone was watching. Once he was near enough, he slipped his hand into mine for security, gripping it especially tight. "Hey," I said, patting his head. "We're not going back to the zoo. Is that what you're worried about?"

The moment he looked in my eyes, I knew it was.

After checking again whether anyone was nearby, I started shuffling Raja across the sidewalk. The moment we were in the open, though, he broke from my grip and hustled down the breezeway.

I cursed myself. I'd thought he'd prefer my company to being alone, that he wouldn't make a break for it, but this new Raja was harder to predict. All it would take is for the wrong person to see him and this would all be over. I ran after him, then stopped short.

Raja had crouched behind a bush, and from the sound of it I knew exactly what he was doing. I turned away to give him privacy while he finished, then he ambled back. I held out my hand, but he ignored me, going straight for the backseat. Shrugging, I got into the driver's seat.

But before I could drive away, there was the small matter of the back door, which Raja had left open. Leaning over the seat, I said to him exaggeratedly, "Close the door."

He blew out a long dramatic breath, rustling the hair that hung over his forehead. Then he pulled the door closed and sulkily crossed his arms over his chest.

It was like I was traveling with a preteen. Which, technically, I was.

I put the car in drive and headed to the exit. But this was interrupted by a screech and a thump from the backseat; Raja was kicking the door. By the time I had stopped the car, Raja remembered the handle and was out, tumbling on the pavement. Instantly he was on his hands and feet, wrist-running back toward the motel room. I opened my door and was about to follow when I saw what Raja was after: He'd let that blue stuffed elephant slip from his grasp when he was getting in the car. He picked it up where it was slumping tiredly on the pavement, hugged it to him, and headed back to me.

"Hey!" came a yell from another motel room, the one where I'd seen the guy the day before. An unlit cigarette was in the man's fingers as he leaned over the railing. "What the hell's that?"

Raja stood upright and stared at the man, his fingertips grazing the ground. He kiss-squeaked in confusion, the elephant slack in his fingers. Raja took one step toward him, then back to me, baffled. With the T-shirt and stuffed animal, he was a strange sight indeed.

"Raja!" I called.

"What the . . . ?" the man said, his face pale. "Is that bigfoot?"

Raja wasn't more than four feet tall. He was no bigfoot.

"No, sir, he's just a monkey." I intentionally used the wrong word, somehow less fearsome than *ape*. "Come here, Raja, time to go," I said, as sweetly as possible.

"Hold on," the man said, "I want to get my friend. He's got to see this." He rapped on the window of his motel room. "Ernie!"

"Raja!" I called, opening the car's back door. "It's time to go."

After a moment's indecision, Raja loped across the parking lot and got in. Sweat ran down my arms.

Once Raja was in and the door was closed, I peeled out of the parking lot, making random turns through a subdivision to make sure no one was following us.

There's nothing technically illegal about traveling with an ape, I reminded myself. It was illegal to buy or sell one, but not to have one. There was no reason for that man to call the police.

While I headed toward the interstate, I stared at Raja in the side-view mirror. He sat there glumly, eyes on the window. His stomach growled, and then so did mine. Raja liked to eat throughout the day, and if I had my way so would I. No wonder we were so low on energy. When we neared a fast-food chain, I pulled in. We'd done plenty of drive-thrus when he was little; I had to hope he'd behave himself at one now.

At the sight of the familiar neon sign and bright plastic trim, Raja hooted softly and sat up in his seat, hands on the window. He glanced at me and back at the drive-thru, unable to believe this lucky turn.

By the time we got to the loudspeaker, Raja couldn't keep himself quiet. He bounced in the seat, hooting and squeaking. My sunglasses were out of the seat pocket and then in his hand and then tilted on his face. It was as though he'd decided wearing sunglasses was the only way to accurately reflect the joy he was feeling.

"Excuse me?" squawked the loudspeaker when, distracted by Raja, I forgot to give our order.

"I need four strawberry milk shakes and eight orders of hash browns," I finally said.

"Hello?" the baffled voice said. I could only imagine what my yammering over an overexcited orangutan sounded like through the woman's headset.

I placed our order again and we passed through to the pick-up window.

He loves this food, I figured. *And he deserves a few moments of happiness.*

I sounded like a divorced dad breaking all the rules.

At the cashier, I cracked the window only a little, to minimize the sounds of ape ruckus. I handed over my dad's credit card. There was no doubt in my mind that FriendlyLand would have contacted him. So the question was: How long until he shut off the account?

The cashier ran the card. While she waited for the amount to clear, she sneaked glances beneath her visor, trying to see what the commotion was in the backseat. I yawned and leaned exaggeratedly to shield Raja from view, though his excited squeaks continued.

"It's this cool new British DJ," I explained to the cashier as I fiddled with the radio knob. "He's sampled all these, like, jungle-y, ape-y sounds."

The cashier nodded warily, then handed me bagfuls of milk shakes and hash browns. I passed one of the milk shakes to Raja. When he squeaked in outrage, I passed a second one back. As she saw a hairy orange hand reach for the drink, the cashier's jaw dropped. I waved and pulled away.

It wasn't until I'd already sipped my milk shake that Raja started in on his; he'd always waited to see me eating something before he'd try it. Soon he was happily slurping away and smacking his lips.

I was proud of myself for pulling off a fast-food trip. And that shot of pride was handy, because it distracted me from the fact that I had absolutely no idea what I was doing or where we were going.

I glanced into the backseat and took a long moment to take in the scene. Raja had stopped drinking, and was instead drawing on the window with the milk shake at the end of his straw. I faced forward again, trying to blot the non-dairy disaster from my mind. *I might need to buy some upholstery cleanser.*

For the next half hour, Raja stared out the window. Then he lay down, elephant on his lap. I thought he was sleeping, but when I looked back I saw he was staring at the ceiling. Seeing him so focused on nothing at all kind of freaked me out, so I plugged my phone into the radio and tried different tracks. Raja didn't react to any of them, until I streamed the soundtrack to *Pocahontas*, which had been one of his childhood favorites. Sure enough, he started wiggling his toes, then tossing the elephant and catching it whenever a song hit the chorus.

Sluggish from the milk shakes and hash browns, I stared dreamily in the rearview as Raja played. Movement, sunlight, company: They were such simple ingredients for feeling so content.

When my phone started vibrating, I almost didn't notice it. Then I saw who it was, and jabbed the stereo's power off. I stared out at the road while the little phone icon danced away in my lap. FATHER, MOBILE.

I couldn't put it off forever. I hit the speakerphone icon. "Hello?" I said.

"John."

"Hey."

Raja took that moment to burp in the backseat. It was an unmistakably orangutan sound — lots of lip flapping.

"What's that?" my father said.

"Um, that? Well, jeez." Raja burped again, loudly. "To tell you the truth, it's, um, Raja."

"What do you mean, 'it's, um, Raja'? Do you have *any idea* how much trouble you're in?"

Heat flushed my collar. "That so-called zoo that you sent him to? They had him in a tiny cage in the direct sun. They've nearly been shut down multiple times because of animals dying from neglect. It was a death pit. Raja probably would have gotten sick and died as soon as winter came."

"That was not your call to make, John!"

"I got him out of there. I had to."

"Where are you now? Give me an address. I can talk them into taking him back."

"Uh-uh. No way."

"Where do you think you're heading?"

"I don't know."

"You can't drive around the country with an ape. You simply cannot. And do you think your mother will all of a sudden say, *Oh, yes, we can take an orangutan in now*, like it's even a possibility? You couldn't possibly be so naive. I signed a *binding contract* with FriendlyLand. Do you know that? Are you doing this just to get me into trouble?"

"Have you heard of the ape personhood case?" I asked quietly.

"What the hell are you talking about?"

"This lawyer is saying that apes are self-aware, like people, and that they deserve rights —"

"I'll happily give an ape rights as soon as he calls me up and asks for them. But Raja can't, because he's *an animal*. The property of —"

"If you could see in my backseat right now, you wouldn't say — Hold on." My phone was beeping, so I glanced at the screen. "I have to go. I'll call you back."

"What do you mean, you have to — ?"

I clicked over, still on speakerphone.

"Hello?" I said.

"Hi, John. It's Nancy Jackson, from FriendlyLand. Can you talk for a minute?"

"Dr. Jackson. Of course. Sure."

I pulled over. Raja kiss-squeaked. I'm sure he had no idea what was going on, but he was happy to share in the excitement anyway.

"From the sound of it you still have Raja with you. Let me cut to the chase: I almost didn't call. I still think I'm probably making a mistake. But you've been on my mind since yesterday. You and Raja both."

"How's everything going over there?" I asked. "At Friendly-Land? Are they mad?"

"I don't know," she said. "Probably. I only go in twice a week, and I've been at my private practice since your breakout. Did your parents call the lawyer?"

"My mom is on it."

"Well, if she gets Raja added, that should block FriendlyLand. If they'll listen. In the meantime I called every ape sanctuary where I have any connections. I'm afraid it's not good news, John. None of them can take on a sub-adult male orangutan. He'd endanger the rest of the animals in such close quarters. It would spell disaster for what they're trying to do."

I didn't say anything. I understood where she was coming from, but the sanctuaries were my only option. I had to risk that they wouldn't turn Raja away if I showed up groveling for mercy.

Dr. Jackson went on. "The hard truth is that there is no good place for an ape in the United States. Their home habitats are being decimated, but they have *no* habitat here. Even at a sanctuary he'd be behind bars, serving time for someone else's crime. You're trying to find a comfortable place for Raja that doesn't exist. You can't give him back his mother. You can't give him back his small size and lesser strength, which allowed him to live as if he were a human for his early years. Those days are over."

"And here I was, hoping you had good news," I said.

She laughed grayly. "Have you heard of CITES? It's a treaty organization governing the welfare of endangered species. In virtually all cases, CITES prohibits the transportation of any endangered animal across international lines. But there are occasional, *very* occasional, exceptions. Only once in my lifetime have I known of anyone who succeeded in returning an ape from the States to its home country."

I sat bolt upright. "Back home? Like, to Indonesia? What would I have to do?"

She sighed. "There is a huge amount of bureaucracy to contend with, and unfortunately I don't have the capacity to help you a great deal with it. But the basics are this: You need a senator to grease the wheels with the state department. A sitting senator has little reason to take on that level of liability, so it's a huge favor to reel in. No one I know has managed it. But I figured if your parents were able to smuggle Raja *in* on a flight, they might have connections. I have no idea, of course — they're your parents, not mine. But it struck me as possible."

"Uh-huh," I said, nodding even as my heart sank. "My father's connections. Right. Okay. Got it." He'd lost his job at HappyFoods years ago. He didn't have any money left. And — oh, right — I'd just hung up on him.

"And then you'd have to find a rehabilitation center in Indonesia willing to take him on. Do you know if he's from Borneo or Sumatra? Those are two separate subspecies, of course."

I ran through my memories. My father pointing to a certain bag of coffee, calling it *Raja beans*. "I think he's from Sumatra."

"Unusual. Most are from Borneo. But there is a terrific conservation group on the ground in Sumatra. This is a gray zone in international politics, so there are no guarantees. If push comes to shove, I'll disclaim responsibility for even bringing up the idea.

You came up with this on your own, do you understand? Your first move will have to be to get your parents on board."

"Right. Get my parents on board."

"Let me know once you've made headway, John," Nancy said.

The moment I'd thanked Dr. Jackson and gotten off the phone, Raja kiss-squeaked and pointed to the stereo. I turned *Pocahontas* back on, and he swung his legs in delight. "You think I'm an ignorant savage, and you've been so many places, I guess it must be so . . ."

We resumed our journey, entering Charleston, where the buildings knitted closer and closer until there was no green between them. As civilization hunched in toward us, my palms went chill and sweaty, adrenaline pricking the back of my neck. Picking up on my tension, Raja planted himself in the middle of the backseat, arms folded around the stuffed elephant, pinning it to his chest. His eyes locked with mine in the rearview. It was as if he was saying *help me.*

I love you, I signed.

He kept his hands clasped tight, his golden eyes staring deep into mine. Any human being would have been embarrassed to look at me so frankly, with so pure a need. But not Raja. When we passed through a toll booth, he didn't do his usual curious squeaking and staring, just held tight, eyes downcast. He'd been out of his element in my father's house, but downtown Charleston was even more distant from the jungles of Indonesia. It was as if he knew he was in too far over his head to take care of himself at all now, that whatever happened next was up to me.

Which didn't seem fair to Raja at all.

On the far side of the city, we pulled off at a rest stop and parked in the most deserted spot so I could take Raja into the woods to pee. I'd have expected to run into tons of people stopping us or asking awkward questions, but it was amazing how easy it was to travel long distances without anyone talking to you, even when you were carting around an orangutan. Raja was a creature behind tinted windows, shuttled over to trees to pee when no one was looking. He was kept as simply as most secrets.

When we got back into the car I called my mother.

"John, where are you?"

"We're in West Virginia. I've got Raja."

"Are you okay? What's your plan?"

My mouth opened, but I couldn't think of any answer. There was no plan. That was the problem.

"Oh, John, we're really stuck, aren't we?" Mom said. Her tone was angry, but I was so grateful for that *we*. "What's your nearest airport? I'll fly out to meet you."

"School's not over for you," I said. "You can't just pick up and leave. They'll fire you, and you need that job."

"I don't care," she said. "You can't do this on your own."

"We're okay," I said, not quite believing myself. I leaned back and ruffled Raja's hair. "Listen, there could possibly be a way out of this." I told her what Nancy had told me, that with a senator's approval we might be able to transport him back to Sumatra.

"Even if we somehow managed to wrangle permission, can you imagine how much it would cost to fly him all that way?" my mom asked. "This whole situation was brought on by your father's being bankrupt. I've got only a schoolteacher's salary. We don't have that kind of money."

"I know, Mom. I'm sorry."

She paused a few moments, and knowing my mom I figured she was trying to find something positive to say. "I did call that lawyer, by the way — he was very nice on the phone, and was excited to be able to add an orangutan to his list. Apparently he only had chimps until now. So that small part's accomplished."

"Oh God, thanks," I said.

"As for next steps, I'm not even sure who our senator is," my mom admitted.

"We can look it up on our phones," I said.

Mom let out a long breath. "This isn't how I would have done things, John, not at all. We'll definitely have a long talk about this when you get home. But send me the actual address of the senator — I'll make sure that someone there talks to me, and showing up is probably the best way. Keep your phone on."

"Thanks, Mom."

"Honestly, sweetie, I can't imagine this will actually work. But I'll give it my best shot. For you."

"I love you. Thanks."

Because I didn't know where to go, I kept driving. The sign said the next rest stop was in seventy-five miles, but that one was closed so I had to continue on longer than I'd planned. We were in suburbs when Raja started to grunt, then unbuckled his belt. He rolled to the other side of the backseat and rolled back, a scaled-down version of the pacing he used to do in his trailer. When he started to kick the doors with his good leg, I made sure the child-proof locks were engaged.

I turned up *Pocahontas*, but Raja ignored it and continued to drag himself back and forth across the car, peering through one window and then the other.

"Okay, okay!" I told him.

I found a huge box store that was basically its own freeway exit. The moment Raja heard the turn signal he got quiet and curious, staring at the little green arrows and exhaling in quiet astonishment every time they blinked.

I parked at the far end of the lot. Making sure no one was looking, I walked around the car to the back door that faced away from the store, and brought Raja out. We ducked over to the grassy edge, and I waited for him to pee. But he didn't. He stood there holding my hand, his eyes inscrutable. He let go of me, wrist-walked back to the car, and got in. I had no idea where he'd gone to in his mind.

Once I was sure he was safely inside, I headed toward the store's entrance. The moment my father's car was out of view, the moment I was nothing more than a guy walking through an ordinary parking lot, my shoulders loosened. A woman passed me with her toddler in a race car shopping cart, and I smiled at them as I walked.

I filled a cart with food and water, then got a little nervous when I handed the credit card over and it took a while to authorize. But the transaction went through, and soon enough I headed out into the hot day, pausing and blinking at the exit when the sun blinded me. Loaded down with bags, I made my way toward the back of the lot, my father's car only slowly becoming visible as my eyes adjusted to the bright light. At first I thought they were tricking me, but then I panicked when I realized they weren't.

The car was shaking.

I broke into a sprint, staggering around vehicles, apples and water bottles rolling from my shopping bags as I ran. The customers wheeling carts stopped and stared, but I didn't have a thought to spare for them. Once I was near my car I dropped the bags and threw open the door.

The air smelled horrible — like Raja must have been saving something during his pee break. Before I could react, a giant orange shape lunged out of the back and tackled me, hurling me to the asphalt. I tried to defend myself, casting my arms around my face. Ferocious hands crushed my throat, an immense weight creaked my ribs and lit up my chest. But Raja's mouth was closed, and his head was pressed tight to me. He wasn't attacking; he was hugging.

I couldn't get any breath in. When I managed to suck in a desperate gasp of air, Raja sat up, alarmed. All his weight was now on my pelvis, but at least I could breathe. I gasped and tried to push him off, but despite my size it was impossible. *I'm sorry*, he signed, though he made no move to release me.

A young mother in the parking lot was standing by the door of her minivan, talking urgently into her phone as she gaped at me. A little girl, probably her daughter, was running into the store.

To get help.

"Raja," I gasped. "Get off me. We have to get out of here!"

He didn't move, just wrapped his arms as tightly as he could around my shoulders. By twisting and getting my hands on the car's frame, though, I was able to drag myself out from under him.

I heard a grinding sound as the young mother's grocery cart rolled across the parking lot. She must have let go of it to make her emergency call. When it creaked its way to us and dinged a nearby car, Raja perked to attention, staring up in interest at the blue plastic contraption, loaded with bright goodies.

"No, Raja," I said warningly.

But it was too late. He got to all fours and lumbered across the parking lot.

The young woman started screaming.

"It's okay," I called to her. "He's not dangerous."

But while I saw brother, she saw beast.

At the noise she was making, Raja perked up and stared at her, the cart forgotten. I could see him gauging her, trying to figure her out. He knew he wasn't going to hurt her, so he couldn't figure out what the fuss was. He lifted from all fours so he could stare about on two legs, looking for the menace.

The young mother continued screaming.

"Raja," I said. "In the car. *Now.*"

A sort of wounded confusion on his face, Raja stepped toward her. The woman bolted toward the store, but then Raja picked up his speed to follow her. She froze.

Raja froze, too, eyes dancing as he tried to figure out this new game.

When he took another step toward her, the woman screeched and sprinted back to her van. "It's okay, it's really okay," I called. "Just stay calm."

Screaming, she launched herself toward the open side door. But her body was flailing, and she didn't quite make it. Her head struck the van's frame, and she fell back onto the ground.

Raja paused, making concerned noises, while the woman groggily got to her feet. She'd busted her forehead on the asphalt. Nothing too major, but there was blood. In sympathy, Raja patted his own bandaged thigh. He looked at me. *What do we do?*

"There it is! There it is!" I heard a little girl's voice say.

I turned to see the daughter coming toward us, tugging the hand of a security guard. His other hand was at something holstered at his waist.

"Keep her away," the young mom called.

"Are you okay, ma'am?" said the guard, his voice draining as he saw Raja. He unholstered his gun. "What *is* that?"

"Everything's fine," I said, stepping toward Raja, arms outstretched, palms open.

"Did that thing attack you?" the guard called, once he'd gotten close enough to see the blood on the woman's face.

Eyes wide and rimmed in white, she held out her hands to stop the guard from coming any closer. "Keep my daughter back."

I looked at the guard, who'd started barking at someone in his radio, and then at the woman, her forehead bleeding into her eyes. Raja and I had only seconds before this spun out of control.

Raja was still walking toward her. I called out his name again, but he didn't react. He was waiting for the woman to restart the game.

I took off toward him. Once I was near enough, I slammed my hand down on Raja's shoulder. He whirled, teeth bared. Once he saw it was just me, he relaxed. Though he kept his attention on the panicking young mother, he wrapped his arm protectively around me, giving me some of his weight.

"We're going," I told Raja as I started us toward my father's car. Mercifully, he moved along with me, though his attention stayed on the young woman. "We're going!" I repeated, louder, in the direction of the security guard and the girl.

When I opened the car door, Raja bounded in, and then emerged again. The blue stuffed elephant was in his hands, and he held it up toward the young woman in the van. A peace offering.

"No," I said to him. "She doesn't want your elephant. Back in, *now*."

He read my tone, promptly getting back in the car and dropping the toy onto the passenger seat.

Now that Raja and I were in the car, the young mother stepped toward her van but reeled, striking the ground with her knees and then staggering to her feet, holding her arms out to her daughter.

I settled behind the wheel, the damaged driver's seat creaking at my back. Raja was half in the passenger seat and half in my lap, struggling to keep his hands clasped around my waist. I flailed across his body and managed to get the door closed without crushing his feet.

I started the car and threw it into reverse, Raja whimpering while I backed into the lot. I heard a bang on the rear window, and I whirled, fearing it was the security guard. But I'd bumped the mother's shopping cart. It rolled back toward her van.

Raja kiss-squeaking the whole time, I put the car in drive and peeled out. In the rearview I saw the guard barking into his radio, staring after us. The girl had reached her mother, who wrapped her in a fierce hug. Heart in my mouth, I pulled out of the parking lot and headed toward the highway. My hands wouldn't stop shaking;

I couldn't escape the sight of that mother's bleeding head, the terror in her daughter's face. Caused by me and Raja.

As Raja and I got miles between us and the superstore, I felt the heavy, hot weight in my lap relax. Raja used his hands as a cushion between his cheek and my thigh, and gradually his mouth slacked open and his eyelids smoothed. I stroked the side of his face. Only half an hour after our escape, Raja had fallen asleep. A small miracle.

I was tired and I had no plan. As I drove in circles around an apartment complex, the enormity of our situation brought me lower and lower. I hit the steering wheel whenever the desperation became too much to keep inside, and each time Raja scrunched his eyes tighter and curled his head down into his chest. He had his hands wrapped around his wounded thigh — the bandages were wet and pink; his wound must have started leaking in the scuffle. I got back onto the highway and started scanning for isolated motels where I could patch him up fresh.

I ground my fingers into the wheel until they hurt, some of my tension dissipating by even that minor punishment of myself. I knew I was reaching my edge. The only thing that kept me from my hatred of myself was the weight in my lap. I'd done so much wrong, I was sure of it; but in that moment I felt an odd moment of rightness within the wrongness, because Raja and I were together.

NINE

After a point I was driving without any awareness of where I was going, or any awareness that I didn't know where I was going. Too much of my mind was elsewhere. I just obeyed lights, turned and stopped and turned again.

For a while after he woke up, Raja signed *I'm sorry* over and over. Then he sprawled half in the backseat and half in the front, his shoulders over the gearshift and his legs dragging on the backseat floor. He watched the world outside the windshield for a while, until his breathing slowed again. Scenery and company had always been enough to set his world right.

Eventually I had to pee. I found a big bookstore, parked my car in a shaded spot around back, rolled the windows down slightly so Raja had air, and left the softly snoring ape while I went in to use the bathroom.

When I came out, my pulse quickened when I saw there were two kids with skateboards staring into the car. They held their boards to their chests like shields as they murmured to each other.

"Hey," one of them said as I approached. "Awesome. Is that thing yours?"

"Yep," I said, phone tight in my fist. I hoped they were talking about the Toyota — but it wasn't the type of car that got that sort of attention. "It's mine."

"What *is* it?"

I gritted my teeth. Yep. Definitely not the car they were gawking at. Raja was at the back window, ignoring the boys but staring up at the bookstore's neon sign. He always loved bright things. His T-shirt had ridden up his torso so that it was around his neck, like some guy showing off his abs at the beach. "Oh, you mean that? He's an orangutan."

"An orangutan? Like, a monkey?"

"An ape, but yeah."

"Are they expensive?"

"Trust me, you don't want one. They're cute when they're little, but it's a whole other story now."

"I still want one. I'd take care of it. Can we pet him?"

I looked around the parking lot. No one was around right now, but the last thing I needed was to cause a scene or for one of these boys to bring his friends or parents over. "Nope," I said. I decided I'd go for the big guns, and held up my hand with the missing finger. "He bit this off. You don't want to pet him."

"Holy crap," the other boy said. "It *ate your finger*? And you still drive it around in your car?"

Huh. The boy was right, though I'd never thought of my choice that simply.

"We need to skip school more often," the boy's friend said. "Because this is *awesome*."

"Question. If I may. Did he spit out your finger, or did he eat it?" the first boy asked. He was turning out to be on the nerdier side of the skateboarder spectrum.

"Jeez," I said. "I guess he ate it. I mean, that wasn't why he bit me, but he swallowed it, so . . . yeah."

"So you're, like, literally part of him."

His friend guffawed and slapped him on the shoulder. "Dude, that's so wrong."

"No, I guess it's true," I said. "Look, guys, I gotta go."

They pressed their faces against the glass, and Raja fixed his gaze on them and brought his face even closer, so that only the window separated them. The glass soon fogged. Raja lifted his hand so his finger was outstretched, E.T.-style. It was curved and knuckle-y, a little witchy. The boys gasped but held near. Showing them my wound had worked; neither of them was about to reach through the gap and touch Raja's hand. "You should really leave the window cracked more," one of them said. "Dogs die in hot cars."

"He's not a *dog*," the other boy said.

"I *know*. But that doesn't mean he can't die in a hot car, dumb butt."

Raja moved to the other rear window and then back. A rumbling sound came from the backseat, low and gurgly. "What was that?" one boy asked.

"Oh, man," the other one said, overjoyed. "He just pooped!"

"What?" I said, then cupped my hands against the glass so I could see in better. "Oh, no. Raja!" He'd left a stream of chunky orange goop along the backseat. He had a tendency to poop when he was stressed out.

"Huh huh, you're going to be in so much trouble," the other boy chuckled.

"All right, guys," I said, sighing. "It's been fun, but I've got to go."

One tapped on the window. "Aw, man. See you later, big guy. If you ever want to give him up, I bet I could convince my mom to let me take him."

Raja grunted at the boy tapping on the window, then turned to examine his own poop, butt high. "Ha!" the other boy said. "What the hell's he doing? That's so awesomely gross."

I clicked the front door unlocked, got in, and locked it again. Muffled by the window, I dimly heard the boys laugh when Raja crawled over the back of the passenger seat to sit beside me, setting the elephant in his lap and buckling the belt over them both.

I sighed, peering into the rearview as I opened the window. "Raja, it reeks in here. What am I going to do with you?"

As I turned the engine on and backed up, those words hung in my mind. *What am I going to do with you?* Indeed. Question of the hour.

I parked on a service road that had zero curious skateboarders. To keep Raja occupied, I picked a cartoon to stream on my phone. I wasn't sure what he would like out of the free options, so I chose a Chinese cartoon that was a knock-off of *Pocahontas* called *Green Tree Canoe Princess!* It had bright colors, and I figured that would be enough to do the trick.

Sure enough, he was transfixed. While he was distracted I took some fast-food napkins and cleaned up the poop as best I could, dropping the stinking mess into a dumpster before hitting the road again. He kept watching his cartoon while I drove, occasionally giving a rasp of concern or pleasure or shaking the screen. When the movie finished, Raja dropped the phone, letting it clatter to the car's floor. I pulled to the side of the road and picked it up. One voice mail — I hadn't heard the call over the rattling soundtrack.

I thought it might have been Mom, but it was someone else. I sat bolt upright and listened. "John. It's Nancy Jackson again. I wanted to let you know I've looked into a couple more things. We should talk. Can you call me as soon as possible? I'm shorthanded so I'm the one doing rounds today, but I'll have my cell with me. Thanks."

Raja still grumbling beside me, I hit RETURN CALL with trembling fingers.

"John, hi," Dr. Jackson said. I heard panting in the background, barks and whines. Like Raja's, but more frantic. "Sorry," she said, "I'm next to the dog cages. Can you still make out my voice?"

"Loud and clear," I said. Raja must have heard the dogs on the other end, because he forgot about the cartoon, leaning forward between the seats and pressing his face toward the phone, his expression curious and hopeful.

"How are you two doing?" Dr. Jackson asked.

"Not so well, honestly," I said. "Feeling sort of lost here." I considered telling her that Raja had indirectly injured that woman in the parking lot. But I worried that she wouldn't be willing to help me anymore if I did.

"I'm sorry to hear that," Dr. Jackson said. "But you two are healthy and okay? You're safe?"

"Yeah. I'm not sure where I'm going, though." I ran my hand along the orange hair low on Raja's back.

Dr. Jackson paused. "Well, here's a possibility. One of the big-animal vets I used to work with is at the Jacksonville Zoo. Turns out the primate center in Leipzig, Germany, has been trying to get a female bonobo from the Jacksonville Zoo to diversify its breeding population. It's a tricky procedure, since transporting an ape is technically contrary to CITES. After two weeks of effort, they got approval. But now it turns out that bonobo female is pregnant, so she can't be transported after all."

"Okay . . ." I said. I couldn't tell where Nancy was going with this. My mind went in all sorts of ridiculous sci-fi directions, imagining some invention that would allow Raja to mate with German bonobos and get sent to Leipzig.

"So the transfer is dead in the water," Dr. Jackson said. "But the paperwork is not. Do you follow?"

"You could . . . change the name to Raja? Do they have other orangutans in Leipzig?"

"He wouldn't go to Leipzig. The requests are specific in some ways and broad in others. The important thing is already accomplished: The request is approved. I could ask my friend to amend the type of ape and the destination."

"You mean to Sumatra?" I said. "Where Raja is from?"

"Precisely."

My heart surged, tears studding my eyes. "Dr. Jackson, I don't know what to say. What do I have to do? Just tell me what I have to do!"

"The permission was granted for a departure from Dulles Airport on June twenty-seventh. Five days. The airport is getting prepared, and the member countries of CITES have been notified, so that part is all taken care of. If you're willing to do this, maybe one of your parents can get an amendment letter from the senator's office, and a transfer of obligation from the zoo. They should be willing, because then they'll no longer be defendants in a court case. If that works, I'll email Orangutan Rescue Sumatra and introduce you. We don't even know if they will accept him, of course — there are four thousand ways for this to fall through, so please try not to get your hopes up yet. It helps that Raja was born in Sumatra, so you can argue that you're repatriating him. There's some precedent for that, though those orangutans had all been smuggled to other countries in Asia."

"Wow," I said. "Thank you for doing as much as you can. My mom can try to get the amendment done. I'll send you her contact info. And if there's any way I can help, any way at all, tell me."

"Of course," Dr. Jackson said. "I'll get right on it. In the meantime, you need to lay as low as possible."

Raja had lost interest in the phone, and had started flipping the glove compartment handle instead. All my remaining cash was in there — good thing I'd locked it. "Thank you," I said to Dr. Jackson, laying a hand over Raja's in an attempt to stop him from breaking the car. "Thank you so much."

"John?" she asked. "Do you have a place to go?"

"Well . . . not really," I admitted. "My father's moving this weekend, and he's sort of the problem here. He's why Raja wound up at FriendlyLand in the first place. And my mom lives across the country."

"My house is tiny," Dr. Jackson said. "But my son's off at college, so you could use his room. And I could clear the garage out so Raja would have a place to be. Just for the couple of days it will take before the flight's arranged. *If* it's arranged. You should ask your mom, and have her call me. As long as she's fine with it, it's okay by me."

"You'd do that for me?"

"Look," she said, "just because I work for FriendlyLand doesn't mean I'm heartless. You and that charming orange young man need a place to go."

"I don't know what to say except thanks," I said.

"I'll text you my address."

After the call, Raja and I sat in the parked car. I stared out the windshield, lost in thought, Raja lying on his back in the rear, drumming his fingers on his chest. I was trying to hold back the hope surging in me, the hope that could so easily wind up dashed. But I couldn't help it — the chance that there could be a way out, that Raja could have somewhere to go, somewhere to *be*, made me want to sing. So I did, tapping my hands on the steering wheel and whooping nonsense.

Excited by my excitement, Raja started making his own

frenzied noises, gooseflesh standing up on his cheeks. I slapped
him on the bottom of his feet. He sat up, surprised, laughing in his
raspy, near-silent way. "Tomorrow," I said, "we'll start your diet to
get you in shape. But for now, it's time for more milk shakes. We
deserve a celebration. You might be going home."

PART FOUR

EVERY MOVING THING THAT LIVETH SHALL
BE MEAT FOR YOU.

— GENESIS 9:3

For another sunrise and sunset, he and his mother didn't move from their perch in the tree. Then, the following morning, she made her sluggish, halting way down, using her grasping feet and one good hand, keeping the injured one high in the air.

Once on the swampy ground, she collapsed flat. Although he was still worried, he also loved the feeling of being crushed between her and the moist, cool soil, nearer to his mother's body than he could ever be without the pressure of the earth pushing back. She slurped at the brackish water of the slow river, gulping and gulping as if she could never get enough. He wriggled out from under her and took a drink alongside her, watching her expression to make sure he was doing it right.

As they made their slow, labored return up the tree's trunk, he had a good view of his mother's hand, swollen to the size of a jackfruit. The fingers looked shrunken and stubby, like her red and plumping palm was slowly consuming them.

That sundown his mother fell fully asleep for the first time since the bite, not squealing and shifting at all during the night. Come morning she hiked him to her and he eagerly wrapped his arms around her coarse orange hair. They began their one-handed way through the treetops. His mother was back.

As they traveled through the jungle, time again stretched, and he was no longer aware of separate days and nights. Instead, he returned to his old work: remembering where food was. The corridor of purple berries leads to the plain with the brown shoots. The sweet yellow-green leaves are on the other side of the lagoon from the pineapple bush. Someday he would need to know this for himself.

One morning, they woke to a crashing sound as a tree fell somewhere out of sight. He was excited, making soft hooting sounds. His mother tucked him close and sped through the treetops. No direction. Just away.

TEN

Raja really liked presents. Well, who doesn't like presents? But Raja *really* liked them. When we first put him in the backyard, I'd bring him something new to play with every few days. A sturdy yellow dump truck, a basketball, a squeak toy, a plastic bat, stuffed animals of all kinds. What he loved most about each gift was the unwrapping. Sometimes he'd rip the paper to shreds, but other times he'd carefully undo it, and spend a long time studying the design before he'd remember there had been a present beneath.

Once he got acquainted with a new toy, he'd pace back and forth in his enclosure, dragging his foot so it made a shallow trench in the dirt. Then he'd line up his toys in the trench, from the tallest one down to the shortest. The spacing was exact — the toys looked like sugar buttons down a Christmas cookie. I'd come home from school to find him in his tire swing, leaning over the side while he rocked in the air, admiring the order he'd created.

As he got older he started giving gifts back to me. Once he'd mastered the timing of my arrival at the enclosure gate after the school bus had rumbled by, I'd come outside to find him standing in the center of the fenced area, hands behind his back. Then, when I got near enough, he'd hold forward his present. Of course, options are slim when you're living in an enclosure, so he'd have to give me something I'd already given him. I'd receive one of his toys, roughly draped in torn wrapping paper. He'd make his pleased raspy noises while I removed the paper and saw my gift.

He was very shrewd about what he gave me. It was always whatever toy he liked least at the moment. The dump truck after the wheel fell off. A lion after he had plucked out its eyes. The plastic bat once it had dented and cracked, pebbles rattling around inside.

As a kid I'd been amazed that Raja and I were exchanging gifts — that after I did something nice for him, he'd do something nice for me. But I was overlooking what was right in front of me: Raja was making his own line of toys, deciding what was kept and what was given away. He was a thinking creature giving himself something to control, when he had no power over the rest of his own life.

As I drove with Raja toward Dr. Jackson's address, it came to me that I'd been raised with a kidnapping victim. He'd been taken from his home and plopped into mine. I hadn't done it, and I was through blaming myself for that part. But though I hadn't committed it, I still grew up with the victim of a crime. I'd called him my brother, when there might have been another orangutan in the wild who'd thought of him as a brother. When there'd been an orangutan in the wild who'd thought of him as her baby.

He'd been taken from the life he deserved so he could serve as an accessory in mine. And now we were on the road, driving through the night, chasing after our one hope of setting it right.

It rained on my way to Nancy's house, so I rolled up the windows. When I did, I realized what an assortment there was to the stink in the car. The underarms of my Fruit of the Loom T-shirt, on its third day without a wash; Raja's poop, the scent of which I hadn't quite managed to get out of my father's backseat despite a stop at an auto shop for vinyl cleanser; coffee and soda and spilled milk shake; blood.

Halfway through our journey, Raja climbed to the front and set himself up in the passenger seat, buckling the seat belt neatly over his belly. I stole sideways glances at him as I drove. He'd be staring out the window, but once he became aware of my attention he'd turn to me, his golden eyes meeting mine. Something complex would pass between us, something rich with history and beyond words.

Eventually I needed a break from driving, so I took a random exit off the interstate, pulling off along side roads until we were driving through patchy isolated fields. I got out and opened Raja's door. Watching me for cues the whole time, he stepped out. I faced away from him and peed into the grass. Once I'd finished and turned back around, I was surprised to find Raja bounding over from where he'd wandered. It must have made him confused and anxious that I'd faced away; he needed the comfort of a hug.

I sat on the trunk of the car, cracking my back. Raja soon joined me. With an orangutan intently following my every move, I pulled out my phone and, squinting to make out the screen in the bright sun, searched *orangutan + Sumatra*.

Critically endangered. Habitat loss and poaching make imminent extinction likely. They used to range throughout Asia, but as humans spread they've been confined to a shrinking portion of Sumatra, and the pockets of rain forest that make up their habitat are shrinking fast. They might be the first apes to go extinct in the wild.

I imagined orangutans in China thousands of years ago, looking down from the trees to see the first humans arriving, the beginning of the end.

One fact jumped out: Young orangutans spend years with their mothers in the wild. How old had Raja been when my father brought him to me?

I didn't really know.

We got back in the car, and I started driving again. Soon enough, my phone guided us off the interstate and onto a narrow road that passed through a state forest. Nothing spectacular, just acres of scrubby trees, but Raja was fascinated. He squeaked in pleasure, bowing low in the seat the better to see the treetops. Maybe he was looking for orangutans. I wondered, though, if he even knew what an orangutan was; he might not remember his own kind at all. Could he climb high in unfamiliar trees without falling? Could he survive without drive-thru milk shakes? If I managed to get him back into the jungle, would he walk up to the first human he saw, even if it was a hunter killing orangutans?

"Hey, Raja," I said, putting my arm around his shoulders, "do you even think of yourself as an ape?"

In response, he made a cup out of his hands and face-planted into it. *Let's go for ice cream.*

Sumatran jungle, scrub forest in West Virginia — it seemed impossible that they could both exist in the same world. I put *Green Tree Canoe Princess!* back on but Raja was uninterested, instead staring out the window at the blurring trees. We skirted the edge of a state park, winding around scrubby hills. Our car startled flocks of wild birds that would burst into the air as we passed. Raja got excited each time, lowering himself onto the floor mat so he could look up and watch where the birds went.

My phone told me to turn down a narrow dirt driveway. After a shady bend I came to a trim wooden house surrounded by a chain-link fence. Dr. Jackson must have heard my car approach, because she came out and stood at the gate. I rolled down the window and was immediately blasted by hot afternoon air. "Is it okay to unlock the doors?" I asked. Raja was already trying his, working the handle back and forth. Good thing he'd never quite been able to figure out car locks.

"Of course," Dr. Jackson said. "No one else is around."

Raja bounded out of the car as soon as I unlocked his door, crouching behind a pine tree and taking a long pee. His wounded leg, I was glad to see, wasn't giving him too much trouble — though the bandage was still on, he was able to put weight on both feet when he squatted.

Already sweaty, Raja stood beside the car, one hand on the hood. He glanced at me for approval, then, after I smiled encouragingly, took a step toward Dr. Jackson. Stuffed elephant dragging in the dirt, he stared at the muddy grass of her front lawn, then predictably lifted his foot and examined the bottom, checking to see whether the mud had become part of him.

"Welcome, John," Dr. Jackson said. "Good to see you. You know, without the police involved."

I smiled grimly, trying to bar the memory of pistols and shouting, the red mist of Raja's blood. "Hi, Dr. Jackson," I said.

"Welcome to my home," she said. "It's not much, but at least it's secluded."

At that moment a brown-and-black blur bounded through the house's doggie door. Barking its head off, it raced to the fence, skidding into it with a clatter. Raja mastered his fear for a moment, but when the dog started barking again he bolted for the car. He was soon shut in the back, peering fearfully through the rear window, stuffed elephant staring out right beside him.

"Sorry," Nancy said. "That's Allie, my mutt. She won't hurt him."

"He's always been a coward around dogs," I said. I rapped on the car window. "Come on, strong heart!" Just like my coach would tell us before we hit the field.

Allie the mutt sat at the fence, tail thumping the earth, eyes traveling between Dr. Jackson and Raja. "Maybe we'll leave them to figure this impasse out," Dr. Jackson said. "Raja will pluck up his courage and come out on his own once he gets hungry, I bet. Come on. Grab your bag, and I'll show you the house."

I got my duffel out of the trunk, but paused at the fence when I saw Raja still watching Allie, nervous and intent. "I think I'll stay out here for a few more minutes," I said. "I don't know if Raja is ready to be left alone." I didn't say the other thing I was thinking: *There are* tigers *in Sumatra. If he's scared of a dog, how is this ever going to work?*

"Okay," Nancy said. "I've brewed some iced tea. Back in a minute."

As she went inside I stood at the fence, watching Allie the mutt beam love at Raja and Raja beam fear at Allie the mutt. Tail thumping, tongue lolling; eyes narrowing, fists clenching. When Nancy came out and saw that the standoff was still going, she shook her head, a smile light on her face. "This is familiar from the apes I worked with during my internship. Courageous around people, gutless around dogs. Raja's typical. Nice T-shirt he's wearing, by the way."

As Dr. Jackson handed me an iced tea, Allie gave up on Raja and threaded my legs, her mud-colored hair stiff against my bare shins. After I petted her, she leaped happily around me, paws at my waist, sloshing my iced tea to the ground.

"You have a nice home," I said, gesturing around. It wasn't what most people would consider a nice home. Tiny peeling house, overgrown lawn, broken clay pots, smells of rot and growth. But it felt so *much* like a home. That's what made it nice.

"Thanks," Dr. Jackson said. "It was me and my son here for a long time, but he went off to college in January. So it's been a little empty since then. It will be nice to have someone else in the house for a few days."

Now that the dog was focused on me and not him, Raja was brave enough to crack the door open. He took a step out, an orange foot all that was visible behind the car door. Then Allie yipped and Raja vanished back into the car, slamming the door shut.

"I'm sorry Raja's being such a scaredy-cat," I said. "He's had a rough few days."

"He certainly has," Dr. Jackson said. "Poor guy."

Once Allie had calmed and was sitting at Dr. Jackson's feet, Raja emerged from the car. He stayed cautious and low to the ground, nose to a pothole puddle left from the rain. He looked up and around, expression both nervous and curious.

"I talked to her earlier today, but you should call your mom," Dr. Jackson said. "I know I'd want Daniel to call right when he arrived at the house of someone I hadn't met."

I nodded.

"Do you want me to dial her on my home phone?" she offered.

"No, I'll do it," I said, girding myself.

Dr. Jackson looked at me closely. The shadow of something familiar passed over her features. This happened to me in other places: at the DMV, with the cable guy, strangers sitting next to me in the barbershop. I look full-grown, so people forget that I'm young. Then it hits them all at once. "John," she said. "I don't mean to add to the pressure, but I need an honest answer from you. Do you want me to cancel all of this? Is too much going on for you to handle?"

I watched Raja pick up a long pine needle and swat it across each cheek, like a makeup brush. It *was* too much in too short a time. But like hell was I backing down. I couldn't see how that was an option, anyway. "No," I said. "I'm not canceling."

"Tell you what," Dr. Jackson said. "I'll bring Allie inside, and you can call your mom in privacy out here while Raja calms down. Then we'll see about settling you in. My nearest neighbor is a mile down the road, and off on vacation anyway, so don't worry about Raja getting himself into trouble. Let him wander wherever he likes."

"Thanks," I said. Once she'd gone inside, I took my phone in hand and sat on a rickety wooden picnic bench out front, my chin resting in my palms. Hot splintered wood prickled through my shorts. Raja busied himself uprooting weedy grasses growing around the table legs. When he saw me watching him, he dropped a handful of green blades and lifted himself to the tabletop. He lay flat on his back, reached out, and began to sift through the sparse red hair on my knee, as if there was some invisible thing to be tracked down between hair and skin. The simple act of his grooming me made my heart lighten. Raja knew what to do, through some basic orangutan magic.

I dialed my mom.

"Hello?"

"Hi, Mom," I said. "It's me. Sorry I only texted earlier. But I'm free now."

"John! Thank the Lord. What's happening to you? Where have you been?"

"Well, right now I'm sitting on a picnic bench, next to Raja." I drummed my fingers on the soft white skin on Raja's thigh, and he jerked. Then he drummed his fingers on mine. It tickled me, like it had tickled him.

"Start at the beginning," she said, her voice tense.

Once I'd assured Mom that Raja and I had safely arrived, she calmed down, slowing me down for more information whenever I rushed the story. "I've spoken to Dr. Jackson a few times," she eventually said. "She's lovely. I don't like the idea of your staying with a stranger, but she seems to care about animals a great deal. And Raja."

"Yeah, she's been great." I waited for Mom to ask how Raja was, but she didn't, so I barreled on. "Did Dr. Jackson tell you about the amendment, that there might be a way to transport Raja back to Indonesia?"

"Yes, she did. I spent all of today at Gillprin's office. The senator wasn't there, but her assistant called an assistant at another senator's office — long story short, they can change the paperwork. They'll email us the final document in the next day or two."

I'd been running my hands through Raja's hair, but I paused, not sure I could believe what I was hearing. Raja sat up, lifted my hand, and returned it to his head. *I didn't say you could stop grooming.*

"Mom," I said slowly, "does this all mean the plan could actually work?"

"He'll need a travel crate," Mom continued briskly. "Dr. Jackson told me there's a place in Delaware that does them, and they can deliver one to the airport, ready to use."

"Mom," I said slowly. "Thank you. So much."

She paused. "I've spent my life trying to keep you safe and happy. To stop your heart from being broken by what your father did. This is the best next step. So we'll make it happen. It's as simple as that."

"It's not as simple as that. This is huge, Mom. Huge."

"You're old enough for me to tell you that for years, just thinking about Raja has made me feel worthless." I bit the inside of my cheek. I'd never heard Mom talk about herself that way. "Trying to get him back to Indonesia is the best way to feel less worthless. I guess that's what I mean." She was breathing heavily, the beads of her wooden necklace clacking.

I chuckled. "Less worthless. A good goal."

She let out a lovely laugh, tired and genuine.

"I want to go with him," I said, twining my fingers around Raja's. He lifted our hands to his mouth and pretended to gnaw on my knuckle, to get a rise out of me. I sneaked out a finger to tweak his nose, to get a rise out of him. "I've let things be done to Raja for too long, without being there with him."

I thought my mom would fight me on that one, but she didn't. "There aren't any direct cargo flights to Sumatra," she said, "so the only way is to go via Singapore. Then Dr. Jackson said that the orangutan-rescue people can probably do a pickup —"

"Oh my God," I said. "All these logistics. I don't even have my passport."

"More than a passport — you need a visa to go to Sumatra. I'm express mailing the embassy a packet tomorrow to get that under way."

I glanced at my phone. The low battery light throbbed. "I can't believe this might actually happen," I said.

"More than 'might.' Looks like 'will.'"

I searched for words. *I've never left the States. And now I'm going to Sumatra? By myself? With an ape?*

"You'll be comfortable at Dr. Jackson's house?" Mom asked, her voice taking on its usual chirp. "Use my ATM card to buy her a nice gift. She seems lovely. Very touched by the lengths you went to for Raja."

Raja got curious about my ear, sticking his finger in to see what he might retrieve. I batted his hand away.

"You know," Mom continued, "that lawyer I spoke to, the one who is trying to argue that apes deserve human rights? He was a nice man, don't get me wrong, but he was a bit of a kook, too. I mean, what judge is going to believe that an ape is as important as a person? That they are *equal*? We should have mercy on animals, sure. But to say they're people is too far. I can't help but think there are less ridiculous things for everyone to worry about."

"I don't know," I said, clasping Raja's hand tight in mind so he'd stop hassling me. "I think we're taught we're unique on Earth from the moment we're born. That humans have the right to do as we will to other species because of that specialness. I think that causes a lot of problems for the rest of the world."

"We *are* different, John," Mom said. "Fundamentally different. God made man separate from beasts."

"Don't you think it would be weird if God meant us to be better than all the other creatures? Doesn't that seem . . . vain?"

"What I'm trying to get at is that, even if humans are the only children of God, that shouldn't stop us from trying to do the right thing for the rest of creation. To act with mercy whenever we can. Which is what you're trying to do with Raja. Even though you put me through a total ringer at the same time."

Her voice had suddenly turned sharp. We were stepping around an explosive vein in her.

"I don't feel like I have much choice in the matter, either, if it makes you feel any better," I said.

"Have you called your father, by the way?"

"Not lately," I said.

"You should. He's part of all this, too. It won't be pleasant, though. He's furious that you went behind his back. That you took his car. That he's potentially got legal trouble on his hands. Never occurs to him that you've been busy working for a better outcome for what he set up. But then again, he's never been able to see that."

I paused, quiet, feeling as orphaned as usual whenever my mother slammed my father.

"Anyway," she finally said. "Call him."

"The crate, plane ticket, fees, hotel once I'm there . . . that's a lot of money on the credit cards, Mom."

"We'll make it work, somehow."

I was quiet for a moment. I couldn't tell what that "we" meant, and was scared to ask. "Mom. I've never left the country. But now — flying to Sumatra, with Raja. Doing what, going off into the jungle? It's got me freaked out. Now that it might actually happen, I . . . I can't remember what I was saying." My breathing had turned rapid and shallow. Raja pressed his ear to my chest, trying to figure out the mystery of what I was feeling.

"John," Mom said, slow and deliberate, "you didn't think I'd let you do this alone, did you?"

"Wait — you mean you're coming?"

"Of *course* I'm coming. The school year ends Friday. I'll fly out and meet you directly at Dulles. Dr. Jackson will get you there."

A big gaping worry — I hadn't realized how large until now — snapped closed in an instant. My mom was coming. I didn't have to do it alone. "Mom. Thank you. Thank you!"

"Of course," she said. "No way am I sending my son to Sumatra by himself."

My phone vibrated — its battery was low. Something about our conversation, about translating words into ones and zeroes and beaming those into space so my mom's device could instantaneously decode them and she could tell me she'd be coming, all while Raja groomed through my leg hair, triggering some millions-of-years-old pleasure center, left me humbled and quiet by the scale of our world, by both the power and simplicity of it. The line went nearly silent as I listened to my mom chuckle. "I should be grounding you for a year, and instead I'm about to buy two tickets to Indonesia. Go figure."

"Thanks, Mom," I said. "Raja thanks you, too."

"Make sure you two behave and eat your vegetables tonight," she said.

"Yeah," I whispered. I slapped a mosquito picking through Raja's shoulder hair, working its way to his skin. Not to be outdone, Raja slapped me back, then got off the picnic table and started to wander Dr. Jackson's yard, kiss-squeaking in surprise and wonder at each new twig and lizard. "I'll make sure we eat our vegetables."

Mom and I talked a little longer, then said good night. When I ended the call, I looked for Raja, but he wasn't in sight. I checked around the car, on all sides and below it. No orangutan.

I heard scuffling, pebbles against soil, grunting. Following the sounds, I went around the back of the house and found Raja locked in combat with Allie. The dog growled. The orangutan squeaked. I broke into a run, worried that I'd find Raja's teeth clenched around Allie's neck. But then I recognized Raja's raspy sigh of pleasure. He and Allie separated for a moment, then lunged at each other again. They rolled in the dirt. Allie disengaged and pranced a circle around Raja, eyes manic with joy at having made a new friend.

Dr. Jackson had cleaned out her garage, dumping lawn tools and storage boxes into her backyard and putting an old quilt in the corner for Raja to sleep on. She brought me to her son's empty bedroom, where she'd made the bed with fresh sheets, but one look at that quiet room and I knew where I preferred to be. All I had to do was ask, and she put a cot and sleeping bag in the garage.

After Dr. Jackson had examined Raja's wounds and replaced the bandages, Raja positioned his quilt beside the cot, as if he was going to sleep on the ground. The moment the lights were out, though, he climbed into bed with me. Years ago, we'd slept in a comfortable double bed in an air-conditioned bedroom, but now we were wedged together on top of the squeaky canvas. Despite the heat, despite our uncomfortable position and the stink of orangutan breath, I slept through the night easily.

It was Raja's breath that woke me up. It had been hot in the garage while we were falling asleep, but the temperature had dropped during the night and he'd wrapped himself tightly around me for warmth, his lips inches from my nose. Orangutan breath: more effective than smelling salts. I startled awake, snorting and flailing.

Rolling out of the cot and onto the floor, I gasped in fresh air. "Jeez, Raja," I said. "Brush your teeth sometime, would you?"

While Raja grunted and stretched in the cot, I smacked my tongue around my gummy mouth. My breath couldn't have been much better than Raja's. I listened at the door leading to the house, but heard no sign that Nancy was up. Judging from the blue-gray dawn light leaking through the window, I assumed we were the only ones awake. I pressed the glowing button to open the garage door so we could go outside. "Hey, Raja," I said. "It's time to start our spring training."

He lumbered out, taking my hand for support while he groggily stared up at the pale disc of early sun. When he stepped forward he startled a group of sparrows, which took to the air. He watched in wonder as they rose.

For a while we sat together on the picnic bench, in sleepy companionable silence, like old, old friends who had nothing they needed to say to each other. "I don't want you to be embarrassed in front of the other orangutans," I said, "so we've got to work on your wilderness skills."

Raja stared at me.

"Let's start by getting rid of the T-shirt," I said. When I went to remove it, he dutifully raised his arms to help me.

"Better," I said, casting the T-shirt to one side and walking to a pine tree and slapping the trunk. "Come on, climb up. I've seen you do this."

He continued to stare.

"Well, I don't know how this tree-climbing thing exactly works, either," I said.

Raja rolled off the bench, face-planting in the dirt. Then he slowly got to his feet and made his way over to the tree. He placed a hand on the trunk, then slowly and deliberately peeled off a piece of bark and studied it diligently, like he'd come across a missing copy of the Constitution.

Meanwhile, I used my phone to look up videos of orangutans climbing trees. Those guys seemed really good at it, letting go of one branch with a hand, then grabbing the next with a foot before releasing and grabbing the next with the other hand. They totally out-Tarzaned Tarzan. I looked dubiously at Raja, who was examining his belly button for lint.

Raja returned to the picnic table bench, feet properly under it, hands on the top, like he was waiting to be served lunch. He watched the videos with me, rasping in pleasure at the sight of other orange apes.

Knowing that Raja learned best by imitating, I went to a pine tree and tried one foot and then the other against the trunk. Reaching for a branch, I tried to pull myself up. It broke, dropping me onto the ground and spraying me with wood chips.

Disappointed in me, Raja lumbered to the car, opened the passenger-side door, and got in. Placing the elephant on his lap and clicking the seat belt over both of them, he reached a hand out and closed the door. He stared at me through the window and pointed to the steering wheel. *What are we waiting for?*

"Come on, Raja," I said, slapping the trunk again. "Tree!"

He scratched under his arms.

"All right, then," I said, fishing the car keys out of my pocket. "Milk shakes!"

ELEVEN

By the time Raja and I were on the freeway approaching Dulles
Airport four days later, my father's car was pretty much ruined. It
reeked inside, but that was the least of its problems. Spilled food
and drinks had given the upholstery a modern-art vibe, and all the
passenger-side vents had been broken by prying orangutan fingers.
But soon I'd be meeting up with my mom as she arrived from
Oregon and then flying far away, the car stashed in long-term
parking with the keys in the mail to my father, and the mess would
be out of my mind. He could deal with it.

My father. Oops. I had three voice mails from him on my
phone, all unheard.

We followed Dr. Jackson's car. Raja had permanently gradu-
ated himself to the front seat, and sat next to me. It looked a little
like I was taking him off to his first day of college. He had a polite,
worried air, both he and his elephant as clean as I could get them
under Dr. Jackson's garden hose. In Raja's case, it meant his hair
was soft and flat in places, wet in others where it hadn't yet dried
under the car's vents, and sticking straight up in still others. He
looked less like an orangutan than a well-loved chew toy.

Dr. Jackson had brought Allie in her car, and the dog was
in the backseat, feet on the headrest as she stared back at Raja,
tongue lolling. He kept his eyes on her, grunting with pleasure at
the sight of his friend across the whizzing asphalt. Halfway to the
airport, Raja finally discovered how the radio's volume knob
worked, and between stare-downs with Allie he enjoyed rolling the

volume of *Pocahontas* to ever-higher levels, rasping in pleasure at the racket.

Once we reached the airport, I followed Dr. Jackson's car down service roads until we were outside a hangar marked SPECIAL CARGO. I slotted my father's car in beside hers.

My mom was standing in front, arms crossed, the same worried look on her face as if I'd taken a hit on the football field. A familiar black suitcase, white luggage sticker bright in the sun, was beside her. The moment I got out of the car, she ran to me and wrapped her arms around me. "Oh, John," she said. "I'm so glad to see you."

Then it seemed to come back to her that I'd jailbreaked an orangutan. She stiffened and released me, staring at Raja. He stared back at her through the windshield, quiet and curious. Of course he remembered her, but it had been a long time since they'd seen each other. He stayed buckled in.

Dr. Jackson opened her door and stepped out. The first thing she did was peer in my side window, smiling at Raja. She might be more comfortable with animals than with people, I realized.

Not true of my mother. "Dr. Jackson?" she asked, extending her hand warmly.

"Mrs. Solomon," she said, taking my mother's hand and shaking it. "It's so lovely to meet you."

"I'm gonna . . ." I said vaguely, then got back in the car so I could be beside Raja.

Immediately he leaned over and hugged me. Not out of affection, exactly, but more because he needed reassurance. This new environment, and seeing my mom again, had clearly thrown him.

I stroked his back while I watched Mom and Dr. Jackson get acquainted. "Ready, Raja?" I finally asked.

He released me, stared into my eyes and then out at the parking lot. His hand reached for mine, and I felt his fingers clamp down painfully hard. There was something distant in his expression, and I realized that he'd been in an airport years before, maybe even this one, back when he'd arrived in a barrel packed into a HappyFoods corporate jet. Was he remembering that? Had he been too little?

When I got out of the driver's-side door again, Raja surprised me by unbuckling his seat belt and rolling out after me, on my side of the car.

"Wow. He's gotten so big," Mom said when she saw him emerge, hand soon in mine. Allie barked behind the closed car door, outraged to be apart from Raja, the nails of her paws clacking against the glass.

"Raja's feeling a little clingy," I said.

"I can see that," said Dr. Jackson. "Well, the crate is inside the hangar, so we'll have to walk him in eventually. I'll go check in, and come back for you two. Shouldn't be a minute."

When Dr. Jackson buzzed the button by the door, a security camera above swiveled to face her. Raja stared at it in interest.

Raja, my mom, and I stood outside and watched a plane approach over our heads. As it neared the runway and the roar got more intense, Raja cried out and clutched me, wrapping both arms tight around my waist. Underneath it all was the constant drone of Allie's barking.

"Was your flight okay?" I asked, lamely.

"John. What's going to happen to us?" Mom asked, hand nervously around the base of her throat.

"It's going to be all right," I said, because it felt like I was supposed to.

Another plane roared overhead, making Raja cry out again, even harder this time. "Hey, Raja," I said, hoping to distract him by bringing him to Dr. Jackson's car. "Want to say good-bye to Allie?"

Raja let me lead him by the hand to Dr. Jackson's backseat. The window was down so he could dangle his hand in. He jerked and whipped it out when Allie nipped excitedly, then he chortled and put his hand back in. This time he petted her head, looking at me to make sure he wasn't messing up.

"You're doing fine, Raja," I said. How would he cope with flying across the world? Would he be excited or terrified? But I took a cue from Raja and banished those concerns from my mind. He wasn't worried about that right now. He was too busy playing with his friend.

My mom's phone buzzed, and she fished it out of her handbag. "You've got to be kidding me," she said when she saw who it was.

I had my suspicions, but before I could stop her, she'd accepted the call.

"Let me tell you where I am," she said crossly. "At Dulles Airport, with the orangutan that you consigned to a life of misery, the one that *your son* has risked his life to save —" My father must have cut her off. She listened for a moment, then said, "Fine, here he is," and handed the phone to me.

I looked at it blankly. There was no one I wanted to talk to less than my father.

Raja took the matter out of my hands, bounding over and seizing the phone and looking at the screen, excited to see what he might find. The screen was no longer lit, though. He peered closely at it, working his lips over the screen. Then my father roared "Hello?" and Raja startled and dropped it.

I was closest, so I picked it up. Drawing up my courage, I brought it to my ear. "Hello?"

"John, is that you?"

"Yeah," I said. "Hi."

"You sounded different at first." I could hear people ordering drinks in the background. Maybe he hadn't unpacked in his new place yet, was spending the day at a coffee shop.

At the sound of my father, my heart got stuck in some low gear, revving away, climbing endless hills. My four-fingered free hand twitched.

He blew static into the line. "I don't believe you."

"What do you mean, you don't believe me? You don't believe that I'm returning Raja to his home?"

"You might look like a man now, but you're not yet. And this proves it. You can't just bring Raja home. It doesn't work that way."

"I'm going to try. Mom's helping."

"Because she loves you. Not because it's the right thing for Raja. Don't kid yourself about that."

"What would you know about what's right for Raja?" I asked. "Everything you've done for him has been wrong."

"I understand that you want to fix things," my father said, voice sharpening. "But all you're doing is raising hopes that will be forced to fall again. It's my job as a father to protect you from that. Do you understand me?"

"What I'm saying," I said, "is that you should *want* to get Raja back home. That it's your duty, too, to try to fix this."

"He would have been fine at FriendlyLand. And if he wasn't, what happened next was my decision to make."

The sight of Raja, flailing his hand around Dr. Jackson's backseat to play with Allie, spurred me forward. "Animals die at FriendlyLand all the time."

"I did wrong by finding him a zoo? Is that supposed to be some kind of joke?"

"I don't think we have anything to talk about," I said.

"Okay," my father said. "No, wait. Don't end the call, John. I . . . I wish you wouldn't try so hard to punish me for giving you what you *wanted* when you were a kid. What you wanted most in the world."

By making this about me, he was really making this about him. Just like when he'd kidnapped Raja in the first place, because bringing home an orangutan made him larger than life, a superhero dad. The needs of others hadn't really entered into it. My father was far less interested in being good than he was in being appealing.

Dr. Jackson emerged, letting the door catch on her foot and stay open. "Everything okay out here? We're ready for you inside."

"There in a moment," Mom said. "John's saying good-bye to his father."

"I don't think we have anything more to say, actually," I said. "We're mailing your car key. Except — one more thing. How did you get Raja?"

My father sighed into the receiver. "Do you really want to know?"

"Yes."

"The same way we got all of them." With that, he ended the call.

My mom gave me a long compassionate look, then nodded to Dr. Jackson. When I took Raja's hand, he gave Allie one last tap good-bye on the window, then walked with me toward the door. We paused when another plane flew overhead. He clung tight to my thigh, burying his face in the fabric of my pants until the plane was gone.

How were we going to pull this off when we couldn't even get into the cargo-office door without him freaking out?

With the aid of Dr. Jackson's gentle coaxing, Raja relaxed enough for me to be able to waddle to the door with him clutching my leg. Mom retrieved his elephant from the car. Rolling her suitcase with the other hand, she and then Dr. Jackson went past. I waited for Raja to remove himself from me before we staggered in, hand in hand.

We were in a small office walled off from the main hangar, all wood paneling and rows of gray filing cabinets. A single desk was planted in the center, with a young woman sitting at it. When she saw Raja walk in the door, she jumped out of her chair and ran into the corner, hands over her face. Worried about whatever monster was causing her such fear, Raja peered around, paying special attention to the upturned chair with its spinning casters.

For a moment all I could hear were Raja's kiss-squeaks and the woman's panicked breathing. "Don't worry, ma'am," Dr. Jackson said. "I told you we were bringing in an orangutan. He's fine. He's not going to hurt you."

"His name is Raja," I added.

Finger by finger, the woman removed her hands from her face. "I didn't expect him to be so *big*."

"His weight is listed on that paperwork," Dr. Jackson said, tapping a folder on the desk. "I told you precisely what we were bringing. He's an orangutan, flying on one of your cargo flights today. Don't you represent Singapore Airlines?"

The woman left the corner and inched to the desk, arms held up defensively in case Raja lunged for her. He looked up at me for guidance. My mom gave him the elephant for comfort and he tucked it under his chin as the woman examined his folder. "Are you John and Theresa Solomon?"

"Yes," Mom said. "That's us."

"Normally animals arrive in crates," the clerk said. "Normally they don't walk in."

"Sorry about that," Dr. Jackson said. "The crate arrived separately, direct from the craftsmen. You should have it somewhere in back, I think."

The Singapore Airlines woman asked us to wait a moment, then disappeared into a cavernous space behind the office. I heard the door lock, then a rattling sound as she tested it. Twice. Raja held still and polite while we waited, his hand in mine as he took in all the details of the room. It was like we'd passed from waiting outside the school to first-day registration. *I love you*, I signed to him.

Raja was too distracted to sign back. *I love you*, I repeated.

I love you, he signed hurriedly, then returned to staring around the room. He took a few steps one way and then another, swiveling on his knuckles, farting discreetly.

The woman returned with two men in blue jumpsuits. They spoke to one another in a language I didn't recognize, probably whatever they speak in Singapore. The men stared in awe at Raja. One made little kissing sounds, like what you'd make to a kitten. Raja stared at him, baffled. He edged away from the strange men and closer to me, so his leg was again flush against mine. He reached out a hand to hold my mom's leg, too. She stiffened, surprised, then laid a comforting palm on the top of his head.

"Which one of you is Raja?" one of the men asked with a smile.

I raised Raja's arm. "The orange one."

"We have the paperwork on file, and your crate is here," the woman said. "We have prepared it on the other side of the door. We aren't authorized . . . Well, we think it would be better if . . . Would you mind being the ones who get him into it?"

"We'll get him there," Dr. Jackson said. "Just show us where to go."

When they opened the door leading into the hangar, Raja hopped into the air, rigid with excitement. Through the door was racket and commotion. Forklifts passed back and forth laden with crates, and a giant sorter rumbled along behind it all, carrying big aluminum containers, the kind slanted to fit in airplane fuselages. Right near the door, a big wooden crate, banded and reinforced in metal, was sitting on the prongs of a forklift.

Raja wrapped one arm around my hips, the other hugging the stuffed elephant close. "Is there any way you could shut everything down for a few minutes, to make it quieter?" I asked.

The guy who had made cutesy kitten noises to Raja disappeared for a moment, and then with a great wheeze the rackety sorter turned off. There were still roaring fans, and a vehicle someone had left in reverse was beeping away, but at least the room wasn't quite as loud. The rest of the staff came over curiously to find out what was going on, forming a semicircle around us.

"Could everyone keep away, please?" Mom asked.

Reluctantly, most of the staff dispersed. Everywhere I looked in the hangar, though, I saw eyes on us.

Even with the three of us in a protective circle around him, Raja was shaking. All his muscles were tensed up. The last time we'd been near crates, I'd tricked and betrayed him, and he was probably expecting a similar betrayal now. To him what was about to happen *would* look like a betrayal, and I couldn't see how to convince him otherwise. That was a very human thing, I realized, being concerned with causes and motives — Raja only knew effects. As I stepped toward the crate Raja resisted, jutting his neck and grimacing. He let go of my fingers and wrist-walked away from me, toward a forklift. Its operator stopped it and stared warily at the ape, shouting something at the woman helping us.

"Where do you think he's going, John?" Nancy asked me, a deliberate calm in her voice.

"I don't know," I said. "He's avoiding the crate. Give me a second."

I walked over to him, but he signed *you poop* and maneuvered farther away. He wrist-walked along the wall, elephant pinched in the fingers of one hand as he ran the other over the corrugated metal. His gaze wandered the ceiling, the doors, checking the positions of everyone in the hangar. Strategizing.

"Raja!"

He got as far as the corner, then stopped. Lifting his head, he listened, eyes wide as he scanned around. I made my way over to him, Mom and Dr. Jackson following. I kneeled in front of Raja. "We're taking you back to where you came from. What's the matter?"

He moved to a wall of what appeared to be crates draped in fabric. He leaned close to it, lips to the covering, making worried little grunts. Then he reached forward and pulled down the curtain.

Behind it was a wall of cages, each with a different animal inside. At the top was a furry creature I couldn't make out, its back against the bars. Below it were monkeys — lots of monkeys. Silver ones with black faces, black ones with orange eyes, gray-haired monkeys with brown fingernails, long-haired creatures whose tails gripped the bars. One near the bottom was obviously pregnant, her belly distended and nipples popping out. In the cage beside her, three babies were clutching one another. All the monkeys looked groggy, weak fingers grasping the bars of the wall, the bars of the floor.

"Where are these guys going back to?" Mom asked Dr. Jackson.

"They're not going back anywhere. These are recent arrivals," she said. "Air France shares this space, and they're one of the only remaining airlines that will transport primates for research. All these guys were captured in the wild and are heading for laboratories throughout the States."

"Oh," I said. I was baffled for a moment, then felt the energy drain right out of me as the implications hit me. Here we were, going through no end of expense and trouble to get one orangutan back to his home country, and in the same hangar were dozens of monkeys recently seized from the wild to become captives, infected with diseases or bashed in the head or sprayed in the face with detergent or whatever human industry had in store. I was swimming against a flood. I felt sad, and I felt like an idiot.

Raja leaned his face in near one of the monkey babies. It seemed barely able to open its eyes to look back at him, and I realized that they all had probably been drugged. The sight of Raja uncaged seemed to awaken something in the baby, and it squealed. It flailed out for Raja's nose, managing to contact it. The instant the baby monkey had Raja's nostril under its fingers, it pulled him close and bit.

Startled, Raja staggered back. The quick movement riled up the monkeys, who began pacing and shrieking, rattling the bars of their cages. One of them peed into the air, a yellow arc striking the cement floor. Poop flew from somewhere else.

"Not good, not good," said Dr. Jackson. She called one of the other employees to help her get the cages covered back up.

Raja bolted, careening headlong through the hangar. Uniformed workers scattering before him, Raja climbed up a stack of crates, sitting cross-legged on top of the highest one. Now that he was a dozen feet up and away, he dabbed at his bloodied nose and managed to find the outrage to squeak angrily at the caged baby monkey. Not long on courage, my Raja.

The workers in the hangar must have been around animals all the time; though they'd all stopped working to monitor the situation, they weren't panicking.

"Any thoughts on how to get him back down?" Dr. Jackson asked me.

"I'm not sure," I said. I opened the crate that had been sent for him. The floor was mesh, with a foot between it and the sawdust-covered bottom of the crate, so Raja could go to the bathroom in the corner and it would drop through. It wouldn't be the most comfortable trip for him, but it was spacious enough.

"I have an idea," Mom said. She unzipped her suitcase and brought out a cloth bundle. Raja watched from his perch as she set it on the crate floor and slowly unwrapped it. Sitting on the mesh was a neat pile of supplies. Two gallons of spring water (Raja would be A-OK with drinking straight from the bottle), a bag of oranges, another bag of apples, two pineapples, and a box whose label said it contained sixteen individual bags of HappyFoods potato chips.

"HappyFoods? Is that supposed to be a joke?" I asked her.

Mom shrugged. "You and I both know those are his favorite."

"Well, if all goes well these will be the last chips Raja will ever eat," I said. "Hope he enjoys them." I looked closer and saw that Mom had even put two magazines in the bundle. I chuckled when I saw they were issues of *Woman's Day*. It didn't matter what the text was, as long as the photographs were colorful. Raja would enjoy the food pictures, I was sure.

"Good work, Mom," I said.

I crawled into the crate, opened the bundle, took out a bag of chips, and crawled back out, positioning myself so I was conspicuously in Raja's view. It was a contest of wills: He stared down at me impassively, pretending not to care as I opened the bag. He gave the smallest kiss-squeak as I pulled a chip out. It became a cry of outrage as I bit down, crunching audibly.

By the time I was eating the second chip, Raja had climbed down from the stack of crates, carefully maneuvering so he never had to release the stuffed elephant from one hand. He wrist-walked over to me and stared pointedly at the bag of chips.

I held the bag so the opening was to him, our sign that it was okay to share, like on that rainy night when Raja and I had both been sick, years ago. He reached in and took a handful that might as well have been the whole bag, stuffing a tumble of chips into his mouth. Another handful went in while he was still chomping the first, crumbs falling from all sides, like Cookie Monster.

When I tossed the bag into the crate, Raja watched it land beside the oranges and magazines, then looked at me. I smiled at him, aware that there was a lie in it, that I was tricking him again, but not knowing what other option I had.

Raja kept probing me. When his golden eyes met mine directly I felt more fully seen by him than by any human in my life. It was like he was navigating back and forth in my heart, sifting and sorting every little feeling he found. Neither of us had a self while our eyes were linked: John and Raja were shared between us.

Then, with a sigh, infinity broke and Raja lumbered into the crate. He sat against the rear wall and faced forward, arms tight around his knees, toy elephant wedged between his ankles. He rocked himself, like he'd done when I'd found him in his trailer in my father's backyard. The elephant stared at me while its trunk sagged toward the floor.

By ignoring the chips, Raja wanted me to know that he hadn't fallen for my dumb trick, that he wasn't a donkey chasing after carrots. He was electing to go inside the crate, with full knowledge that it meant being closed in. Despite all I'd put him through, he was deciding to trust me, and wanted to make it clear that it was his decision.

I love you, I signed to Raja.

I love you, he signed back, his gaze wandering the crate,

something like sadness in his eyes but also a deep, longstanding resignation. Acceptance.

I wondered how he could love me. But he'd said that he did.

He reached out to help me when I struggled with the heavy wooden door, his rough orange fingers over mine. Together, we closed the crate.

PART FIVE

THE QUESTION IS NOT, CAN THEY REASON?
NOR, CAN THEY TALK? BUT, CAN THEY
SUFFER? WHY SHOULD THE LAW REFUSE
ITS PROTECTION TO ANY SENSITIVE
BEING? . . . THE TIME WILL COME WHEN
HUMANITY WILL EXTEND ITS MANTLE
OVER EVERYTHING WHICH BREATHES.

— JEREMY BENTHAM, *AN INTRODUCTION
TO THE PRINCIPLES OF MORALS AND
LEGISLATION*, 1780

He woke to a new smell.

It wasn't rot, and it wasn't freshness. It wasn't sweet, and it was only a little bit sour. It was the smell of something warmed, but not by the sun. The closest thing to it he could remember was the blackened tree he and his mother had once come across, in the middle of the bushes, with the tangy bark. But this smell was in the air itself.

It woke him before his mother, and he left the nest to creep along a branch, nose in the air and eyes darting about. When his mother sensed him gone, she jerked awake. Grumbling, she shifted along the branch, reaching long fingers to snag her son and pull him back. He protested only a moment before huddling in close. His mother went still as she, too, became aware of the smell. She lumbered them off, away from it. The air sweetened as they fled.

Later that day, the smell returned. His mother took them off in another direction, but this time it didn't go away. As his mother hesitated, unsure of where to go, he could see the hot smell now, hanging low in the humid air. In the distance, a plume of it rose into the sky. This was the closest they'd yet been to it, and he no longer found it exciting. His heartbeat quickened along with his mother's.

She picked a new direction, making anxious sighs as she went. She looked for sweetness in the air, but found none of it anywhere now. Only shades of hot sour.

His mother took them along the banks of a river, to places he had never seen before. She tested each branch nervously before putting all her weight on it, and he realized that his mother had never been here before, either.

Then they reached the end of the jungle. He hadn't known it had an end.

There were palm trees here, springing with oily, unappetizing fruit. These trees behaved strangely. Each was a precise distance from the next. There was no other greenery between them, only brown soil. The regular lines of trees continued far in the distance, where he heard strange noises. Calls that were like an orangutan's or a gibbon's, but were also something else entirely.

His mother pivoted this way and that in the last jungle tree. Behind them was the hot smell. In front of them were those orderly palms with their heart-thrumming feeling of not-right. She had to make a choice, for her and her son.

Only there was no choice, not really.

TWELVE

Up until the moment the plane hit the tarmac in Singapore, I thought we were still high up in the sky. My head leaning against the window, all I could see was white-gray haze, even as we taxied. The captain explained over the loudspeaker that there were wildfires in Sumatra, and the smoke was rolling north, all the way to Singapore. Our plane was in the clouds even as it parked outside the cargo terminal. My mom and I could see nothing but each other and the ground beneath our feet as we headed inside.

Raja, Mom, and I had been the only passengers on the plane. There was the flight deck, which I'd been allowed to visit — I even got to sit in the copilot's chair, thanks to looser rules on cargo flights — and then a small climate-controlled area behind it, where Raja's crate was strapped in. Mom and I had backward-facing seats, like flight attendants, right beside him. Mom's and my meals were all prepared and wrapped in plastic, and we got to eat them whenever we wanted. Most of the rest of the time I spent sitting against the crate, eye pressed against a gap in the wood, while Mom read a book. Raja was usually staring back, only inches away. Since I couldn't see the rest of his body, there was something aquarium-like about it, like I was staring into the eye of a whale.

The flight had lasted almost a day. I'd downloaded Teach Yourself Indonesian to my phone before we left, and learned how to say "How are you?" (*Apa kabar?*) and "Yes, ma'am" (*Ya, ibu,* which sounded like "Yeah, boo" and cracked me up to no end). I learned how to say "I am an American man": *Saya orang America.* Orang!

When I got invited into the cockpit, I asked the pilot about it, and he told me the word *orangutan* was from Malay, a language very close to Indonesian, and meant "man of the forest."

John Solomon orang America. Raja Solomon orang hutan.

For long periods during the flight I was able to forget the miracles involved, was just a guy in a seat trying to fall asleep. Then I'd remember that I was six miles up in the sky, hurtling through the air in something heavier than air. Even more startling was when I'd make eye contact with Raja, crouched in the crate beside me. So many miracles had come together to produce this day spent in the skies, returning an ape to the land that had been his before humans had arrived.

We had a few hours in Singapore before the cargo was switched out and our flight continued to Medan. Raja had to stay on board, but Mom and I got off while the other cargo was swapped. The airport was the best. A butterfly sanctuary, free massage chairs, every kind of restaurant you could imagine. We had ramen soup, and it wasn't like instant noodles, it was classy. As I slurped the gritty broth at the bottom I thought what a joyful mess Raja would have made of that soup.

On the TV screens in the airport, all the news was about the smoke. Sumatra is an island that's part of Indonesia, which is a totally separate country from Singapore, but the smoke was drifting north into Singapore's airspace, creating an international incident. The newscaster told us the fires were set intentionally by Indonesian farmers, because the simplest way to convert forestland into farmland was to burn it. Although that was technically illegal, they were clearing out the land to grow more crops. A guest on the program countered that a lot of the companies who profited from the illegal burnings were based in Singapore, so they couldn't get too outraged about the lax enforcement of laws in Indonesia, that it was unfair to blame impoverished farmers when they were at the bottom of a chain that had multinational companies at the top. I wondered if anyone back home had any clue what was going on over here.

It was evening by the time we landed in Medan. The plane flew low over rich, leafy jungle, then touched down on a narrow runway cut out of the greenery. It was like a city had sprouted from the back of the terminal. Raja gave one shriek as we landed, then quieted down once he could see my eye staring back at him through the gap.

Compared to Singapore, Medan's airport looked like something out of an old black-and-white movie, all brick and no glass. *Medan* was painted along the top in 1950s-style lettering, and random tiles had been laid into the cement throughout. The plane stopped in front of a big crumbly terminal, lit by portable floodlights. Someone rolled a staircase up to the plane, then Mom and I disembarked with the crew. As we headed to the terminal, a passenger plane began unloading. We joined its flood, a couple of white people rising head and shoulders over the Indonesians.

As we passed into the terminal, Mom fell farther and farther behind. Finally she stopped to rest beside a wall. I asked her if she was okay and she nodded. "Let's let the crowd pass. Too many people."

I waited beside her, but all the same I was antsy to go find the sanctuary staff who had come to meet us. But even after the crowd had passed, Mom was against the wall, eyes closed. She looked pale. "It's all clear now," I said softly.

She opened her eyes and looked at me expectantly. I realized with a start that she was waiting for *me* to lead the way. I remembered now how on family trips she'd always let my father make every decision, and I guessed she was falling back into that mode. Part of me wanted to say *I might look big, but I'm still sixteen, Mom.* But instead I said, "I think we go this way, Mom."

As soon as we entered the immigrations hall, we were thronged by guys clamoring in Indonesian and reaching for our bags. I shook my head to keep them at bay. The men were all smiles but they never really went away; instead they started switching up the volume, shouting and then whispering, as if that might help us understand their words. I felt like Raja probably did when people tried to talk to him.

You need a visa stamp in your passport to go to Indonesia; Mom had scrambled to take care of it ahead of time. It allowed us to skip the crowd of people bottlenecked in that line. I led the way straight to a guy in front of a wooden stand that said IMMIGRATION. *"Saya orang America,"* I said proudly as I handed over our passports.

He tried but failed to hide his smile.

While he checked our documents, I was tempted to ask him where we could pick up Raja. But Diah, the head of the sanctuary that Dr. Jackson had put us in touch with, had told Mom they would take care of the Raja part of our arrival. All we had to concern ourselves with was getting through immigration. That was plenty enough for me to worry about, so I stayed quiet.

On the other side were lots of guys with signs, waiting to greet people. No women. Since none of the signs said *John and Theresa Solomon* (or *Raja Solomon*, for that matter), we picked a wall, stood against it, and sweated. Well, I stood. Mom was doing more of a slump. "You okay, Mom?" I asked.

She nodded, heavy-lidded. I felt this need to protect her. Her mind was probably filled with worry about the plane tickets she'd put on credit cards, the legal gray zone we were in, how she was flying across the world to save an animal acquired by the man she'd divorced. She looked tired, and older than I'd ever seen her.

Maybe it was nothing deeper than intense lack of sleep, though. It had been thirty hours since either of us had last slept in a bed. My eyes prickled, and my body felt both overmoist and dried out, the sides of my feet puffing against my sneakers. I tried to convince my body to move again; I stretched my legs, crossed one arm and then the other across my chest, like I was prepping for a game.

It was weird, looking so different from everyone around me. That had never happened to me before. It made me feel like a target, like it would be easy for everything to go wrong.

A bell went off, and the luggage belt began to rumble. People lined up, struggling to get their bags through the crowd, and went off into the nighttime world that was honking away on the far side of the greasy exit doors. I already had my duffel, so all I had to worry about was one very important crate.

Where was Raja?

A guy who didn't look much older than I was came running up. "Hello," he said. "You are John and Theresa Solomon?"

I looked around and smiled. "Yeah, how could you tell?"

He held out a hand. As my mom and then I shook it, I noticed his pinkie nail was very long. "Very nice to meet you," he continued. "I am Adhi. My wife is Diah. It is she you have been emailing."

"Nice to meet you, sir," Mom said, a little stiffly. "Can you tell us where Raja is?"

"Diah is excited to meet you. She is home. She will see you there. I am sorry I am late. I was being talking to the . . . to the men who handle . . ."

"The baggage handlers?" Mom interjected. I flushed.

But he wasn't offended at all by Mom cutting in. "Yes, that is it!" he said. "And they do not have our crate yet. But do not worry, they have not finished unloading the plane. Our *mawas* will be coming out last, I am sure. I am going to find informations. You will stay here?"

He ran outside while Mom and I glanced at each other with small uncomfortable smiles. What did either of us know about how things worked in Sumatra? I mean, I wouldn't even know how things worked in *Toronto*. The truth was that we were in way over our heads. Who knew what the people around me were saying. Who knew how the country worked. We were at the mercy of a place we knew nothing about.

A thud brought my attention to the luggage belt — something large was blocking the conveyer. I heard shouting, and could glimpse chaos between the black flaps as suitcases hit the obstacle and tumbled away. Then, with the sound of men roaring and shouting — and one conspicuous kiss-squeak — the object shifted and emerged on the groaning conveyer belt.

Raja's crate. On the conveyer. Like a suitcase.

Adhi was nowhere to be seen, so I turned to the nearest person I thought could help me, a fat porter with a cigarette hanging from his mouth. When I gestured to the crate as it slowly made its way toward us on the struggling belt, the man looked at me in shock. Eventually, though, he nodded. He let the cigarette fall from his lips and widened his stance, like a sumo wrestler preparing for impact. He said something, and though I'd never heard the words before I recognized a countdown.

When the crate came near we each heaved on one side. Raja shrieked from within, his voice hoarse, as the crate tipped onto the ground. The red-faced porter shouted in triumph, looking at me to share the victory, his eyes wide and friendly.

"*Terima kasih, pak,*" I said after racking my brain for how the woman in my language app would say *thank you*.

He looked pleased that I knew any of his language, slapping me on the back and repeating the amazing thing I'd just said to the guys who'd assembled around us. I turned my attention to the crate. Raja was thumping its sides, desperate to get out. Once I managed to meet his eyes between the slats, he calmed.

As a crowd of men accumulated, I felt my face do its usual betrayal and turn red. I didn't have the language to explain what was inside the crate, so all I did was shrug and stand before it protectively. Mom hovered nearby, looking as out of place as I felt.

Luckily Adhi came running back up. "Oh, no," he said. "They have put our *mawas* on the baggage thing?"

The guys slapped Adhi on the back, joking and teasing; he was clearly a known quantity around here. At Adhi's request, a handful of the men crowded around the crate and lifted in unison. Mom and I floated behind as they duck-walked it into the humid night, where Adhi directed them to heave the crate up onto the flatbed of a truck. He passed them each a few coins, then stood at the driver's-side door, gesturing me and Mom into the passenger's side with a wide swing of his arm.

We passed through the jovial men, who patted my back and spoke to me in Indonesian, then got in. Turned out people drive on the left in Indonesia, so the passenger's and driver's sides of the car are switched, but even so, stepping up into the Ford truck was such a familiar feeling ("shotgun!") that for a moment I was able to forget that I was halfway across the world, driving an ape in the back of a pickup off into the Sumatran night.

As we headed out into the streets, the first thing I noticed was that lanes didn't seem to matter. Motor scooters zipped along four abreast, parting to weave between slower-moving trucks and cars before coming together again. Some had carriages hitched to the back, and those wheezed more slowly along the road, engines puffing and straining. People were on foot everywhere, picking their way through the crowded roadways or lounging beside food carts whose vendors ladled soup into cracked ceramic bowls. Only rarely did I see girls or women over the age of nine or ten, and when I did, they were always in the company of men.

"It is too late to drive tonight to the orangutan quarantine center," Adhi informed us. "So if you are okay with this, Diah and me, we will like to invite you to sleep in our home. We travel Raja to join the other orangutans tomorrow. Mrs. Solomon, I would like to tell you our house is humble, but clean. I hope you will like it."

Mom nodded, tight-lipped, while my mind spun. *The other orangutans. Tomorrow.* "That is very kind," I managed to say. *"Terima kasih."*

Adhi and Diah lived in a small, tidy house nestled right in the middle of the bustling sprawl of Medan. After the car pulled alongside a gate, an old hunched man came out and opened it. He gaped openly at the big white guy in the passenger seat as Adhi drove through. Once we'd parked in the tiny courtyard on the other side, Adhi ran around to open the door. After I'd gotten out, he helped my mom.

"Thanks," she said, clearly embarrassed to be treated like royalty. Adhi guided her out with only a delicate hand hovering beneath her elbow, then gestured us toward the house.

"What about Raja?" I asked.

"Sorry, friend," Adhi said, tapping the side of the crate. "We leave early tomorrow, and there is no place for orangutan to be loose here in the city. Once you are inside, I will clean him and give him fruit and new water. He feels safer in this crate, anyway."

Poor Raja, I thought. It was a familiar feeling; I was used to the weight of his suffering. I could shoulder the pain of his being locked away because I'd spent so long doing just that. It was like when I'd had to deal with my parents' constant fighting during the divorce years; the emotional muscles that combated this bad feeling were strong from use.

After I'd gone inside, Adhi ushered me into a narrow room with overstuffed bookshelves and a small desk in the corner, bowing under a yellowing PC. A carpet runner led farther into the house, where I could hear the tinkling sounds of a table being set. A pretty woman in a headscarf stepped into the hallway and smiled at us, eyes downcast.

"This is Diah," Adhi said. "My wife, and the head of the sanctuary."

I felt a little confused. Diah was the boss, but Adhi was acting like the one in charge. I smiled widely to Diah and nodded my head, not sure whether I was allowed to shake her hand. "It's an honor to meet you," I said. "Thank you for helping."

"Hello," said Mom.

"It is no problem for us to make a dinner for four instead of two," Diah said quietly. Adhi sounded like he was figuring out his English as he went; Diah was singing it like a song she'd learned to love.

"You made dinner for us?" Mom asked, warming. "That's very kind of you."

"And thanks for taking on Raja," I added.

"Yes, Raja," Diah said, smiling. "Our first American orangutan! I had thought he would have an American name, like Charlie or George or Kanye. *Raja* . . . this is a word from Bahasa Indonesia. It means 'king.'"

"King," I repeated. I knew that. We'd raided an Indonesian dictionary when we were deciding what to name him. *"Terima kasih, ibu."*

Her smile took on a new light. "You speak Bahasa!"

I tried to remember how to say "no" and had a big Indonesian fail.

"Let me show you where you will both sleep tonight so you can unpack and get fresh," she said. "Then tomorrow you will meet the other orangutans. So will Raja."

• • •

By the time we went to bed, fatigue had settled so deeply into me that it had become irritating, and I think that irritation was what was keeping me awake. At least that was my theory — I had a lot of time to think about it. As I lay there on the cot in the room I was sharing with my mother, eyes open and staring at the ceiling, I tried to sleep. But every time I'd get near, my mind went to Raja in his crate and I'd be fully awake again. I'd been up for thirty-six hours, but he'd been in a cage for almost that much time, and was still in it.

My cot was in a closet in the room where Diah and Adhi's daughter slept when she wasn't off at boarding school. Mom had the bed. My duffel, still packed tight with my clothes from the U.S., sat perkily upright by the door. Mom had fallen asleep right away, and her deep breathing made me get even more irritated at being awake. A rattan screen covered the window, the streetlights shining through it at an angle to make custard triangles on the wall. While I lay there, I watched the faint doubles change shape as they slowly migrated.

As I lay there thinking, I recognized another feeling that was stirring me up. It had been there for a long time, I realized, dull but powerful.

Anger.

Diah and Adhi had stopped their lives to get me and Raja from the airport. Adhi had handed out his own money for tips, never asking us to pay him back — though I'd make sure we did. Adhi and Diah and Dr. Jackson had all taken on such costs to help Raja, even inviting total strangers into their homes. My mom, too, had wrung money from nearly dry bank accounts and maxed out her credit cards to get us here.

All to mend what my father had done in a moment.

He'd thought I'd be amazed by having an orangutan to grow up with. And I *had* been amazed. But my joy wasn't a good enough reason for him to do what he did to Raja.

As the first glimmers of dawn arrived, I could hear Adhi snoring on the other side of the house's thin wall. Not an awful sound, but the sort of whiffles people make when they're sleeping really deeply. I rolled my T-shirt back on — it still smelled like airplane — and then my sweatpants. Slipping my feet into the flip-flops Adhi and Diah had loaned me, I padded as silently as I could to the house's front door. Carefully unlatching it, I crept over to Adhi's truck. I stood on the bumper and eased one leg and then the other over the tailgate.

Raja's crate was still. At first, not wanting to wake him, I pressed my eye against a gap between two of the wooden planks. It was hard to make out much in the near dark, but I could see his shape curled in the corner, a faint bluishness to the black at one edge — that must have been the stuffed elephant. Raja's eyes had been closed, but he must have been shutting out the world, not sleeping, as two new moon glints appeared as he opened his lids.

"Raja," I whispered, lying on the truck bed, pushing aside sharp bits of tools I couldn't identify. "Hi, Raja."

He shifted forward on his hands and knees, bringing his face close to the wood. His breath was warm through the slats.

"You'll be out of this soon," I promised.

He made a sort of whimper that was part yawn. Reaching a finger to the gap between the planks nearest my face, he ran his thumbnail down it. We'd be touching if we could. But we couldn't. "I'll stick here until morning, how about that?" I asked.

Raja brought a finger to his mouth and toyed with his lips, making a long raspberry sound. A kind of *Nothing else is going on, why not do this?* gesture. Clearly he knew even less about what was going to happen to him than I did. I signed *I love you.* Then I settled in.

・　　・　　・

I woke up to Adhi's amused smile, sunlight haloing his head.

"I will tell you a thing," he said, "other Indonesians think Diah and I are crazy for caring too much for the orangutans. But you, you are more crazier than us!"

"Is there any coffee?" I mumbled.

Adhi set about better securing Raja's crate to the truck bed while I went inside to eat breakfast with Diah. She was busy over a wide frying pan releasing jets of fragrant steam. *"Nasi goreng,"* she said. "Fried rice. Would you like some?"

"Yes, please," I said. "How do you say that in Indonesian?"

"In Bahasa, you would say *Saya ingin makan nasi goreng.* But before you eat, I think you should check on your mother. I heard — how should I say this? — many flushes of the toilet early this morning. I thought that was why you slept outside, so you would not get sick, too."

Coffee in hand, I lumbered into the room I'd shared with my mom. She was on her side in the fetal position, eyes shut tight. Much like Raja, weirdly enough. I nudged her shoulder. "Hey, Mom. Are you okay?"

She groaned, her hands on her stomach. "Are you okay, sweetie?"

"Yeah, I'm fine. But what happened to you?"

Her face scrunched up. "What's that smell?"

"Breakfast. It looks delicious."

She shut her eyes. "I think I must be sick." She let out a long breath as her belly gurgled.

"Well, foreign food and all that," I said. "Anything I can get for you?"

She shook her head. "I don't think I can even drink any water. Not yet. You have to go tell them."

I went into the kitchen. Diah looked at me questioningly, and I shook my head. "Not good. I think she's got a stomach bug."

"Your poor mother," Diah said. "Do you think she will eat her breakfast?"

"She won't be eating anything for a while, I don't think."

"At least this means you get a double portion," she said. "You should accept it, because at the field station the food will be much worse."

Except for when I poured yogurt into my coffee by accident, breakfast was delicious. As soon as it was over we crept to the doorway of Mom's room. "Mrs. Solomon?" Diah asked softly.

Mom sat up, but immediately clutched her stomach and lay back down. "I'm so sorry," she said.

"Do not be sorry," Diah said warmly. "*I* am sorry that you are sick on your first day in Indonesia. It is not a good introduction."

"Please don't think this is your fault," Mom said. "It's just my rotten luck."

Diah sat lightly on the bed and laid the back of her hand against Mom's forehead. I could imagine her doing the same thing with her orangutans, how comforting that gentle touch must be to any suffering animal. "Raja can't stay in that crate too much longer, and there's nowhere to let him walk around in Medan. He needs to go to the quarantine. But that's many hours out, and it's nowhere you would want to be while you are sick. I also cannot risk your infecting the orangs out there. So we have a decision to make: whether John will stay here with you or come with us."

"I'll stay, Mom," I said. "What if you get worse?"

"Oh, no," Mom said. "You haven't come all this way to turn back before the end."

"You wouldn't be alone," Diah explained. "Adhi's aunt and uncle live next door, and his cousins are down the road. Ibu can come in to look on you every hour. She will take good care of you. Adhi and I will have our phones, too, if anyone needs to reach us."

I looked at my mom, and knew she'd prefer if I stayed. But she wasn't telling me to stay, because she loved me and knew how important Raja was to me. "I think I'll go, Mom," I said. "If you're sure it's okay."

"Yes," she said weakly. "I'm just embarrassed to have come all this way only to get sick."

Diah made Mom a mug of ginger tea to calm her stomach, then went next door to fetch Ibu while I perched on the edge of the bed. When Adhi's aunt arrived she immediately took charge, switching Mom's blanket to a thicker one and making a fresh tea with some different type of ginger. She lay an expert hand against Mom's forehead and then busied herself adjusting the curtains so the room was darker. It was clear that Mom was going to be in good care. Or at the very least bossy care.

"Thanks, Mom," I said as I stood at the doorway with my duffel.

"For what?"

I shrugged. "For everything."

"Be careful out there, okay?" she said.

I gave her a long hug, then headed out to the truck. Adhi took the driver's seat and Diah the middle, so I squeezed my body into the passenger side, arm and shoulder out the window so I didn't press against Diah and risk offending anyone. Adhi knocked once on the rear windshield, as if we were Raja's chauffeurs asking for permission to start, then pulled out into the streets of Medan.

Adhi drove like there weren't hundreds of motorcycles darting around us; he rumbled forward through the crowded dirt street and let everyone else worry about avoiding us. While we drove, Diah asked me quiet questions, about where in the States I was from and how long we'd had Raja. She asked how Mom and I had gotten him.

"It was all my father, actually, back when I was little," I said. "He worked for HappyFoods, and scouted plantations over here. One time he came back with Raja."

"Ah," Diah said, hands tight in her lap. "HappyFoods."

"You've heard of them?"

"Oh, yes," she said. "I've heard of them. You know of palm oil, yes?"

"Yeah, I know. They operate palm oil plantations out here, right?"

"Yes. The nut of the palm tree, it produces the cheapest oil in the world. This is why many companies want to grow it. Palm oil is in many things we use. Soap and toothpaste and candy and chips. But to build a new palm oil plantation one must first remove a jungle. It requires three years for a palm plantation to begin to provide oil, and to repay that cost they sell the hardwood they cut down from the jungle. Old-growth wood can bring in a lot of money.

"But orangutans cannot live on a plantation. They need the jungle trees intact in order to survive. When they are in the jungle, they are almost invisible in the branches — and if they cannot be seen, they cannot be shot. The jungle is their home, so when these companies come in to knock down the trees, some orangutans either cannot run away in time or climb the tallest trees to hide. They fall with them and are crushed, or they are shot, or they are burned alive. You will meet many orangutans at the rehabilitation center, and they all went through a history of violence like this.

"When an orangutan has a baby, she will climb high in a tree when she senses danger, but once the other nearby trees are all cut down, she will be totally exposed. Raja's mother was probably shot in the tree. Often what happens to the mothers once they are

shot is that they climb down to their killers — they will do anything so that they don't fall and kill their baby. Raja's mother
probably delivered him to them. And they were building plantations for HappyFoods."

The same way we got all of them. That's what my father had said
when I asked how he got Raja. It was happening to orangutans
throughout Sumatra — millions of years of continuous jungle life,
erased in the space of decades.

My gut dropped, and then righted itself. I found my mind
turning familiar cycles of thought that I'd always looped through
whenever the universe's fabric dropped away and showed the dark-
ness beneath: *That's the way of the world,* it said. *If you thought about this all
the time, you'd be miserable. Think about the good stuff in life.* But this time,
those cycles weren't good enough. I stared out the window. Right
by the car were three teenage boys walking through traffic, arm in
arm. All wore T-shirts with nonsense English; the nearest boy's
shirt sported a cartoon watermelon with *Invitation* scrawled over it
in bubble letters. I watched the world outside without seeing it. My
thoughts were on Raja.

While Adhi started yelling at the people in the car in front of
us who had stopped to buy tissue packets from a street vendor,
Diah ran a finger along the side of her headscarf, tucked the fabric
neatly back, secured the barrettes that kept it in place. "John, I was
not trying to make you feel guilty with what I said. You were just
a boy; it was not your decision. But I thought you should know
what Raja came from."

Yeah, I thought as I stared out. *Now I know where Raja comes from.*
Maybe our escape from the police at FriendlyLand hadn't been so
unfamiliar to Raja. Maybe dealing with humans and their guns
had been his mother's final lesson.

Normally it took no work to ignore the things that I had to
ignore to keep myself happy. But now, knowing the violence Raja

came from, the world beneath me felt like it was falling away even as the truck rumbled forward. As we left the bustle of Medan behind, we passed a string of small shops huddled close to the road. Small children scurrying at her feet, a woman set a restaurant table, laying plastic forks along a plastic table covered in a plastic tablecloth printed with *Coca-Cola*. A guy my age hunched at a kiosk, selling cell phone cards. An old woman had a blanket spread out, selling sprouts, oranges, coconuts. Next to her was a cage which had what looked like giant black gourds hanging from it. I was seeing it all, cataloging it all, thinking of none of it. Only of Raja.

Diah followed where I was looking. "Fruit bats," she explained. "I'm from Jakarta originally, and we wouldn't eat them. But in Sumatra they do. Roasted."

A few minutes later we came across chickens pressed tight in a wooden cage, feathers strewn over the ground beneath. While we waited in traffic one was purchased, wrung, plucked. Not that unlike what was happening in those giant windowless buildings in West Virginia, probably, except this time it was out in the open.

Half an hour later, we passed a motorbike with a small trailer hitched to the back. Standing on the trailer was a squealing sow, struggling to keep her balance, legs splayed out for stability. On her back was a dog, clutching her and howling. And on *his* back was a monkey, eyes wide with fright as it hugged tight to the dog's fur. The whole contraption was racing along at least thirty miles per hour. If I weren't seeing it with my own eyes, I'd have thought it was impossible, monkey riding dog riding pig. If the pig lost her balance, they'd all wind up in the street. I wondered where they were going. I wondered why this man had to bring his pig, dog, and monkey to the same place at the same time.

In front of a motorcycle dealership, another monkey sat in a cage, glumly picking at his toenails. When we came to a stop because of more traffic a man came over with yet another monkey chained to his wrist, offering to pose for pictures. Adhi tossed the man a banana we'd bought from a vendor a few minutes before, and we sped along as soon as the traffic allowed.

Monkeys were everywhere in Sumatra, I was coming to realize — as common as cats. There were dogs, too. Some were free, but most were caged up.

"Why don't they let the dogs out?" I asked. "Do they get into trouble?"

"Owning a dog is a status symbol," Diah explained. "The owners of those caged dogs want their guests to see that they have enough money to have one. They own a dog for the same reason some men have one long fingernail — it proves they aren't forced to do manual labor."

Adhi grinned sheepishly and tapped his nail on the steering wheel.

Eventually the village restaurants and vendors fell away, and we were rolling along green fields, alternating with rows and rows of palm trees. "See how evenly spaced they are?" Diah said. "Those are planted African palms. That's what much of Sumatra looks like now."

The orderly trees were pretty — the palms kept lining up to make new diagonals as the truck moved past.

Once we left the city, our truck accumulated some village kids in its wake, giggling as they tried to keep pace. Diah had Adhi slow down and bought a bag of plums for me to hand out. The kids were intimidated by hulking white me, but they eventually got over it and each took one, shouting "U.S.A." before plopping down on the grass to enjoy their treats. They rapidly passed from view. I saved one plum in my lap, to give to Raja.

As we chugged along, a river cut across the road. The ravine wasn't too deep, but there wasn't a bridge, just two planks that someone had laid across. "How do we get to the other side?" I asked.

"Over the bridge," Diah said. "How else?"

"Oh," I said, looking at the planks dubiously. "That's a *bridge*."

Once Adhi had carefully lined the vehicle up so the tires were in front of the wood, Diah and I got out and checked his work. The tires and the planks were basically the same width. I stood in the dirt, arms crossed, while Diah turned away and covered her face. "I can never watch this part."

The fit was so tight that the planks disappeared under Adhi's tires, bending into shallow U shapes under the truck. Diah and I shouted encouragement while I tried to force away visions of the truck tumbling, Raja's crate carried off in the stream below. He couldn't see what was going on, but all the same the pitching forward and backward set him to kiss-squeaking.

Once Adhi had made it to the other side, Diah and I walked across the planks and got back in. Raja made confused grunts from his crate while we once again rolled forward along solid ground. At the peak of a steep incline we passed a trio of women, bundles of greenery bowing their heads. One had a toddler following along, his arm wrapped around her leg. I wondered how far they'd gone with their burdens. How far they had left to go.

We stopped at a solid metal gate, which a man in coveralls came out to open. After we'd rolled through and parked, more workers emerged — three men in coveralls and two women, each in a headscarf like Diah.

After I'd been introduced around, Diah took me on a tour of the human quarters. It didn't last long: There were two low and damp cinder-block buildings, draped by overhanging trees. One of them, Diah explained, was the kitchen and dining room. I'd be staying in the other. She offered to show me to it, but I said I'd wait, because I wanted to be back at the truck when they brought Raja out.

It took all of the men working together to maneuver the crate to the ground. Raja must have been pacing as they did, as the crate's balance kept shifting from side to side, the men breaking into shouts every time it nearly toppled. Orange fingertips appeared here and there behind the slats.

In a soft but commanding voice, Diah directed the men in Bahasa. "Raja's new quarters are ready," she explained to me. "We'll put the crate alongside so he can enter directly."

I nodded, then followed behind as the men hauled the crate. Diah had plenty of time to explain the purpose of the quarantine center as we made our slow progress. "Orangutans are susceptible to almost any disease that could strike a human, and a few more as well. Almost all of them arrive with parasites and diseases, and we have to get those out of their system before they can infect the others. That takes a few weeks, which is why we have the quarantine here. Once they're through with quarantine, we can bring the orangutans back into the forest."

As the rest of the site came into view, I saw what looked like an orangutan prison. A few dozen apes were in individual cages, thick metal bars above, below, and on all sides. There was an open space beneath each cage, where orangutan poo could fall through and be hosed away. As we passed, they pressed their faces into the gaps between the bars, trying to spy the new arrival. They made kiss-squeaks like Raja's. Some held out their hands and stared into my eyes, hoping for a caress. Diah instructed me not to touch them, not until I'd been decontaminated.

"They look lonely," I said.

"Yes," she said. "It would make them all happier if they were in one big cage, and if they could interact with us. But then they would make one another sick, and become used to human contact. This is dangerous, because then they would approach people who might come into the jungle, people who would like to harm them. We need them to spend time only with themselves. This way we can make their isolation period as short as possible and get them back into the wild. So they are sad and lonely while they are here, yes, but it is for the greater good."

"Raja will be isolated, too?"

"Yes. I am afraid so. Remember: Orangutans are not as social as chimps and gorillas. They spend most of their adult lives by themselves. They don't mind the solitude as much as a human would."

I wondered if that applied to Raja, or if I'd trained him to expect company.

The crew lowered Raja's crate to the ground near a group of cages. They shared walls, so the orangutans could come near each other and reach arms through if they wanted.

"At least we don't have to put Raja in complete isolation at first," Diah said. "Since he hasn't been around other orangutans for years, that means there are many diseases we can be sure he is not carrying. So he gets to be alongside other orangutans for now, even though he has his own cage. His neighbors will help educate him on how to be a good, proper orangutan, as well."

I didn't know what a "good, proper orangutan" was, but I was pretty certain Raja would never be one. Hopefully his neighbors would be fine with a farting, improper orangutan instead.

The quarantine workers lined the crate up with the cage's sliding door. But something was clearly wrong — the men called Diah over. She exchanged words with them, then waved me over.

"Your crate, how does the door open?" she asked.

"Just . . . out. You know, like a door."

She nodded and said something to the men in Indonesian. "The crates we use have up-and-down gates so we can transfer the apes more easily. But we'll figure something out."

Under Diah's guidance, the men eased the crate back a few feet. One of them unlatched the door and, after warning his colleagues, worked it open.

The wood cracked as Raja kicked the door, knocking it from the hinges. With another kick the door was wide open, the attendant on his back in the dirt. Raja busted through and whirled, his teeth bared as he made a low groan, in a way I'd never heard him do. The men shouted and scattered, one of them running into the clinic. I whirled, terrified he'd return with a weapon.

Raja whirled, too, making his low cries until he finally saw me. He rushed in my direction, and at the sight of his one hundred pounds bearing down, I yelped. He slammed right into me, knocking the wind out as we rolled in the grass.

I heard Diah yelling, and saw feet in my peripheral vision as the men scurried about. It was all I could do to breathe. I was seeing bright flashing lights, and my nostrils filled with Raja's scent. He was caked in some fluid, and it took me a few moments to realize it was stale urine. We were both soaked in it, and something else, too. Probably poop. It wasn't Raja's fault — he'd been cooped up in a cage for two days; of course he'd made a mess. Despite the fact that it was designed to keep his waste away, some of it had probably sloshed onto him.

I managed to maneuver so we were embracing on our sides, so Raja's full weight was no longer crushing me. He was trembling, his strong muscles shaking my own body, jolting me fiercely enough that it left me numb and rickety. I held Raja and was held by him, only barely aware of his stink, of the relieved shouts of the staff, of a woman giggling somewhere. At that moment, those humans lived on a distant shore.

Slowly, Raja's trembling subsided. He still kept his head buried in my chest, but I was able to sit up and see Diah. She was standing near, amusement and something deeper and sadder on her face. "He loves you," she said simply.

I closed my eyes and nodded. "He's sort of my brother."

"This isn't going to be easy for either of you."

"I know," I said. I thought of how to phrase what was on my mind. "I'm worried that we're *too* close, that he's gotten too used to me and other humans to make it with other orangutans."

"We'll give him a chance to adapt. That's all we can do. Now, to get him in his cage — you know him best. Will he let you walk him in, or do you want help?"

You know him best. I staggered to my feet, Raja unsteadily coming up with me. The staff gave us a wide berth as we lumbered over to the cage, about the size of my old bedroom. He seemed almost relieved to enter it. Yet another cage for Raja. Whatever his fate, maybe this would be the last one he'd ever have to be in.

Once we were in his new cage, I fished in my pocket for the plum I'd been saving. It was crushed and gooey, but I knew that would be no problem for Raja. He took his time eating it, slurping the tart skin first and only then moving on to the sweet flesh. After he'd eaten, I sat beside him on the sun-warmed bars, staring out at the sanctuary while he breathed into my chest, eyes closed. After a while, he lifted his head and stared out with me. There was plenty to see. Around the corner were the isolation cages, each with its own young orangutan. At a hundred paces was a giant cage with many orangutans in it, their orange color screened and muted by the layers of meshing they used for sleeping. I wondered what Raja was seeing through his golden eyes, if he was seeing versions of himself or strange animals. Did he think he was a human being, or an ape? Had he thought until now that he was the only one of his kind, destined to be alone on the planet? Maybe the sight of these orangutans brought something like relief.

In the cage next to us, not ten feet away, was a large male orangutan. His cheek flaps made his face almost a perfect circle, broad and glistening with perspiration. He turned in our general direction, but didn't meet our eyes.

"That's Gorgon," Diah said, standing on the other side of the bars. "Our longest resident. He lost his home and wandered into a village. They tried to shoot and eat him, but a kind logger took pity on him, quit his job, and drove ten hours through the night to bring him to our door. We got him into surgery and started removing air pellets — he had dozens in him. We got most of them out, but he's still crippled and fully blind. He will never be leaving here. But Gorgon lived a long time in the jungle, and I hope he might be able to teach Raja a few things before he goes to the forest. Raja can watch how he swings on the top of his cage, can see that he always has two hands on the bars. Gorgon's a strong, smart orangutan. He will make a good teacher."

Raja and I looked at Gorgon, who stared severely into the air over our heads. He didn't look like the sort of teacher who would be grading on a curve.

"Gorgon never shows affection to anyone, human or orangutan, but he is my favorite. Anyway. Let me show you your room," Diah said.

I thought Raja might give me trouble when I tried to leave, but he was transfixed by Gorgon and didn't protest as I got up. As I crept across the bars, Raja's attention remained on his new neighbor. This fascinating creature, so strange to him for being so alike. Diah locked the cage behind me.

"I stay in the city with Adhi each night, and most of the staff members live with their families in nearby villages," she said as we walked. "So in the evenings there will only be you and one guard and the *mawas*. It will be very quiet, but maybe you will like that after busy America."

Diah brought me to the back of the maintenance building and pushed on a door, which came right off its hinges. She stared at it for a moment, surprised, then shrugged and handed it to me. I put it to one side, then peeked in. The room was basically a closet with a mattress. The walls were damp concrete, a large spider and its web entombing one corner of the ceiling. My duffel hunched accusingly in a corner. *Where have you brought us?*

"I warned you it wasn't much," Diah said.

"It'll be fine," I assured her. "Thanks."

"I'll give you some time to unpack," she said, then ducked out.

Unpacking. Right. There was nowhere to put my clothes, just a rickety bedside table and a lamp. I pulled them out anyway and put them in a loose stack on top of the duffel, the only clean thing in the room. I sat on the bed, letting out a long breath. The mattress sagged enough to bump the floor, and when it did, something skittered away and out the door. I only caught a glimpse, but I was pretty sure it was a scorpion.

I put my head in my hands, ground my palms into my eye sockets. I'd spent the day worrying about how Raja was going to adjust, but now that I was alone I realized that this was all maybe a little overwhelming for me, too. Maybe a lot overwhelming. I took a few long breaths. I reminded myself that, however bad I had it, Raja had it worse. I'd be returning to the States in a few days. Raja's new world was his for good.

I played a game on my phone, to give my mind somewhere else to be for a few minutes. As soon as I'd recovered enough, I returned to Raja's cage. He was leaning against the bars, as far as he could get himself from Gorgon. He face-planted into his palms, like when he wanted to go for ice cream. He probably wasn't gunning for ice cream specifically, but his meaning was still clear: *We go.*

I signed back: *I'm sorry. No.*

His next sign was one I hadn't seen for a while. *Little poop.* The equivalent of *bummer.*

Next Raja took his hand and made the shape of an elephant trunk in front of his face. Of course — his toy. I tried to think of where I'd last seen it. The crate. It was still right next to his cage, so I went over to it and looked in. What remained of the stuff Mom had gotten together for Raja's journey was still in there. Raja had arranged everything in a pyramid in the corner.

The stinking elephant. It wasn't a real creature, but the protective feelings it brought out in Raja were real. Raja's affection for it was misplaced but important, all the same. I brought the elephant to Raja's cage, pushing it through the bars. He wrapped his body around it and tucked it in close.

I walked alongside Gorgon's cage and sat on the other side of his bars, staring at the hulking male. "He looks nice, Raja," I lied. Truth was he looked like a drill sergeant reincarnated as an orangutan. Raja was a perky little rag doll compared to him.

I rested on my side of Raja's bars while he rested on his, our forearms intertwined in the in-between space, the elephant crushed into the bars. By the time Raja was asleep and I'd headed back to the human zone, Diah and Adhi had left for the day. The one guard on duty greeted me from the kitchen area as I passed. We tried to have a conversation, but it soon became clear that his English was even worse than my Indonesian. He pointed to a pan of crispy rice on the stovetop; feeling lonely and overwhelmed, I served myself some and ate it quickly, despite the quaking in my worried stomach. I rinsed my plate and holed myself away in my moist little room, propping the door up as best I could. I might have been sixteen, but as I sat on that lonely bed in the jungle, I had a pure and uncomplicated six-year-old's feeling: I missed my mom.

I moved the lamp closer to the bed, but it flicked off and refused to come back on. So I lay on the bed in the dark and read on my phone. Or technically read; whole paragraphs would go by and I'd realize my thoughts had been elsewhere the whole time. Raja was right there, a few hundred feet away on the other side of the wall, having his own thoughts while he lay in a corner of his cage. From Raja my thoughts spiraled further: to Mom lying sick in Diah and Adhi's house, to my father . . . somewhere. They existed.

I put the phone down and shut my eyes, trying not to think about the scorpion I'd seen earlier that day. I couldn't see it anywhere but, like Raja, like me, like everyone, it had to be *somewhere*.

I woke up the next morning to the smell of cat pee. I opened my eyes to see a stray tomcat yowling at me from the other side of my bedroom, glaring at me with crusty eyes puffed to slits. When I sat up, the cat pointedly lowered its hindquarters, peed on my stack of clothes, and escaped through a broken window. The last thing I saw was his knobby short tail. I scrunched my nose at the stench. I'd be smelling like cat pee my whole time in Sumatra. Awesome.

Nothing to be done about it, though. I ate some crackers I'd snagged from the airplane and then headed out to the orangutans. Raja was already up, sitting at the door of his cage. When he saw me, his eyes lit up and his fingers flurried. *I love you. Ice cream.* My heart quaked, though I knew that this was sort of like dropping a little sibling off at summer camp: Getting Raja used to being separated was an important part of all this.

"Morning, Gorgon," I said dryly as I approached the cages. The blind old orangutan lifted his head and sniffed the air, baring his teeth in my general direction. "I see you're in your usual good mood."

Raja and I groomed each other through the bars of his cage. I picked out bits of sleep from the corners of his eyes, and he helpfully removed a beetle that had been crawling on my shirt. He held it between his fingers, watching the legs flail. Then he crushed it and ate it. It sounded like he was eating a sunflower seed.

Once he became bored with me, Raja got brave enough to approach the orangutan next door. Gorgon went perfectly still as Raja rolled over the bars that made up the floor of his cage, coming to rest right near his neighbor. Raja lifted a trembling finger and brought it toward Gorgon's face. At the last minute he chickened out and pulled back, but then curiosity got the best of him and he tried again, this time getting as far as tapping Gorgon's elbow. The blind ape jerked, making an irritated squeak and pulling himself up the bars of his cage, far from Raja.

Raja looked at me, amazed. *Did I make that happen?*

"I think you startled him," I told Raja. "He's blind, remember."

Raja stared at Gorgon. I maneuvered so I could see his face. I expected to see fear, but instead I saw he was delighted at the power he had.

Eventually Gorgon came back down, and Raja approached again, pressing his body against the bars so he could reach Gorgon's foot, giving it a fierce yank. Gorgon squeaked, rolling away while Raja rasped in pleasure. I guess Raja's role around here was going to be Grade A pest.

I spent the morning with him, watching Raja come up with more and more ingenious ways to annoy Gorgon. Eventually, though, Gorgon started returning Raja's touches. By noon they had their hands through the bars, calmly scratching through each other's hair. They looked like old men who had been coming to the same park bench for decades.

"Oh, good, they're friends," came Diah's voice. I looked up and saw her approaching with a wheelbarrow full of fruit.

"Hi," I said. "Yeah, I think they are."

"You smell like a cat," she said, smiling as she came near.

I sniffed my shirt. Right. Yuck.

"Good morning, Raja," Diah said. "How was your first night in the Orangutan Marriott?"

He saw the mounds of fruit in her wheelbarrow and squeaked in excitement, pressing against the bars and reaching out.

Instead of giving him a fruit, though, Diah took some chunks of melon in hand and tossed them so they landed between the bars that formed the roof of his cage. Raja looked up, baffled, then back at us. *Why would you do that?*

"In the jungle, most fruit he eats will be in the trees," Diah said. "He's too used to finding everything he needs on the ground — he needs to start looking up for food. Here — toss some melon onto Gorgon's cage."

I took a few pieces and hefted them rapid-fire, football practice muscles creaking into use. Gorgon heard the food ring against his cage and immediately took to the bars, lifting himself up to retrieve the melon.

Raja watched carefully, then looked up hungrily at the melon on top of his own cage. "Come on, Raj," I said, pointing at the fruit. "Go get it!"

He tentatively took the bars in his hand, looking at me for guidance. I nodded encouragingly.

He climbed and flailed through open air, finally contacting a piece of fruit. It fell down, and he returned to the bottom to retrieve it. Inelegant, but mission accomplished.

I felt totally proud and totally undone. The ending was beginning.

Diah looked at me with searching eyes. "What is the word in English for when something tastes unpleasant and good at the same time?"

I thought for a moment. "Bittersweet," I said.

"Yes, that is it," Diah said, nodding. "Bittersweet."

Diah took me to the office to call my mother, but the satellite phone was down when we got there. "It happens often, unfortunately," Diah said. "The network will be back up in a few hours. I saw your mother last night, and she wants you to know she is fine. Ibu is taking good care of her. Come, there's someone I want you to meet."

Diah took me back to Raja's cage and brought me around the rear. There, in an adjoining cage, was a small huddled form I only gradually realized was an orangutan. She was missing most of her hair, and one side of her face was a web of hardened tissue. But when she heard us approach and looked up, I saw she had the sweetest expression. Yearning.

"That's Gaia," Diah said. "I just moved her out of isolation and into here before her release. Farmers torched her home swamp, and she got badly burned trying to escape. Then the tree she was in fell and crushed her leg. They'd assumed she was dead and discarded her — a schoolgirl found her in a garbage dump and called us."

Once Gaia knew she had our attention, she held on to her feet, so she was in the shape of a ball. Then she rolled around her cage, faster and faster, only stopping once she was back near us. Diah watched her tenderly, then reached out through the bars to scratch the scar tissue on her back. "I think that part must be very itchy for her," Diah explained.

I heard a familiar kiss-squeak and saw that Raja had approached us within his cage. He sat at the edge, feet dangling, and stretched out a hand so he could join the grooming. Eventually he got bored and started pulling at Gaia's sparse hair instead, until the smaller female squealed and rolled away.

Diah had to go feed the other orangutans, but I stayed back to hang out with Raja, Gaia, and Gorgon. After a few hours I headed back to the buildings, hoping to reach my mom on the satellite phone. I found Diah at the wood table in the dining area, studying a calendar, brushing tiny ants from each date as she examined it.

"Oh, good, John," she said. "Come join me. I am trying to figure out our release-trip schedule."

I sat down next to her and looked at the calendar, its corners curling in the humid air. "Raja is an unusual case," she said. "He is not an infant like most of the orangutans we receive, but he also does not have any experience in the wild. Once his blood tests have come back, he can be released. But release is not our only option, you understand."

I nodded, waiting to hear where this was going.

"Raja could stay here and be safe for the rest of his life. Or we can bring him into the wilderness with the next batch of release orangutans, and hope he learns quickly enough from his fellows to survive."

"What do you recommend?" I asked.

"It is not an easy choice," Diah said. "As Raja's family, I think you and your mother should be the ones to decide. Here is what it would look like if we brought him to the wild: We're planning on releasing three younger females tomorrow or the day after, depending on travel conditions. If we brought Raja, too, that would make a total of four orangutans. Males will not generally help each other, but I hope that the females will have tolerance for . . ."

". . . a clueless American?" I offered.

Diah smiled. "Yes. They might help him along. Wild orangutans spend five years with their mothers, and by the time they go off on their own, the young ones have mental maps of which trees are fruiting at what times of the year. It is hard for released orangutans to catch up if they never had mothers teaching them how to survive out there in the first place."

I nodded. Calling Raja unknowledgeable was an understatement. All I'd taught him how to do was play video games. "I think I should call my mom and see what she thinks," I said.

"This is a good idea," Diah said. She looked at the satellite phone's screen. "And we are in luck." She dialed and spoke to someone on the other end in Indonesian, eventually switching to English. "Hello, Mrs. Solomon," she said. "I have John here." She passed the receiver to me.

"Hi, Mom. How are you feeling?" I asked.

The answer was garbled, but after she gushed about how glad she was to hear me and know I was okay, I thought she said she was still weak but feeling slightly better. Praying she could hear me better than I could hear her, I told her the situation. "So what do you think we should do, Mom?" I said. "Keep Raja here in quarantine for life, or give him a shot out in the jungle?"

"Sweetie," Mom said, "it's a hard choice, isn't it? But I think . . . you would feel terrible if something bad happened to Raja out there, wouldn't you? Wouldn't it be better to have him in safety, rather than risking that?"

I thought about what she was saying. I wished we could let Raja decide, but that wasn't possible.

It would feel better to keep him safe — much better than it would feel if I found out that Raja had died, after it had been my choice to put him in danger.

But my family had gone through years making decisions based on what was easiest at each moment, what would decrease pain in the day-to-day, even if it meant willfully looking away from what was really there. After all this time, I could let Raja spend the rest of his life in a cage, without ever having another chance to be free. But that didn't really feel like a choice. "I get what you're saying," I told my mom, "but I think it's time he had his shot out there."

"That's what I imagined you'd say," Mom said. "It's not what I'd choose, but you've fought so hard to get this far. I won't put up a fight. If it . . . doesn't work, then at least he had his chance."

Yes. At least he had his chance.

THIRTEEN

The release team arrived early the next morning in an enclosed truck whose interior had been specially fitted with padded restraints. So the journey would be less stressful, Diah had tranquilized the orangutans, carefully dosing each one with a sweet, drugged fluid. She started by loading two of the females, directing the staff to drag them out of their cages one by one to maneuver them into the truck. It was startling and strange, the sight of these sleeping apes limp in the arms of men, mouths lolling and fingers pointing to the earth.

Raja would be next, followed by Gaia. Under the roar of the dawn insects, I waited beside Raja's cage for his tranquilizer to set in. As he started slumping, Gorgon and Gaia tugged him into the corner that adjoined both their cages and nervously groomed him, one of Raja's hands in Gorgon's lap and the other in Gaia's. They kept trying to groom their way to the root of Raja's strange behavior as his head began to bend forward, his eyes taking longer and longer to open each time he blinked. Gaia reached out to pry Raja's eyes open, but once he'd slumped forward she couldn't quite reach.

Gorgon's blind eyes, the even gray of rainclouds, stared into the distance. But I knew he was focused on Raja: When the staff heaved Raja's limp form out of the cage and toward the truck, Gorgon held his new friend's hand for as long as possible, his fingers trailing in the air even after Raja was gone. For her part, Gaia climbed to the highest point of her cage so she could watch Raja for as long as possible. Before he disappeared from view, she signed a rough version of *you poop*. She was a quick study.

As I watched them load Raja into the truck, my heart did tight little flips. I was pretty sure we were doing the right thing for him — but all the same here I was, watching him be tricked, restrained, brought to yet another new place with no say in the matter. I comforted myself that at least this would be the last time.

I went back to Raja's empty cage and picked up the stuffed elephant. Despite its oily dirtiness, I held the elephant up to my face and breathed in Raja's smell. Then I put it in my room. Raja couldn't have it in the wilderness, so I'd be bringing the toy back to the States with me.

I paced while Raja was loaded in and secured. Adhi and Diah asked for my help with Gaia, and I jumped at the opportunity, glad to have something to occupy myself. The tough girl had resisted the tranquilizers the longest but now she, too, was getting sleepy. Gaia collapsed right at the entrance to her cage, as if to make her transfer as easy as possible for us. She was small enough that I was able to carry her on my own to the truck, Gorgon sniffing in our direction as yet another neighbor was carted off.

We loaded Gaia in back and got into the truck's cab. Adhi was in a surly mood — we were running late, and it turned out that going to the release site meant missing days of wages at the gas station where he also worked. But Diah wouldn't have been allowed to drive with me on her own — or drive a vehicle at all in the conservative Aceh province. Diah filled me in on all this as we rolled through the nearby village streets, heading for the congested main road with our ape cargo. There were so many new and unfamiliar things to see — it was as much as I could manage to keep up my side of the conversation while looking out the window.

After a few minutes of uncharacteristic griping, Adhi fell quiet and concentrated on the road as he plodded the truck forward, ignoring motorcycles and dodging potholes as best he could.

"You must be familiar with Aceh from the news in the United States," Diah said as we bumped along the dirt road that stretched north from Medan. We passed buffalo tilling fields, mosques rising from the middle of nowhere, their minarets of hammered tin wavering above fields of green and yellow.

"I haven't heard of it," I admitted. This place sounded like a sneeze.

Diah frowned, and I realized I was supposed to have heard of Aceh. "It is the northernmost point of Indonesia. While orang-utans used to be everywhere in Sumatra, because Aceh is most strictly vegetarian Muslim, the people here have been the slowest to hunt orangutans. So most of those who remain in the wild are in the north. It used to be one of the most dangerous places in the world, because the Acehnese wanted to separate from the rest of Indonesia. There were many terrorist attacks. I am from Java, so for a long time it was too risky for me to travel here — outsiders were targets."

"They can tell where you're from just by looking at you?"

She laughed. "Yes, of course. I would rather be from Aceh, actually. They are a beautiful people, with heart-shaped faces. Not stumpy-short like the Javanese. Adhi is from Aceh."

She placed two delicate fingers under her husband's chin and turned his face so I could see his profile. They'd never displayed affection in front of me before — though the move would have been nothing back in the States, I flushed like I'd walked in on them in the bedroom. Adhi gave a small embarrassed smile and tilted his chin away.

I wanted to tell Diah she didn't look squat at all, but was pretty sure I'd screw it up, so I moved on. "So what happened? How come we're able to travel to Aceh now?"

"It is a terrible reason. Do you remember the great tsunami in 2004?"

I shook my head again.

"Well, it affected a lot of Asia, but Aceh got hit the worst. Many thousands of people died, and the countryside was devastated. Many of the separatists, they were washed away. Literally, you could say? And for those who remained, suddenly having a central government to help them recover did not seem like a bad idea. So, like that, it became safe to travel here. Still, if we have to confiscate an orangutan being held captive in Aceh, I hide in the car. We do not want to make it look like outsiders are taking their property."

"Those confiscations happen often?"

"About every two weeks we get a call. Those are just the orangutans that we hear about, of course. Many are hidden in cages, being fattened up to be eaten. We will never know about them."

"How many orangutans are left?"

"In Sumatra? About six thousand. In Borneo there are more, maybe fifty thousand. The Sumatran orangutan will probably be the first ape to go extinct in the wild."

My mind went to Raja, how he was heading right back into danger. "They will definitely go extinct? Even with the work you're doing?"

"The *tripa* swamp is still being converted into palm oil plantations. Two million hectares a year are being lost. Until that is reversed, the orangutans will continue to lose their habitat, and without habitat they cannot survive. Indonesia is a poor country compared to those in Europe or America, and the dollars those companies offer for palm oil are too attractive for our government to turn down. So the swamps continue to burn."

The conversation was laying me low. I placed my hand over my mouth, holding up my chin as I stared out the window at the countryside rolling by. I thought about Raja in back, invisible and yet *there*. Totally ignorant about what was to come, but counting on me to make it happen. And how much more did I know about what was to come, really? Next to nothing. I was out of my depth. Which meant Raja and I both were out of our depth.

Except for the occasional village, the view outside was a stream of plantation crops separated by desperate strands of overgrown jungle. After a few hours, the road narrowed to a single lane, and we would pass broken-down vehicles blocking the way, forcing us to detour through the muddy shoulder.

Somewhere past noon, Diah's phone buzzed. She listened intently, asking terse questions in Indonesian. When she ended the call she talked to Adhi for a while. He looked at his watch, then the fuel gauge, and nodded.

"We have someone to pick up," Diah said. "Or something to pick up, depending on how you think of these things."

While Adhi navigated back-country roads, Diah made half a dozen calls. Eventually our truck rumbled along a dirt road only barely wide enough for us to pass, branches scraping the windows. Stump-filled clearings appeared through the tree line, until the forest view turned to open land peppered with fresh and oozy stumps.

"Logging," Diah said.

"Illegal?"

"They were probably granted permission by the government. But that permission comes from bribing an official. So. Legal, yes. Illegal, yes."

I started to hear chain saws and men's voices, and then Adhi pulled us into a clearing. There were logging trucks lining the edges, some with only a few stray woodchips and others stacked with pyramids of stripped trunks. A little bird was perched on a fallen tree, a blip of yellow that flitted away as our truck pulled near. Adhi stopped amid a jumble of chained fallen trees. Men with saws were crawling over them, hacking away branches.

A pickup truck was parked at the far end, a man in a police uniform standing by the driver's-side door, cigarette dangling from his mouth. Adhi called out to him, and he shouted something back with a smile and a shake of his head. I wondered if Adhi knew this guy already.

Adhi pulled near and shut off our truck. "Stay in here," he instructed Diah and me. "Whatever happens, you will promise me to stay here?"

We nodded.

Adhi got out and greeted the police officer, clasping his hand warmly. The officer offered Adhi a cigarette, which he accepted. They strolled along the fallen trees, passing out of view.

Loggers stopped their work and trailed after them, dragging chain saws. Though Diah kept her face calm, I could sense her breathing quicken.

"They'll be okay, right?" I asked.

She didn't answer, just clasped her hands in her lap and settled in to wait. The little yellow bird returned, hopping frantically around the gashed earth.

"I can't believe everyone here is letting this happen," I said.

Diah looked surprisingly ticked. "This once happened in America, too. Most of your forests were cut down for farmland. You could argue that Western conservationists want to keep Sumatra in the dark ages, to keep us from having the economic advantages that your own period of forest-clearing allowed you."

"Oh," I said. "Touché."

Long minutes passed, Diah and I motionless in the front seat as we stared out at the logging camp. The little yellow bird gave up and flitted away even as an egret soared in, stood on a fallen tree, picked at something it found in the trunk, then flew off. Fuzzy little flies batted the windshield, a hushed patter.

Diah leaned her ear against the back of the seat, then returned to facing forward, nervously tapping her fingers on her lips. "I can't hear any motion from the orangutans in back, but the tranquilizer won't last too much longer. As you can imagine, it will be better if they don't wake up while they're still in the truck."

She toyed with the door handle, and I could tell she was considering risking going after Adhi. Before she could, though, he came back into view. He and the policeman were dragging an orangutan by a chain. It was cinched tightly around her waist, and she faced the logging camp as she went, clawing at the earth with her hands and feet while Adhi and the policeman heaved. She squealed, once turning as she tried to bite Adhi. He jumped out of the way, scolding her, then continued to drag her to the truck.

"They told us she was a baby," Diah said.

This ape was small, but even I knew that she was no baby. As she got closer, I saw she was nearly bald. A big chunk was missing from an ear, and her jaw hung strangely loose.

As Adhi neared, Diah leaned across me and rolled down the window, calling out something in Indonesian. Adhi responded in bursts while he tried to keep the female under control. Finally

Diah turned to me. "She looks small, but this is an adult orangutan — look how dark her face is, and there is no white hair left
on her eyelids. She cannot go in back, because Raja and the females
have been quarantined, but this one has not. She will have to go
back to the rehabilitation center before she can be released. That
means she has to stay in the front of the truck with us, at least for
the next hour. Are you comfortable with that? Please be free to
say no."

I wasn't so comfortable with it, actually, but because I knew
saying so would mean leaving this orangutan behind, I nodded. I
looked at her small angry eyes, the fresh gouges her fingers had left
in the earth.

Diah fished a wrinkled bath towel from under the seat and
tossed it out the window to Adhi. With one hand, he slowly reeled
the orangutan in. Her jaws snapped furiously the whole time.

"She's learned to fight," Diah said. "It would not come as naturally to an orangutan in the wild."

Adhi's other hand had the towel, whipping it open. Once the
orangutan was near enough, he managed to swaddle her, and
hugged her tight.

For a moment she was more frenzied than ever, and my miss-
ing finger throbbed. But then something unexpected happened.
Swaddled in Adhi's arms, the orangutan calmed and went limp.
She stared out from the soft cotton as Adhi hefted her in the air
like a sack of sand. He jerked his chin at my door. I opened it.
With a grunt, Adhi placed the orangutan in my lap.

She was heavy, her weight pressing my body deep into the
truck's seat. Springs jutted into the backs of my legs, and immediately it felt like I had to pee. But at least the orangutan was mostly
still. I faced her forward and wrapped my arms tight around her,
like I'd once done with Raja. She smelled like cigarette smoke.

"She'll keep still," Diah said. "Nothing in their world presses an orangutan to move fast, and in their inner hearts they want stillness more than anything else. Just hold her tight."

With the door open, I could see that the loggers had lined up to watch the scene. When they saw big white American me, one of them shouted in surprise. Adhi slammed the door closed and hurried around to the driver's side. He started the car, while Diah peered deep into the young female's eyes, as if measuring something she found there. "Are you okay?" she asked me, her eyes never leaving the orangutan's.

"Yeah, I'm fine," I said.

"They've been beating her," Diah said as Adhi turned around and headed down the dirt road. "She's missing teeth, and her jaw broke and healed on its own. It's in bad shape."

Still strangely calm, the orangutan looked directly up so she could see into my eyes. I brushed a tentative finger along the underside of her chin. She ignored me, instead shifting her gaze to the dashboard. The one fingertip that emerged from the towel twitched. I ran my own along it.

"She's got smoker's breath, too," I said. It was really stinky — if she'd been a cartoon, she'd have been breathing out yellow-brown.

"Not all that uncommon, either." Diah sighed. "The loggers probably taught her to. We have had a few orangs arrive hooked on nicotine. But at least she seems to like you. *Mawas'* capacity to move on after being wounded, to stay open . . . it always inspires me. When I was a veterinary student in Java, I met my first orangutan at the Jakarta zoo. He did the same thing. He had been captured and placed in a small cage for his whole life, but all he wanted to do was nuzzle his captors. In its terror, the mouse will go to the cat for help."

I stroked the fuzz on the top of the orangutan's head. She closed her eyes, maybe in pleasure. "She's very warm," I said.

Diah laid the back of her hand across the orangutan's forehead. "I imagine it's mostly sunstroke. I'd like to get fluids into her as soon as possible."

I continued to stroke the orangutan's chin, taking in her narrow golden eyes, her wide mouth, her flat and hairy nose. Her lips parted as she shifted in my lap, and I saw that Diah was right: All the teeth on one side of her jaw were missing.

As we drove, clouds began to knit in front of the sun, and by the time we passed a simple wooden sign at the side of the road, it was too shaded for me to see what was written on it. "We're entering a national park," Diah said. "You'll still find swamps burning here, too, but this is technically government land. It's in here that we release the orangutans. We chose a territory that didn't already have a wild population — much better to keep the released ones together and not risk spreading disease."

The jungle knitted in tight as we drove. The road had once been paved, but the few remaining bits of asphalt worked better as obstacles than pavement. After one bend we came across what I thought were branches in the road, but they turned out to be snakes sunning themselves. They scattered as the truck rumbled near. Then, around the next bend, we disturbed a trio of skinny chickens that ran off into the brush.

"Is someone keeping chickens out here?" I asked.

"No," Diah said. "Those are wild chickens."

Wild chickens. Huh. Who'd have thought? As soon as the chickens had disappeared, a creature poked its head out of the foliage, and then departed. He'd had a beautiful chocolate-brown face, and drew himself away through the canopy on long, graceful arms.

"That's a gibbon," Diah said, noticing my attention. "One of the lesser apes. I have a soft spot for them. There's this old joke: The chimp tried to be a boxer, the gorilla tried to be a sumo wrestler, the gibbon tried to be an acrobat, and the orangutan tried to be a gibbon but couldn't make the weight."

"Did you see the gibbon?" I asked the orangutan in my lap. But she didn't react, and I realized she'd fallen asleep. "Oops, sorry," I whispered.

Eventually Adhi stopped the truck along a pullout, beside a dinged-up old school bus. "We have cut a few trails to get from the road to our camp," Diah explained, "and sometimes school field trips use them. We will pass some students on our way in. They will be curious, but I do not imagine they will be brave enough to come too near the orangutan. Do you think you can carry her? We will return with help for Raja and the rest."

"Yeah, I can manage," I said. Waddling through the wild jungle with a forty-pound orangutan in my arms — what could go wrong?

I got my feet onto the rim of the truck, then Adhi helped me down. The orangutan woke and shifted in the towel, her feet digging into my hips as she tried to leverage herself higher up my torso. Face toward mine, she was actually helping me by distributing her weight more evenly, like a backpack with waist straps. Orangutans had clearly figured out what they were doing over the last few million years. I lightly laid a hand over her foot, pocked with burns and scars. "You're going to a better place now," I said. She responded with a stinky sigh in my ear.

"How's the path ahead?" I asked Adhi as I picked my way forward, semi-blind. The orangutan wasn't exactly tiny, and she was blocking most of my view.

"Pretty clear," he reported. "I'll let you know if there are any big logs or holes."

Depending on how I tilted my head, all I could see was the sky, or the back of the orangutan's head, or the world of the swampy floor. Enormous ants trekked in columns across the wet, peaty ground. Bright green plants grew in clusters that made them look like big open mouths, flies buzzing at the corners of their lips. Lizards with black lightning bolts running down their backs darted from underneath my sneakers moments before my weight came down.

We turned a bend and walked headlong into a school group, all young kids around nine or ten. They wore matching uniforms, the girls in headscarves, the boys with bare heads, all sitting on a row of moss-slick logs as they listened to their teacher. At first they didn't notice us, and we took a break to watch. The teacher pointed to a bird hopping between branches, giving it a name. He peeled a piece of bark from a nearby tree and held it out to the children to smell, making sure each kid got a turn. The whole time the kids had their phones out, taking pictures.

Diah started us moving again, and I returned my attention to the swampy ground. We kept a fringe of trees between us and the schoolchildren, and I hoped we might escape notice. But then I heard ripples of delight from the group, and turned to see they were all on their feet. Some had hands over their mouths, frozen in shock, but the rest had their phones out, snapping pictures. The teacher stood in front, bouncing on the log, unable to contain his excitement. In the same tone he'd used for the bird and the bark, he gestured my way. I pivoted so they could see the orangutan better. The teacher asked me something in Indonesian while kids kept photographing.

I didn't understand, of course, but luckily Diah was there to speak for me. *"Tidak, pak,"* she answered. *"Orang America."*

"Wait," I whispered to her through a gritted smile, "it's *me* they're all excited about?"

"You're probably the first white person these kids have met," she said. "So smile big."

I did, and at that slight encouragement, the kids went full tilt. I was surrounded by schoolchildren throwing peace signs, making funny faces, cell phones clicking away. After they'd all had a chance to take a picture, Diah warded them off. The teacher patted my shoulder energetically, joy bursting from him, and shook his clasped hands in prayer at me. Then he herded the schoolchildren back toward the bus. I toddled along with the swaddled orangutan.

The camp was three large tents, a cage, a folding table covered in radios and other electronics, and a rain tarp. A narrow home base of tech, dwarfed and shrouded by the surrounding jungle. A generator hummed nearby, and an electric light lit us up in shades of gold. Out of a tent emerged a woman, younger and taller than Diah, with no headscarf. She greeted Diah energetically, then gestured toward me. Diah said something back in rapid Indonesian.

Diah introduced us, but in the ruckus of getting out from under the orangutan's grip and shaking the woman's hand, I missed her name. "Sorry," she said energetically, "my English not good!"

"Better than my Bahasa Indonesia, I can guarantee!" I said.

She looked at Diah in confusion, and while Diah translated for her the woman nodded and bobbed her head at me. Then they went right into the examination of the orangutan I was holding. On Diah's guidance, I lowered her to the table, and the vets started tracing the wounds on her limbs and torso, cataloging the scars on her face and mouth. She lay still, not calm as much as run-down, her head to one side. As her arms were lifted and scrutinized, as her mouth was opened and prodded, she kept her eyes on mine. I was where she'd decided to place her heart for the moment.

Adhi introduced me to two men in the same blue coveralls the workers in the quarantine center wore, and held out a spare uniform and a surgical mask. "Ready to go get the orangutans from the truck?"

The sky began to mist down as we left the clearing. I looked back through the glossy semi-rain and saw the orangutan had turned her head so she could watch me go. Her fingers curled, as if to wave good-bye as inconspicuously as possible. Her wistful expression made her look a little like young Raja, staring after me when I went off to school.

As we opened the back of the truck, I was glad to see the orangutans were still laid out flat, Raja snoring away in the center. Adhi and one of the men got Gaia, one taking her shoulders and the other her legs. Raja was next. As I got my arms under his torso, I realized he'd definitely lost some weight on his journey; he was still fat, but I could tug him along the truck's bed with less effort than I'd have expected. Some extra orangutan padding was a good thing, I figured — Raja could work off his milk shake weight while he figured out how to forage on his own. The other worker got his legs, and we staggered out onto the swamp trail.

And, like that, Raja was back in the jungle. After all these years, it was really happening. Could he possibly be ready for this?

By the time we'd reached the clearing, Diah and her colleague had placed the orangutan I'd carried in a cage, to keep her separate from the release apes. They laid out a tarp, where we arranged Raja and Gaia. Workers returned for the remaining two females while I sat heavily on the bench, winded. The orangutan from the logging camp watched me from her cage, squeaking, her rain-soaked hair flat along her face. She really did seem focused on me above all other people. Maybe it was my red hair.

Diah emerged from one of the tents, thermos in hand. "So," I said as I accepted a capful of fragrant green tea, "what happens now?"

"We deliver Raja and the ladies to their new homes and wait for them to wake up," she said, sitting on the bench and looking down at the three orangutans on the tarp, misty rain bejewel-ing their hair. "That will be in another hour or two, I would say."

Raja looked like me on a Saturday morning, enjoying sleep a bit too much. His fingers and toes curled and uncurled, his lips now and then pulling back from his teeth. Knowing I'd never again see him sleeping, I tried to memorize every detail of how he looked. That was one way we'd always been uneven: I knew which good-byes were long, and which were temporary. He had no idea that sometime soon he'd wake up and I wouldn't be there — ever again.

"There are two locations where we can place orangutans," Diah said. "One is a wild zone of *tripa* swamp. That is where we are sending two of these females. The other is an island we have made. A haven for orangutans who can't survive without monitoring. That is for Raja and Gaia. They will still have much land to wan-der, but we will be able to keep an eye on them. That is because of a grant from the U.S. Fish and Wildlife Service. We owe a lot to protection money from the United States."

"We're going to start with the two females," Adhi said, com-ing over to share the tea. "Papua and Kalimantan. Want to come?"

"Do I!" I said.

His nose wrinkled. "Yes. Do you?"

"Sorry. That's an expression in English. Yes, I would definitely like to come."

I tried to explain my nonsensical native language to Adhi while Diah fetched me a musty orange poncho from one of the tents. As I put it on, the rain went from misty to torrential. Pulling the hood over my head, I positioned myself at Papua's legs, an ankle in each hand. Adhi got under her shoulders, and two of the other workers took hold of Kalimantan. Slipping and sliding in the mud, we started along the jungle trail. Absorbed by the rain and the broad green plants all around us, the sunlight was as dim as if we were deep underwater. The ground was peaty and soft, each footfall squishing deep into the surface, black water drenching my sneakers.

After a few minutes we took a break, two dozing orangutans heaped unceremoniously in the center of the trail, four wet and sore humans sitting on a log and rubbing their arms.

When I looked down, I saw there were these small gray worms that were obsessed with my feet. They inched toward my sneaker and reared in confusion whenever I lifted my foot. Like they were tasting the air. "Check these guys out," I said to Adhi. "Friendly worms."

"Yes," he said. "Don't let the leeches reach your skin."

Instantly, I tucked my feet under my legs. "I thought leeches were only in the water."

"These are land leeches. They don't carry disease, but are not too pleasant, either. They sense your heat. They have two mouths, to make sure they can get you one way or another."

I looked down at the fascinating little gray creatures, one mouth on the ground and one dabbing the air, trying to find my blood. I shuddered. Suddenly I felt ready to move on.

After we'd hauled the orangutans for maybe another twenty minutes, the trail widened into a clearing. The swamp was all around, under us and above us — from everywhere the sound of dripping and slushing water. The noise of the cicadas was as constant as a pulse.

We placed Kalimantan and Papua at the base of a broad leafy tree. Adhi kneeled beside them, took a small plastic kit out of his bag, and filled a syringe with fluid from a glass bottle. "A small dose of adrenaline," he explained. "They are vulnerable when they are sleepy. We could wait for them to wake up, but Raja and Gaia are already coming out of sedation back at the camp. We need to keep moving."

He jabbed one orangutan's thigh, then filled a fresh syringe and injected the other ape. Wordlessly, Adhi gestured to the rest of us, pointing the way we came. We silently passed behind the tree line and watched.

Kalimantan was the first to wake, groggily sitting up and staring around. She flicked her lips away from her teeth and back down, a move I'd often seen Raja do when he was anxious. After climbing a few feet up the tree's trunk, she looked down and seemed to notice Papua for the first time. She dropped back down and mouthed the other orangutan's arm hair, tugging on her shoulder. Papua sat up, greeted Kalimantan with a quick embrace, and followed her up the tree.

"There are still a few tigers left in Sumatra," Adhi whispered. "The orangutans are much safer in the trees than on the ground, so it is their instinct to climb. They might spend days and days up there without ever coming to the forest floor."

Papua held on to a branch with one hand, let it bend near the next tree over, then grasped that trunk. Kalimantan mimicked her, following her friend through the canopy by bending trees until they were out of view.

I felt bad for my poor Raja, who'd never have the instinct to climb a tree if he woke up in a strange place. He'd have wrist-walked around the ground, looking for milk shakes and stuffed animals and DVD players. Once upon a time he'd known what to do, I assumed, until we'd drummed the wild impulses out of him.

"There aren't any tigers on Raja's release island, are there?" I asked.

"No," Adhi said, smiling. "No tigers on the release island."

We were back at the leech clearing when Adhi stopped us, nose in the air. He barked something in Indonesian at one of the other men. He paused, sniffing, and nodded. Then I smelled it, too: woodsmoke.

Adhi stalked into the trees, stepping over and between brambles and vines to make as little noise as possible. The other men followed. Trying to banish leeches to the back of my mind, I trailed behind.

Soon the smoke was visible, wafting low through the trees, weighted by the rain. We slowed, then came to a stop behind a thick bush. Adhi and his colleagues dropped to the soil, and I lay myself beside them.

Methodically making their way between thick reeds, men were using flaming brands to set fire to the grasses. Some reeds were black but extinguished, doused by the rain. Others had caught, though, and were smoking and smoldering.

"Stay here," Adhi cautioned.

I watched as he and the other men stepped into the scene. The fire-starters froze, momentarily surprised, then began shouting and backing up. Adhi and his colleagues yelled back, Adhi pointing in the vague direction of the base camp. The men pointed in the opposite direction, wherever they'd come from. One took a folded piece of paper out of his pocket and handed it to Adhi, who read it in the rain, quivering with indignation, before hurling the paper to the ground and stomping on it. Muttering curses, the fire-starter retrieved the paper and took back up lighting the grasses. He mimed a gun and fired vaguely in Adhi's direction.

Adhi and his coworkers stormed out of the clearing. I unsucked myself from the muddy ground and followed as they hurtled back through the swamp. Adhi was shouting in Indonesian, occasionally switching to English. "They have no chance!" he said. "We just released those two, and the swamp is burning already."

I asked him what was happening but he didn't respond, hurtling over fallen trees and splashing through deep puddles. Adhi was already shouting for Diah before the camp had come into view. She looked up from where she was leaning over Raja and stared into Adhi's eyes, bewildered as he shouted at her in Indonesian. Then her own eyes widened and she, too, began shouting.

I headed over to Raja. He was awake and blinking, lying on his back. When I stroked his hair, he sluggishly reached his arms around my neck. "It's okay, Raja," I said, pretty sure I was lying.

Diah slumped at the table. She'd come out from under the tarp but hadn't even bothered to put her poncho on. "What's happening? What can I do?" I asked.

"This is protected area," Diah managed to say. "Already most of the swamp is gone, but this small area is *protected*. They should not be able to do this here. But all it takes is one politician who wants some money, and then it is done. They have *permission* to burn the swamp and plant palms. With that paper, the *police* are on their side. We will be *shot* if we defend our project. It is the corporations that are behind this, the corporations that are making the money from this, but they get local farmers to set the fires so that it cannot be traced back to them."

"So these guys can, what, burn down this whole swamp?"

"They are granted a piece at a time. They have a new acre to burn. But that is how it has always worked so far. One more piece given away, another piece of money, until all the swamp is gone, and the orangutans with it."

"How do we stop them?"

"I am out of favors. I am the irrational witch who wants to keep the people poor by preventing them from using the land. They will not listen to me. I do not have the power to make them listen."

I stared into the swamp's edge. Somewhere out there Kalimantan and Papua, after losing their parents and painstakingly being nursed back to health, were trying to survive on their own. It would be hard enough for them without someone setting fire to their trees. Here, too, was Raja, under my very fingers, waiting for his turn to be released, even more stacked against him. There were these terrible gears grinding under the surface, too large and heavy to be stopped. What chance did any individual have against that?

FOURTEEN

The rain hadn't broken by the time Diah, Adhi, and I had loaded Raja and Gaia into the boat. As the tranquilizers wore off further, Raja seemed to have entered a blissed-out state; he had his mouth open wide, teeth to the sky, blinking in astonishment whenever a raindrop hit his eye. If he could speak he'd have been slurring *Dude, look at the sky! The colors are so awwwwwesome.* Gaia was still sound asleep, her hands wedged between her knees, eyes shut tight. Last to bed, last to rise. She was getting soaked by the rainwater accumulating at the bottom of the boat, but we had no dry place to move her.

We'd borrowed a wooden fishing boat from a local village. Its owner came with us, the elderly man expertly navigating the reed-choked waterways. The Island for Misfit Orangutans was deep in the national park, and we spent over an hour passing down small rivers and tributaries before Diah announced that we'd arrived. This island looked no different from many of the other ones we passed, but apparently this was home.

Raja's home. Without me.

"The orangutans who already live on the island have recently been sighted on the other side. It takes them three days to go from one end to the other end as they search for food, so this way Raja and Gaia will get their bearings and make each other allies before they meet any of the others. They might decide to go in separate directions, but we chose to release these two together because they seem to like each other. They're both working with disadvantages, and can use all the help they can get."

I looked at the rain-soaked orangutans, at the wet hair parting in various spots and revealing gray-white skin, at the rivulets of water tracing Gaia's network of scars. Raja stared at me in bliss, blinking heavily as Adhi directed the fishing boat to a clump of reeds at the shore. I was certain Raja had no idea what the future held — maybe the future itself was a concept that was foreign to him. Or maybe he thought he and I were going to stay here together. Either way, Raja was in for a surprise, and there was nothing I could do about it.

Adhi stepped out and immediately sank into muck up to his thigh. "In case you wanted to experience the other kind of leeches," he announced, grinning.

"Awesome, thanks," I said, gritting my teeth.

Adhi tested the various grass clumps until he found one that didn't give. The fisherman hopped to shore as Diah and I took up positions on each of Raja's feet and worked to ease him over the side of the boat. After a countdown, we heaved. Raja went over the side and tipped into the grass, the boat rocking mightily as he did.

Brackish river water sludged over Gaia, still at the bottom of the boat. She inhaled some and startled awake, snorting and sneezing. Diah laid a hand on the orangutan's scarred back until she calmed. The young female peered around, looking peeved that we'd woken her. Then she saw the trees knitting the open sky above her, and squeaked. Freedom. Without another pause she was up and out of the boat, using Raja's belly as a stepping stone in the process. He grunted and sat up, then watched curiously as Gaia tested the lower branches of a tree and started to climb.

After a few groggy attempts, she seemed to decide climbing was too much to handle for the moment and slid back to the ground. She kept her arms around the tree, though, turning her head against the bark to stare at us. Not to be shown up, Raja wrist-walked to the other side of the same tree and wrapped his arms around, too, in the process landing his fingers right in Gaia's face.

Diah watched them, hands on her hips. "I don't think we're going to need any adrenaline shots for these two," she said. She pointed into the jungle canopy. "And look — there are some budding vines, and ripe shoots. They won't have to travel far to eat for the next few days. That is good, because if orangutans don't eat for more than a day, the parasites in their intestines wander out and can get into their hearts."

My own heart did a pitter-patter at that. My poor Raja. "Hear what she's saying, Raja?" I said. "Keep eating." Eating enough had never been a problem for him before. But then again, the era of pizza bagels was over.

Diah turned to me. "John, it's time to say good-bye."

I looked at her, startled, and saw her lips were in a firm line. She was making this sudden so it would be easier for us, like a doctor sticking in the needle before the countdown was over. I stared at Raja, wiping rain from my brow.

His hands were still in Gaia's face. She complained in a series of outraged squeaks, nibbling at his fingertips until he removed his hands. The moment he looked up the tree, Raja absently put his hands back into Gaia's face, setting her to squeaking and nibbling all over again.

Raja usually had an acute sense of what I was thinking. Where we'd always been different, though, was that because Raja only really knew about the present, good-bye didn't mean anything to him. There was no *See you later*: I was either here or I wasn't. So, instead of good-bye, I signed *I love you.*

He signed a sloppy *I love you* back. Then he got distracted by rapping the top of Gaia's head with his knuckles, rasping in excitement when she protested and fought back.

"They have a lot to figure out," Diah said. "We should go and let them start."

As we got into the boat Gaia stood and watched us, swaying on two feet. She seemed to have more awareness than Raja did of the significance of what was happening. Raja, ever the follower, mimicked her and stood on his two feet, too.

As we assembled in the boat, they watched us, clutching each other for solace as the loud motor started. They made no move to try to join us. By the time we were a dozen feet from shore, they were investigating the ground, poking around the mud. When we turned the corner and branches finally blocked the view, they were off climbing palms. We were the ones leaving, but they were the ones who disappeared first.

On the way back to base camp, I wound up in the front-most position of the fishing boat, so it was just me and the pelting rain and a triangle of water parting and spreading under the prow. It didn't feel like we'd released Raja. It felt like we'd ditched him.

As we put-putted through the swamps, Adhi pointed out a long black snake coiled around a branch. It was way bigger than any snake I'd ever seen in the States. That monster would have no trouble killing Raja. Then Adhi pointed out a long toothy crocodile laying on a log in the water, mouth open, teeth sharp. It could easily kill Raja. As we passed, it slipped into the black water. That water could also kill Raja.

From here on out, if he got into serious trouble, that would be it. There would be no rescue.

How could I leave my brother to that?

I was on my feet before I was aware of what I was doing, standing in the rocking boat and looking back.

"John?" Diah asked. "What are you doing?"

I visored my hand against my forehead so I could see through the rain. "I . . . Do you see him? Is Raja there?"

"He's long past," she said, baffled. "John, please sit down. It's not safe for you to stand in the boat."

Because of Diah's quiet calm more than any deliberate decision, I sat back down. I swiveled so I was facing toward her — and, somewhere in the trees back there, toward Raja. "Can we turn around? This is a mistake."

Diah shook her head. "No. Turning around now isn't an option."

I nodded. Part of me was relieved that there was no room for me to waffle and punish myself — and Raja — further. Maybe to make sure I didn't do anything crazy, the fisherman gunned the engine, setting the boat to vibrating. My thighs went numb where they thrummed against the wooden seat, and my mind went to a Jet Ski video game Raja and I used to play. If you went off the course and into rough water, the controller would vibrate. That was always Raja's goal, to get the controller to vibrate as much as possible. I'd be laps and laps ahead, while he was heading into the white water, pushing harder and harder against an invisible wall at the far edge of the game world. I faced forward in the boat.

He was going to wake up without me. I was going to wake up without him.

He wouldn't wake up alone, though. Gaia would be there. I remembered how, when she thought Raja was leaving her behind, she'd signed *you poop* to him. I wondered what other signs he might teach her. *Little + sleep* for nap time. *Little + Raja + thank you* for video game. They'd have to come up with some new game for that to refer to, though. No PlayStations out here.

I wondered, too, what new signs they might come up with. If Gaia had a baby, what they'd teach it. I'd never know. It was all up to them.

For their survival, I'd have to count on Gaia knowing enough about what to eat and what to avoid to keep them both alive, and that she'd be patient enough to keep a fat male with zero street skills around. I imagined them bickering in the jungle when Raja invariably screwed up. *You poop. No, YOU poop.*

There were no parents to guide them, but maybe two young orangutans could teach each other. Like how Raja and I had once taught each other, figuring out our shared lives as best we could.

Back at the quarantine, I didn't have much to pack. The staff had admired my shirts, and Diah had told me that manufactured clothes were hard to come by in the small Sumatran villages, so I left most of my clothing behind as gifts. My nearly empty duffel bag was cinched down and ready for the drive back to Medan and Mom when Diah ducked into my room. "Ready to go?" she asked.

I nodded, shouldering the bag and wedging a blue bedraggled blob under my arm.

"Are you really carting that thing all the way back to the States?" Diah asked.

It was grimy, one-eyed, stinky. But it had been Raja's. He didn't need it anymore, but maybe I did. "Yep," I said. "Think they'll give me trouble at customs?"

Last stop before I left was the cage of the quarantine's newest intake, the young female from the logging camp. I gave her a piece of pineapple — a rare treat — as a good-bye.

When we got back to Diah's house, I found Mom in slippers

in the kitchen, cooking with Ibu. Turned out they'd started switching off meals: Indonesian, American, Indonesian, American. At the moment, Mom was introducing Ibu to spaghetti with meatballs. Though she was still a little pale, Mom moved easily and greeted me with a big hug. "Feeling better, huh?" I said.

She didn't answer, just hugged me tight. I felt my shoulders relax under her grasp. She knew what I'd been through.

As we got ready to go to the airport, she didn't even blink when she saw that I was planning on carrying a stinky toy elephant back to the States. She gave it a little pat on the head.

Our flight had an extra security check leaving Medan, and the guard looked at me curiously when I placed a stuffed animal on the conveyer. I didn't even shrug, just nodded vigorously. *Yes, it's mine. Is that a problem?*

The return was a commercial flight this time, which meant more meals and more snacks. As soon as I finished the first dinner I asked the flight attendant if she had any extra trays to spare. Meals in the jungle had been rice and greens, and I felt I could eat for days to catch up.

For the day and a half it took us to get home, I'd forget about Raja for a few minutes, then have the trembling realization that he was somewhere, that he *was*. That he and Gaia were on that island that was now thousands of miles away. That I had the luxury of flying away, while Diah and Adhi were the ones still working every day to keep orangutans safe.

I couldn't get over how simple and so impossible it was, that so much of the world could be invisible and also present. That while I watched a movie on the plane, palm oil companies were still burning and cutting. That pigs and cows and chickens were still crammed into those windowless buildings I had driven past in West Virginia. My heart said that none of those things were real, that the only things that existed were the ones I was seeing right now. But this was one place where the heart was not the wiser organ. It was the job of my brain to remind my heart that sometimes what it felt was true was not — not really. That injustice often comes from not forcing our feelings to stand up before reason and account for themselves.

Raja was out there. It was unreal, and it was true. Even as our final plane touched down in rainy Oregon, as we passed through a land of lighted signs, of automated kiosks with the screens speaking a language I speak without thinking about it, of trim gray carpet and drinkable tap water, I knew Raja was out there somewhere, with or without Gaia, living at the mercy of his environment in a way I would never live at the mercy of mine. My survival would never mean eating whatever fruit I could track down and drinking whatever water looked cleanest and hoping for the best. Safety nets were layered under my life; Raja was living over open space.

I imagined a plane like mine passing over Raja's island. He'd stop to listen; all the orangutans would. Even the cicadas would go silent at the mystical machine roaring overhead.

After we picked up the car from long-term parking, a few swipes of Mom's credit card got us home. I fell asleep as soon as I got into my own bed, and spent the next few days in a kind of stupor. The easinesses of my once-familiar world shocked me: Tomcats with knobs for tails didn't creep in during the night and pee on me; I didn't wake up to fire ants swarming my ankles; I could go for hours unaware of my body because I wasn't uncomfortable. Our food didn't have insect turds in it, and our logs weren't crawling with leeches.

And there was no Raja.

After a couple of days, a poster tube arrived from my dad. There was no note attached, but as I pulled it out, I knew it was a sort-of peace offering. It was the blown-up image of me and Raja that had been on my old bedroom wall. The only thing I'd set aside to keep from my father's house.

As I tacked it up, I remembered the rambunctious little ape I'd once known, so different from the Raja now living off in the swamps. Before I left Sumatra, Diah explained an Indonesian word to me — *merantau*. She said it was hard to translate into English, but it meant something like hitting a dead end and leaving one life to live another one elsewhere.

Raja had been safe in that trailer in my father's backyard. But now, I had to believe, he was something else. He was free. This was a more dangerous existence, but also a better one. The way Diah described it, every living creature should have a right to *merantau*, although it could mean leaving loved ones behind, although it could mean death. Even if Raja soon died in the jungle, I'd still have to believe I'd done the right thing for him.

I knew life in the wild wasn't always noble or happy. It could be ruthless and brutal and unfair. Raja could have been bitten by a snake moments after we left him. Or he could be fine. I imagined Raja in a patch of wild swamp, poking through muck, farting and snorting and doing all his usual Raja things. That might be the truth.

I would never know. In my deepest heart, I didn't think I'd be hearing anything about Raja ever again.

Because he was free.

A Q&A WITH
ELIOT SCHREFER

Q: This is your third novel about apes, but *Rescued* feels markedly different from your previous two. How did you come up with this particular story?

A: There are a number of qualities that make orangutans different from bonobos and chimpanzees, the two species of apes I wrote about before. One is that they are slightly less closely related to humans, and you can tell — they're a much more mysterious animal. Another is that they live in Asia, not Africa, and so had earlier and more substantial contact with the West.

One of the first orangutans I read about was Jenny. Early in my research, I came across a picture of a young ape brought back to England from what were then known as the Indies (modern-day Indonesia) in the early nineteenth century. At that time, the Indies were Europe's primary source of spices and coffee, and "gentleman collectors" traveling on merchant ships would sometimes return with exotic specimens. If those animals were lucky enough to survive the sea voyage, they'd be put on display in one of London's zoos, which was just what happened to Jenny.

Jenny was displayed in chaste clothing, given a tea set to drink from and a Bible to leaf through. People came from far and wide to see the animal who looked like a person. Queen Victoria visited and was repulsed, calling Jenny "frightfully, and painfully, and disagreeably human."[1] Charles Darwin had also been struck by the

---

[1] Jones, Steve. *The Darwin Archipelago* (New Haven: Yale University Press, 2012), 2.

Portrait of Jenny, the first orangutan at London Zoo. Printed by W Clerk,
High Holborn, in December 1837.

uncanny resemblance when he'd visited Jenny's mother a few years earlier — but rather than revulsion, he felt wonder. After the visit, he marveled in his notebook about her intelligent expression, how she showed "passion & rage, sulkiness, & very actions of despair." He concluded that "man in his arrogance thinks himself a great work, worthy the interposition of a deity. More humble and I believe true to consider him created from animals." Twenty-one years later he published *On the Origin of Species*, detailing how man might have evolved from other animals rather than having been created separately. Of course, taking from humans their privileged position as God's most special creation led to an uproar that is still playing out in biology classrooms today.

I couldn't get Jenny out of my mind. I wondered what she must have gone through, taken from her home as an infant and brought to a foreign and cold place. The urge to dress her up showed our thrill at the idea that another creature might have human characteristics. Even the name of the orange ape comes from *orang* and *hutan*, Malay words that translate as "man" and "forest."

It seemed to me that Jenny's treatment at the London Zoo revealed much more about human nature than it did about orangutan nature. I started imagining a contemporary version of Jenny's story, and realized that a captive ape's situation was similar to the plight of a kid during a divorce, getting swept along by the needs of powerful parents, at risk of being seen for what he represents instead of as a child with his own needs. That's where John entered, and the story took off from there.

Q: You journeyed to Indonesia in the summer of 2013 to research orangutans for this book. What did you discover while you were there?
A: I've now visited conservationists working with bonobos, chimpanzees, and orangutans, and I've been so impressed by how

accommodating they've all been. Most orangutans are from Borneo, with only six thousand left in Sumatra. But it was Ian Singleton, the director of the Sumatran Orangutan Conservation Programme, who wrote back enthusiastically right after I emailed him, and was gracious enough to invite me to come and spend some time at their orangutan quarantine in the jungles of northern Sumatra.

My journey was a lot like John's, minus the ill mother. I flew via Singapore to Medan, the capital of Sumatra, and then hitched a ride into the jungle on the quarantine center's fruit truck. The compound is a fenced-in stretch of thick jungle where the orangutan orphans — victims of Sumatra's deforestation — are brought.

SOCP's mission is the rapid and effective rehabilitation of the young apes. It means the orphans are, to be frank, somewhat miserable while they're there: They're kept in isolation cages for their first months, then introduced to socialization cages, and finally brought back to the wild if they have prospects of surviving out there. It makes for a grim, almost prisonlike, environment — but it's the best thing for the orangutans. If they were all frolicking together throughout the quarantine, it would have been a much more charming experience for human visitors like me, but meanwhile they would have been spreading diseases and learning to live on the ground instead of in the trees — which is lethal for an orangutan in the wild. They need to keep to the treetops to avoid their worst predators.

Q: So orangutans are very different from bonobos and chimps?
A: There was one afternoon when I was doing a circuit of the orangutan sanctuary, handing out pieces of fruit. I ran out before I could give a piece to the last orphan, but she seemed not to mind. When I came back around half an hour later, I heard a *phhbbt* and

then felt spit on my neck. She'd waited to get her revenge! But she'd never shown any anger on her face. It was the strangest thing, trying to read her poker face. I wouldn't say orangutans are any smarter than bonobos and chimps, but they're certainly wilier. Raja's extraordinary escape from his trailer is modeled on a very similar feat managed by an orangutan at the Wanariset rehabilitation center in Borneo.[2]

Bonobos and chimps spend their time in groups, and so they have a vested interest in showing their feelings — it's really important for the welfare of the community that everyone knows if someone's angry or happy. Orangutans, however, spend most of their time foraging in solitude. Except for mothers and children, who spend a number of years together before the young ones go off on their own, orangutans have little need to show feelings on their faces.

As a result, they're these mysterious and unknowable creatures. That's why people who spend time with orangutans often talk about their apparent wisdom, like they're hairy orange yogis. It's easy to imagine they're having deep thoughts, because they have quiet smiles and long penetrating gazes. But who knows what's really going on in the mind of an orangutan.

Unlike chimps and bonobos (and humans!), orangutans are also relatively uninterested in domination. An orangutan is a creature whose motto would be *Live and let live.* I spent the second half of my Indonesia trip taking a refitted fishing boat into the Borneo jungle to visit the orangutans of Camp Leakey, and felt perfectly safe sitting on the dock next to a two-hundred-pound male. No way would I have risked doing the same with a chimp or a bonobo.

As Shawn Thompson writes in *The Intimate Ape*, orangutans "are the most sensitive to [lack of interest] and also the best at

[2]Russon, Anne E. *Orangutans: Wizards of the Rainforest* (Richmond Hill: Firefly Books, 2004), 212.

hiding it."[3] Their undemonstrativeness is why John and Raja's closeness is so crucial. John knows Raja well, but it's hard for others to get a read on the ape — which is why it's so important that John be the one to eventually come through for him. No one else really gets Raja.

Q: Why are you so interested in writing about apes?
A: Apes are a great testing ground for our beliefs about the natural world in general, because they're the animal that most blurs the line between human and not-human. A lot of the qualities that we assume give us a unique position in the world (awareness of self, capacity for a range of deep feelings, use of tools and language) apes also share. It's much harder to claim that humans are essentially different when you're around an ape, and it's interesting to think about how most of Western culture, with the primacy it gives humans, developed in early human societies that didn't have exposure to apes or monkeys.

It's even simpler than that, though: The basic fact is that when you look into an ape's eyes, it's very hard to argue that there isn't consciousness there.

That being said, I don't think animals should need to be nearly human to be worthy of our mercy. All they need is a capacity to suffer — which virtually all of them have. The way an orangutan can muddy the human/animal divide is important, as a charismatic ape can serve as an ambassador for other animals that are more difficult to relate to, and more invisible in our society, including those used for research or the ten billion land animals annually raised and slaughtered behind closed doors for consumption in this country alone.[4]

---

[3]Thompson, Shawn. *The Intimate Ape* (New York: Citadel, 2010), 87.
[4]Safran Foer, Jonathan. *Eating Animals* (New York: Back Bay Books, 2010), 15.

Turns out it's difficult to really get animals directly into view. I still feel like I'm looking at them only sideways most of the time.

Q: What are the specific problems that orangutans are facing in their homeland?

A: Orangutan fossils have been found as far north as China. Forty percent larger than the surviving orangutans of today, those prehistoric apes were probably watching from the trees when *Homo sapiens* first arrived in Asia. But now orangutans are restricted to ever-shrinking parcels of swamp in Sumatra and Borneo. As is true across the globe, apes survive only in the rare pockets of jungle considered undesirable enough until now to resist agriculture and economic development.

Global manufacturers have increasingly turned to palm oil as the cheapest to use in their products. Once you start looking, it shows up everywhere. There's palm oil in grocery store products from toothpaste to margarine, and 83 percent of it comes from Indonesia and Malaysia.[5] Unfortunately for the orangutans, palm oil is a crop that can be grown in plantations on former swampland. Multinational corporations set up smaller local companies, hiding their accountability, then burn tracts of land, using the initial sale of the hardwood to fund the setting up of a palm oil plantation, whose trees take three years to finally bear a cash crop. Indonesia has lost an average of 7,500 square miles of forest every year since 1996.[6]

Orangutans, who used to keep to themselves in the treetops, are now starving from the razing of their former food sources. In desperation, they wander into plantations and are attacked by

[5]Morris, Desmond. *Planet Ape* (Richmond Hill: Firefly Books, 2009), 257.
[6]Ibid.

workers ordered to protect their crops. The results are usually grim — sometimes orangutans are burned alive where they're cowering at the top of a palm tree, or they're beaten if they try to escape on the ground. Leuser, one of the orangutans I met at SOCP, went blind after he'd been shot sixty-two times by an air rifle when he wandered into farmland. He inspired Gorgon in this book.

Q: So, what can readers do to help?
A: The physical evidence of logging and deforestation is found in Indonesia, but that's only the end result of a chain of decisions by multinational companies, including many American ones. Certain nonprofit organizations are working to establish protocols to hold companies accountable for the deforestation they are funding in the jungles of Sumatra and Borneo. New programs like Debt for Nature allow debt forgiveness for impoverished countries in return for protecting their natural habitats.

If orangutans can't be seen, they can't be shot, but they need surviving hardwood to hide in. Protecting their natural habitat is the simplest bet for their continued survival. There are plenty of online petitions going around to pressure corporations — including many based in the United States — to only use palm oil that has been sourced responsibly. They work, too: In 2013 a petition to Kellogg's managed to get the food giant to commit to sourcing its palm oil only through sustainable sources.

On the smaller scale, we can all look at our own purchasing habits. It's consumption that drives the destruction of orangutan habitat. We can make sure we don't buy products that contain unsustainable palm oil. When we're buying something made from hardwood, we can make sure it has the Forestry Stewardship Council (FSC) label, which confirms that it has been harvested responsibly.

We can also avoid zoos that don't keep animals in conditions that are near to natural — and avoid animal circuses entirely, as well as airlines that fly captured primates from their home countries and into medical testing. (It was consumer pressure that got China Southern Airlines to stop transporting lab monkeys in 2014 — Air France is now the only major carrier willing to do so.)

Also, consider adopting an ape! No one's going to mail you one (and trust me, that's in no one's best interest — especially not the ape's!) but you can financially care for one of the primates housed in sanctuaries around the world. Check out:

World Wildlife Fund (www.worldwildlife.org/Gifts)

Jane Goodall Institute (www.janegoodall.org/chimpguardian)

Friends of Bonobos (www.lolayabonobo.org)

Save the Orangutan (www.savetheorangutan.org/help-us)

ACKNOWLEDGMENTS

There's no way I could have written the Sumatra portion of this book without Ian Singleton's generosity in hosting me at his group's quarantine center. He's rough-and-tumble, kind, and resourceful. The orangutans (and I!) are very lucky to have him as an ally.

Most of my time on-site was spent with the quarantine staff. Yenny Saraswati, the head vet, was an inspiration. Her compassion for her charges is obvious to human and orangutan both, and her ape patients melt around her. I kind of did, too. Shout-out to the daily staff, who shared their rice with me and tolerated my twenty words of bad Indonesian.

Of course, *Rescued* takes place primarily in the United States, and for my research into the situation of apes that have been trafficked into the West I counted most on Patti Ragan, who founded the Center for Great Apes. She was very generous with her time, joining me on the phone from her sanctuary in Florida. She's done terrific work taking in apes that have been discarded once they were no longer of use in the entertainment industry, or released after spending years in medical testing. She told me of the very rare cases when apes have been repatriated, and I don't know what I would have done without her guidance. There's a reason she's beloved within the ape-conservation community.

To all my writer friends who read drafts, thank you! Donna Freitas, Marie Rutkoski, Daphne Grab, Jill Santopolo, Marianna Baer, Anne Heltzel: This book wouldn't have made it without you. Of course, my mom remains my best line editor. Eric Zahler: Thank you for journeying with me down watery Borneo ways, and for sharing my love for our adorable orange buds.

David Levithan, my longtime editor: Once again, your thoughts and insights were so essential to getting to the heart of this book. (And once again, you wisely chopped out a main character — Nina will join Luc's baby sister from *Threatened* in the great character waiting room in the sky.) The rest of the team at Scholastic — you've become such powerful, positive presences in my life. I'm so glad I get to call you guys home.

Richard Pine, my agent: You are such a fighter, and I consider myself very lucky to have you on my side of the ring.

There are so many terrific sources on orangutans and Indonesia. Here are the ones that were most useful to me:

On Orangutans

Among Orangutans: Red Apes and the Rise of Human Culture, by Carel van Schaik

The Intimate Ape: Orangutans and the Secret Life of a Vanishing Species, by Shawn Thompson

"Language Garden," by Susanne Antonetta. Published in *Orion* magazine.

Orangutans: Wizards of the Rainforest, by Anne E. Russon

Planet Ape, by Desmond Morris, with Steve Parker

Reflections of Eden: My Years with the Orangutans of Borneo, by Biruté M. F. Galdikas

Thinkers of the Jungle: The Orangutan Report, by Gerd Schuster, Willie Smits, and Jay Ullal

Orangutan Island, DVD. Animal Planet

On the Human / Animal Relationship

Animal Liberation: The Definitive Classic of the Animal Movement, by Peter Singer

Between Man and Beast, by Monte Reel

The Bonobo and the Atheist: In Search of Humanism Among the Primates, by Frans de Waal

Eating Animals, by Jonathan Safran Foer

Dominion: The Power of Man, the Suffering of Animals, and the Call to Mercy, by Matthew Scully

On Indonesia

The Animal Estate: The English and Other Creatures in the Victorian Age, by Harriet Ritvo

A History of Modern Indonesia, by Adrian Vickers

The History of Sumatra, by William Marsden

Merchant Kings: When Companies Ruled the World, 1600–1900, by Stephen R. Bown